T0200811

Titles by Jenn McKinlay

Library Lover's Mysteries

BOOKS CAN BE DECEIVING	A LIKELY STORY
DUE OR DIE	BETTER LATE THAN NEVER
BOOK, LINE, AND SINKER	DEATH IN THE STACKS
READ IT AND WEEP	HITTING THE BOOKS
ON BORROWED TIME	

Cupcake Bakery Mysteries

SPRINKLE WITH MURDER	DARK CHOCOLATE DEMISE
BUTTERCREAM BUMP OFF	VANILLA BEANED
DEATH BY THE DOZEN	CARAMEL CRUSH
RED VELVET REVENGE	WEDDING CAKE CRUMBLE
GOING, GOING, GANACHE	DYING FOR DEVIL'S FOOD
SUGAR AND ICED	

Hat Shop Mysteries

CLOCHE AND DAGGER	COPY CAP MURDER
DEATH OF A MAD HATTER	ASSAULT AND BERET
AT THE DROP OF A HAT	

Bluff Point Romances

ABOUT A DOG
BARKING UP THE WRONG TREE
EVERY DOG HAS HIS DAY

Happily Ever After Romances

THE GOOD ONES

HITTING THE BOOKS

Jenn McKinlay

BERKLEY PRIME CRIME
New York

BERKLEY PRIME CRIME
Published by Berkley
An imprint of Penguin Random House LLC
1745 Broadway, New York, NY 10019

ISBN: 9780451492685

Berkley Prime Crime hardcover edition / September 2018
Berkley Prime Crime mass-market edition / July 2019

Printed in the United States of America

Cover art © Julia Green / Mendola LTD.
Book design by Laura K. Corless

*For my aunt, Nancy Gould, whose laugh delights me,
whose sparkling blue eyes light up every room she enters, and who
always tells the funniest stories and bakes the
best cookies. I love you very much.*

Acknowledgments

This series has been such a delight to write. Libraries have always been and will always be my favorite places to explore. I am so grateful to all of the librarians and library workers in my life for making it a much more interesting journey. I have to thank my editor, Kate Seaver; assistant editor, Sarah Blumenstock; and my agent, Christina Hogrebe, for being such a wonderful support system. The books get done because these ladies have my back and keep me on target. I would also like to thank the amazing sales and marketing team at Berkley for getting the books out there and the art and production department for creating such stunning covers and page designs. You are all brilliant and I feel very fortunate to work with you.

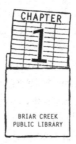

CHAPTER

1

BRIAR CREEK
PUBLIC LIBRARY

H e was whistling. At five o'clock in the morning, the
man was whistling. Lindsey Norris grabbed an extra
pillow and plopped it over her face, making a sandwich
out of her head. It blocked out the chipper sound coming
from the bathroom, but it also made breathing a challenge. She shifted and tried to make an air duct for her
nose and mouth without letting in any sound. Sucking in
a breath of cool early morning air, she tried to get back
to her blissful unconscious state.

Her brain refused to be lulled. It was too busy being
irritated. What sort of person whistled first thing in the
morning? Her boyfriend, Captain Mike Sullivan, that's
who. The man woke up *before* the sun rose every day,
even on days he didn't have to. It was positively unnatu-
ral. Lindsey had moved into Sully's house several months

ago, and while she loved him and she loved living with him, there were just a few things that made living together a bit tense, not the least of which was Sully's egregious habit of greeting every day whistling like a songbird at sunrise.

A former navy man who owned his own boat touring and water taxi company, Sully was used to being up and out before anyone else. Lindsey was not. She was the library director for their small town of Briar Creek, and as a public servant, she kept bankers' hours, with an evening and rotating weekends thrown in just to keep it interesting.

Great, now her mind was on work. Lindsey did a quick mental rundown of her day, hoping that by thinking it through, she could put it aside and fall back to sleep. She had a meeting at nine o'clock with the library board, which had been in transition since its last president had been murdered. She hadn't yet gotten a read on the new members and what their expectations of the library were. Mostly, they seemed relieved after every meeting to still be alive. She wasn't sure what that said about her as a library director. She decided to bring muffins and hope that relaxed them a bit. After all, everyone liked muffins.

At lunch, she had a crafternoon scheduled. This was a weekly Thursday meeting where they shared lunch, did a craft, and talked about a book. Lindsey wasn't a crafty sort, so this week's string bracelets were not really her thing, but her library assistant, who was in charge of the craft, assured her that the worst that could happen would be that she'd suffer a small burn. Lindsey made a mental note to put some antibiotic pain-relief ointment in her purse.

Lastly, she had a late meeting with the mayor to discuss making the library a more environmentally friendly space by changing out the current lighting with more energy-efficient LEDs. The mayor was all about the bottom line and never welcomed ideas, even good ones, that would cost money in the immediate election cycle. His ideas for the future didn't run much past getting reelected. She was going to have to come up with a compelling reason for the change to get him to listen to her. Maybe she could convince him that this would get him the youth vote in the next election.

Today was definitely a "look professional" day. Pity. She would have preferred to wear her book-lover pajamas to work, comfy flannel pj's covered in a repeating pattern of eyeglasses and flying books. It was April in Connecticut, still on the chilly side in the morning, but the afternoon would be warmer. Her navy blue business suit with the pencil skirt and tailored jacket would work. She wondered whether she'd gotten her jade green blouse back from the dry cleaners—that would lighten up the severity of the suit but still give her executive polish.

How much time had passed since the whistling started? Why hadn't she fallen back to sleep? Could she fall back to sleep now? Lindsey tried to gauge her level of tiredness. Her brain was fully engaged; sleep was going to remain a memory for the rest of the day. Darn it.

Her nose twitched. What was that smell? *Mmm. Coffee*. She peeked one eye out from under her pillow.

Freshly showered and shaved, Sully was approaching with a steaming mug of coffee in one hand. He carefully put it on her nightstand. The man brought her coffee; that was the definition of *true love* in Lindsey's book. His unfortunate whistling was immediately forgiven.

She reached out from under the covers and grabbed his hand before he could escape. He allowed her to pull him down, and he crouched beside the bed and peered under the pillow.

"You awake in there?" he asked.

Lindsey tossed the pillow aside. "Good morning."

Sully studied her with a small smile on his lips. "Good morning. I can't believe you're awake."

"Really?" she asked. She didn't mention the whistling.

"What time did you finally put the book down last night?"

Lindsey glanced at the floor, where the book she'd been reading had landed when she'd fallen asleep. "One thirty, maybe two."

"In the morning?" Sully asked. He ran a hand through his reddish brown hair, making the curly waves stand on end.

"I was suffering from OMC syndrome," she said.

"OMC, is that some sort of insomnia?"

"Sort of. It stands for *one more chapter*."

"Book nerd," Sully teased. Then he leaned forward and kissed her on the nose before standing up.

Lindsey yawned. "Yes, I am, and I have no read-grets, not even for missed sleep. The book was that good."

"Is that another made-up word?" he asked. Lindsey

nodded. "Fine, then here's one for you. If you don't get moving, you're going to have to break the read-o-meter to get to work on time. It's already eight fifteen."

"What! I thought it was five. You always get up at five."

"Not today," he said. "I have a late boat tour, plus I was tired because somebody keeps their light on into the wee hours of the morning."

"Gah!" Lindsey lurched from the bed, dislodging her dog, Heathcliff, from where he was resting his head on her knee. She grabbed the hot mug of coffee and slurped some as she hurried into the bathroom, slamming the door behind her.

"**Y**ou look awful, like someone left you out in the rain, tossed you on the floor of their car, where you were stepped on for a few months, and then they stuffed you in the book drop and pretended they had no idea how you got into such bad shape," Beth Barker said. She stared down at Lindsey, who was sprawled on the couch in the crafternoon room at the back of the library.

"Gee, thanks," Lindsey said. She opened her eyes and glanced at her best friend, who was also the children's librarian. "That means so much coming from a woman who is dressed like a pigeon."

Wearing an oversize gray sweatshirt that had big, round eyes and a beak sewn onto the hood, Beth flapped her arms, which had been fashioned into wings, and then clasped them in front of her in a begging pose. "Please, can I drive the bus? I'll be your best friend."

Lindsey snorted. No one could act out Mo Willems's *Don't Let the Pigeon Drive the Bus!* better than Beth.

"You're already my best friend," she said. "Which is why I forgive you for saying I look awful."

"It's a book hangover, isn't it?" Paula Turner entered the room, pushing a cart full of craft materials. "Was it *A Tree Grows in Brooklyn*, our discussion book today?"

"No, I finished that one a few days ago. This was one I picked up on the way out of work last night. I couldn't put it down," Lindsey admitted.

"That's the worst—the best, but also the worst," Beth said. She plopped down on the couch.

Lindsey draped her arm over her eyes. It wasn't that she wished her friends would go away exactly, but she had almost managed a fifteen-minute power nap. She had read somewhere that fifteen- to twenty-minute naps could refresh a person without sending them into such a deep sleep that they were groggy all day. Oh, how she wished for that right now.

"What was it? A thriller, romantic suspense, murder mystery?" Paula asked. She tossed her thick blue braid over her shoulder while she set up the large table at the side of the room. "I'm looking for a good read."

"Thriller," Lindsey said. "But the author killed off one of my favorite characters at the end, and all I could think was *No, take me instead!*"

"I hate that," Nancy Peyton said as she entered the room. "It destroys me when an author kills off a character I'm fond of, especially in a series."

"But sometimes it has to be done," Violet La Rue said

as she followed her best friend in. "You have to trust the author to be true to the story they need to tell."

"Not if it breaks my heart, I don't," Nancy insisted. Her bright blue eyes sparked with a fierce light as she tossed her short bobbed silver hair as if emphasizing her point. "I will break up with an author over something like that."

Nancy Peyton had lived in the village of Briar Creek all her life, making her a true Creeker. She'd been married to Captain Jake Peyton, and when his boat went down in a storm, she had never remarried or left her home, choosing to make their captain's house into a three-family apartment building. Lindsey had rented the third floor from her before she moved in with Sully.

Nancy's partner in crime in all manner of shenanigans was her best friend, Violet La Rue. Violet had retired to Briar Creek after a long career on the Broadway stage. With her dark skin and warm brown eyes, she was still a great beauty; and with her silver hair scraped back into a bun at the back of her head, her cheekbones dominated her heart-shaped face, which had delivered famous lines from the likes of William Shakespeare and Sam Shepard to appreciative audiences all over the world.

"You're being thick," Violet said. "Think of all the great works of literature and how they would be different if the author didn't follow their vision. Take *Romeo and Juliet*—it had to end the way it did."

"Did it?" Lindsey asked. "Couldn't they have communicated better and ended up living together in some faraway land? Then again, maybe it would have ended exactly the same if they'd gotten married and Juliet discovered Romeo was a morning person who whistled really loudly while he shaved, and one morning she just snapped."

The room became quiet as her friends stopped talking to stare at her.

"What?" she asked.

"You and Sully have been living together for six months, right?" Violet asked. She sat in an available armchair by the couch, and Nancy did the same.

"Something like that," Lindsey said.

Nancy exchanged a look with Violet and nodded. "It's over."

"What? No!" cried Beth. "How could it be over? It took them forever to get together." She bounced forward on the couch and reached for Lindsey's hand, looking devastated. "I mean, if you and Sully can't make it, Aidan and I—"

"Are still in your honeymoon phase," Violet interrupted. "Relax. You're fine."

"Oh, thank goodness." Beth sagged with relief and dropped Lindsey's hand. "I've barely gotten used to being Mrs. Barker. I'm not ready for things to go sideways on us."

"Sully and I are fine," Lindsey insisted. "It's just that living with someone, even an awesome someone, is—"

"Annoying, irritating, exasperating, all the *-ings*," Nancy said. "I remember the first few months I was married to Jake, I fantasized about clobbering him with a frying pan more times than I can count."

"Communication is the key," Violet said. "But that's

just what I've been told. I was married to my career, so I'm not really a go-to person when it comes to relationship advice."

"What about you, Paula?" Beth asked. "You and Hannah have been living together for the same amount of time as Lindsey and Sully. Is she getting on your nerves, too?"

Paula glanced at Lindsey. She cringed and shook her head. "Sorry. But maybe I'm getting on her nerves. I'll check and get back to you."

Lindsey laughed. "Thanks, but I wouldn't want to stir up any trouble. Probably, my reading until two in the morning gets on his nerves, but Sully's too polite to say anything."

"He is very nice," Nancy said.

"And he's a man," Violet said. "They have different expectations."

The two women exchanged another glance, and Lindsey turned to Beth, who shrugged. She and Aidan Barker had gotten married just a few weeks ago, and she'd been walking on clouds ever since. In other words, she was useless.

"All right, people, I have the craft supplies set up. Where is Ms. Cole? Isn't she in charge of food today?" Paula asked.

"The lemon—er—Ms. Cole was in the staff lounge last I saw," Beth said. Ms. Cole was the newest member of their crafternoon group. During the first two years that Lindsey had worked at the library, Ms. Cole had been full of disapproval, and her puckered disposition had caused Beth to dub her "the lemon."

But they'd been through some dire times at the library, and Ms. Cole had softened toward her fellow librarians and had actually asked to join their book club and invited them to call her Ginny. The new name didn't take, however, and she remained Ms. Cole to them—and occasionally, when she was being particularly rigid, she was still the lemon. But there was affection there now, too, which made all the difference.

"She was loading up a cart full of food," Beth continued. "I really hope she made her charlotte russe to go with the book. I love that ladyfinger, raspberry-gelatiny goodness that she made for the last holiday staff party."

"Should we start on our craft then?" Paula asked.

Beth popped up from her seat first, and the ladies made their way to the craft table.

"Are we late? I tried so hard to get here on time, but babies have their own schedules." Mary Murphy, Sully's younger sister, hurried into the room with a baby in a sling across her chest and a padded bag the size of a small car strapped to her back.

As if she knew she was the topic of the conversation, the wee person strapped to Mary's front shoved a tiny fist into the air and then let out a not-so-delicate wail.

"Josie's here!" Nancy clapped her hands in delight.

Simultaneously, she and Violet rushed forward as if they were in a race to see who could get their hands on the baby first. Given that Violet was the taller of the two women and her stride longer, she beat Nancy by a grabby hand.

Mary plopped the baby into Violet's arms and dropped

the bag onto the floor. She then collapsed onto the couch, looking like she didn't intend to move for the rest of the hour.

Both Beth and Paula moved forward to get in line for their turn with the baby. Lindsey did not. She loved little Josie Murphy—after all, she was Sully's niece and hands down the cutest baby Lindsey had ever seen—but Lindsey was not really a baby person. She didn't have any younger siblings, just her older brother, Jack, and had never babysat while she was growing up. While a clean, sleeping baby was an adorable thing to gaze upon, when they got messy or wailed, she found them somewhat terrifying.

She backed up to allow the others access to the baby. Little Josie did not seem to mind being passed around like a hot dish at the dinner table, but still, Lindsey knew what was coming. Someone was going to try to hand her the baby, and Josie, knowing full well that Lindsey should never be entrusted with such a delicate being, would begin to wail, desperate to be rescued. And Lindsey could not blame her one little bit.

She turned away from the group and studied the scene out the window as if she were tracking an incoming storm from the bay. Short of running out of the room, this was her best defense against having the baby passed to her. Just the thought of holding the infant made her hands start to sweat, which convinced her that she'd drop the baby and she'd smash like an egg. No, Lindsey figured she'd wait on the holding thing until Josie was walking or talking or, even better, driving.

Big white fluffy clouds filled the sky. Lindsey scanned them for any distinctive shapes. She saw one that resembled a dragon, but she'd noticed that big cumulus clouds always looked like dragons. The early afternoon sunlight danced on the water in the bay. She gazed at the pier. Sully's tour boat was out, taking visitors around the Thumb Islands, an archipelago of over a hundred islands of all sizes that filled this small coin pocket of Long Island Sound.

She saw Dennis Greaves and Sam Holloway, two of Briar Creek's retired residents, across the street in the town park that was on a narrow patch of land between the town beach and the main road. They were sitting at their usual picnic table, enjoying a game of checkers as they did every day around lunchtime.

Lindsey knew Dennis was a big Tom Clancy reader, while Sam came into the library only if he was looking for car-repair manuals. He was always fixing up vintage cars, and the library had manuals going back into the nineteen-twenties. The only reason Lindsey hadn't thrown them out was because Sam used them every now and again.

Across from Sam and Dennis, Theresa Huston, the local tennis coach, was power walking through the park in her bright turquoise running suit. She was one of Lindsey's favorite patrons, as they shared a love of poetry, particularly Emily Dickinson. Lindsey waved, but she doubted Theresa could see her.

A pack of five bicyclists pedaled down Main Street, interrupting Lindsey's view of the park, and her gaze shifted to a group of women down on the small town beach. They were having a picnic with their toddlers, who were racing up and down the sand, kicking inflatable balls almost as big as they were. Adorable. She recognized most of them from Beth's story times and wondered whether they'd just enjoyed her portrayal of the Pigeon.

Seeing all of the activity, Lindsey felt her sleepiness lift. Spring was here and summer was coming. The sound of tree frogs would fill the nights, and the days would get longer. It was hard to sustain a grumpy mood in the face of such happy activity.

She started to turn back to the room when she caught a movement out of the corner of her eye. A car was speeding down Main Street, going way too fast for the pedestrian-friendly area. Lindsey glanced back at the park and saw Theresa step into the crosswalk, where pedestrians clearly had the right-of-way. Lindsey's heart thudded in her chest. She had the sick feeling that the car wasn't going to stop.

She glanced to the right, thinking surely the driver would see Theresa and slow down, but he didn't. Instead of hitting the brakes, the driver sped up. Horror flooded Lindsey as she realized Theresa was going to get hit. She cried out and slapped her hands against the glass window as if she could push Theresa to safety just by willing it. She couldn't.

With a sickening, bone-crunching thud, Theresa was struck by the car. Lindsey watched as she collapsed back onto the sidewalk and the car took off.

Dennis Greaves and Sam Holloway abandoned their

checkers game and raced across the grass as fast as their geriatric bones could carry them. The women on the beach gathered their children and stared wide-eyed at the park above them.

Lindsey spun away from the window and ran from the room, yelling, "Call nine-one-one. Theresa Huston was just hit by a car."

CHAPTER
2

BRIAR CREEK
PUBLIC LIBRARY

Lindsey dashed down the hallway. She was forced to take small steps since she was in her pencil skirt and heels, which was just as well, as she had to swerve around two patrons in a tug-of-war over the latest Stephen King novel and a mom pushing a stroller with twin babies. Then she was out the main door and running down the sidewalk with Beth on her heels.

When they reached the street, they stopped to check both ways, and Beth, gasping for breath, asked, "What happened?"

No cars were coming. Lindsey cut across the road, not bothering to use the crosswalk.

"It was a hit-and-run," Lindsey said. "Theresa stepped into the road, and a car came out of nowhere and hit her and then sped off."

"Oh my God!" cried Beth.

Together, they reached Theresa. She was lying on her side, curled up into a ball and rocking ever so slightly back and forth. She was gasping and panting, and high-pitched moans were coming from her throat. Dennis and Sam were kneeling beside her, looking as if they were afraid to touch her but wanted to comfort her.

"Theresa, we've called an ambulance. What can I do for you?" Lindsey crouched down beside the woman.

"My leg," Theresa cried. "Oh, my leg. It hurts. It hurts so bad. I think I'm going to be sick."

A sheen of sweat had beaded up on her skin, which was a sickly shade of gray.

"I think she's going into shock," Dennis said. "I saw this when a buddy of mine had his arm blown off in Vietnam."

"Her leg is definitely broken," Sam said. "Look at the weird angle of it."

Lindsey glanced at Theresa's shin and felt her stomach lurch. It was bent forward. Shins weren't supposed to go that way. She felt her own stomach roil and knew the pain Theresa was feeling had to be excruciating.

"I think I'm passing out," Theresa said. Her eyes rolled back into her head, and her entire body relaxed.

"Oh, crap!" cried Beth. She hunkered down beside Lindsey. "Is it okay if she passes out? What if she also hit her head? There could be a traumatic brain injury happening, and passing out would be a definite no-no."

"You're supposed to raise a person's feet when they pass out," Sam said.

They all glanced at Theresa's leg. Lindsey shook her head. No one was willing to touch it and risk causing more damage or hurting her.

"She's breathing," Dennis said. He moved closer so he could see the rise and fall of her chest. "I say we let her be, but maybe you should talk to her—you know, reassure her."

"It's going to be okay, Theresa," Lindsey said. She brushed back a hank of thick dark hair from Theresa's forehead. "We're here, and we won't leave you until help arrives."

Theresa blinked twice, and Lindsey took that to mean she could hear her. A shudder rippled through Theresa's body, and her teeth were chattering.

"Here, she might be cold from the drop in her blood pressure." Sam unbuttoned his wool cardigan and handed it to Lindsey to drape over the injured woman.

The sound of a siren was just audible, and Beth said, "I'll flag them down."

She jumped up and stood on the side of the road, shoving the hood off her head so she looked less like a pigeon and more like a person. She bounced up and down and waved her arms. The ambulance driver homed in on her and pulled over. In seconds, two EMTs, a male and a female, were out of the vehicle and tending to Theresa and her leg.

Lindsey stepped back to give them room. She stood with the others as they watched the man and woman go to work checking Theresa's vitals and preparing her to be lifted onto the stretcher.

"What happened?" the woman asked. She glanced up at the group while she opened her medical kit. Her name tag read *Annie*.

"Hit-and-run," Lindsey said. The words fell like stones falling from her mouth. A hit-and-run, here in Briar Creek in the middle of the day. It seemed so unthinkable. So unlikely. She glanced up at the sky. The same fluffy white clouds she'd been admiring before were rolling by, but suddenly they felt ominous instead of pretty. She shivered.

"Ma'am, can you hear me?" the male EMT said to Theresa. "I'm going to have to move you just a bit."

Theresa whimpered, and Lindsey turned her head away. She couldn't bear to watch. She noticed the others did as well.

"Keep everyone back!" The order was barked from the sidewalk, and Lindsey saw Emma Plewicki, the chief of police, directing one of her men, Officer Kirkland, to keep people away from the area.

It was then that she noticed a crowd had gathered across the street. This was not surprising, given that everyone in the small town kept track of everyone else. This community closeness had seen them through hurricanes, blizzards, summer tourists, and property-tax hikes.

"Lindsey, what happened?" Emma demanded as she joined them.

"Theresa Huston was struck by a car when she stepped off the curb to cross the street," Lindsey said. "It appears her leg is broken."

"And the driver?" Emma asked.

"Sped off," she said.

Emma's lips compressed to a hard, thin line. Emma Plewicki was a good-looking woman with a heart-shaped face, a head of thick, glossy black hair, and a curvy figure that distracted from the raw muscle beneath the swerves. And most of the time she wore a wide, warm smile that greeted the residents of Briar Creek even while she mediated their difficulties. That smile was gone right now and in its place was a look of cold fury. Emma took crime in her town personally.

"Can you describe the car?" Emma asked. She pushed her narrow-brimmed police hat back on her head and surveyed the scene, taking in the tire marks on the road and the bent iron fencing that encircled the park. Officer Kirkland was standing on the far side of the road, keeping the gawkers over there while asking questions and canvassing the crowd for any information.

"It was a sedan, four doors, white," Lindsey said. She glanced at the others. "Right?"

Dennis nodded but Sam shook his head.

"It was a two-door," Sam said.

"No, it wasn't," Dennis argued.

"Oh, what do you know?" Sam asked. "You were about to lose to me at checkers."

"I was not! I was about to triple jump you for a king."

"Puh."

The two men looked like they were about to square off for a shoving match. Lindsey eased her way in between them and sent Beth a desperate look. She gave Lindsey a slight nod to let her know her message had been received and slid in between the two men as well, creating a nice two person buffer.

"I only saw the back of the car. It was definitely white," she said. "Honestly, I just followed Lindsey when she ran out of the building. I wasn't even sure what was happening."

"We're about ready to roll out," Annie, the medic, said to Emma.

They loaded Theresa onto a stretcher. Her right leg had been braced, and she was strapped down. Annie held up Sam's sweater, and he took it from her with a nod.

"That was quick thinking," she said.

Sam shrugged like it was no big deal, but Lindsey could tell he was pleased to have been able to help.

"I'm going to follow them," Emma said. "Lindsey, can you give me a quick rundown of what you saw?"

"There's not much to tell. It happened pretty fast. Theresa was walking through the park. She stepped into the road to cross the street, when out of nowhere this car appeared, and before she could get out of the way, it sped up and hit her."

Emma frowned. "You're certain it sped up when Theresa stepped into the crosswalk?"

"Positive," Lindsey said. "I was standing in the back room of the library, looking out the window, and I had just turned away when I saw the car out of the corner of my eye. That's what made me look. While I was watching, I heard the engine rev as the driver sped up."

"I saw it, too," Dennis said. "I even said to Sam, 'What's that fool doing?'"

"He did," Sam agreed. He pushed back his baseball cap and scratched his head. "Is Ms. Huston going to be all right?"

"I don't think we'll know for sure until she's had some X-rays," Emma said. "Back to the vehicle—was there anything distinctive you remember about it? Dents, mismatched tires, broken windows, bumper stickers, anything?"

Lindsey shook her head. The others did the same.

"Did anyone get a look at the driver?" Emma asked.

Lindsey glanced at Sam and Dennis. They'd been closer than she had, but they were elderly and she had no idea how good their eyesight was. Plus, like her, they had probably focused on Theresa and not the car.

"Sorry. I didn't get a good look," Sam said.

"Me neither," Dennis said. "Hell of a thing to have happen."

"We're taking her into New Haven," the male EMT said to Chief Plewicki. He looked as if he was about to say more and then thought better of it. Instead, he helped lift the stretcher into the back of the ambulance and shut the doors.

Lindsey suspected he'd been about to tell them how badly her leg had been broken. He didn't need to. She doubted she'd get the visual of that weirdly bent leg out of her mind for a long time to come.

"I'm right behind you," Chief Plewicki said.

She turned and strode toward her squad car.

"Theresa! Oh my God, Theresa!"

They all turned toward the street to see Liza Milstein

pushing through the crowd with two students about the same age running beside her. She was a petite young woman in her early twenties with light brown hair that she wore in a ball on top of her head. She was clutching a stack of textbooks in her arms, and her backpack was unzipped and hanging off one shoulder as if she'd been interrupted in the middle of her studies and hadn't bothered to put her books away. A set of headphones dangled around her neck, but she seemed oblivious to all of it as she ran toward them, looking frightened.

Meredith Lane and Zach Stoliwicz were right behind her. Lindsey had come to know all three of these college students, along with Toby Carter, who wasn't with them at the moment, as the four students had formed a study group that met in the Briar Creek Public Library two years ago when they began commuting to college in New Haven.

"Theresa—is Theresa Huston in there?" She waved her hand at the ambulance. Liza was panting for breath, and Zach grabbed her backpack before it fell to the ground.

"Maybe," Emma said. She paused beside the distraught young woman. "Are you family?"

"No, maybe, sort of. Is she all right? What happened?" cried Liza.

Emma gave her a hard stare. "Unless you're family, I'm not at liberty to—"

"She's my tennis coach, and she's engaged to my father. That makes me soon-to-be family. You have to let me see her!"

"She has a right to know," Meredith said. She supported her friend by putting an arm around her shoulders.

Emma hesitated. Larry Milstein, Liza's father, was well known in town, as he owned one of the largest furniture franchises in the country and was always good for a donation whenever the town was having a fund-raiser for new school equipment or a new cruiser for the police department. Emma nodded at the driver, and he opened the doors.

"Liza." Theresa lifted her head with a wince. She glanced at the young woman standing by the open door. "I'm all right. Please don't worry your father. I'm fine."

"Worry him?" Liza said. "Look at you—he's going to go mental."

She didn't wait for an invitation but climbed into the ambulance. She turned around and took her backpack from Zach with a quick nod of thanks.

"You don't have to—" Theresa protested.

"Yes, I do. I won't leave you alone," Liza interrupted. She glanced at the driver and scowled. "Can't you see she's in pain? Let's go!"

Liza's command got everyone moving. The driver shut the door and hurried to the front of the vehicle.

"All right, I'm off. If any of you think of anything you feel is important, call me," Emma cried over her shoulder as she dashed to her squad car.

"Of course," Lindsey said.

They stood motionless as the ambulance flipped on its lights and sirens and sped out of town with Chief Plewicki right behind it. The silence that followed their departure felt heavy, as if a large hand were pressing down on the small seaside community, pushing out the air and making it hard to breathe.

"I have lived here all my life," Dennis said. "And I have never seen anything like that. A hit-and-run, can you believe it? Right here in the center of town in broad daylight."

"What is wrong with people?" Sam agreed. "He didn't slow down or stop or anything. He had to have seen her. He intentionally swerved into the bike lane to hit her."

"He?" Lindsey asked. "Did you see that it was a man?"

Sam frowned, then shook his head. "He had a hat on. I just assumed it was a man."

"Did either of you recognize the car?" She glanced between Sam and Dennis.

"It was a Chevy," Dennis said.

"No, it was a Honda," Sam argued.

"What sort of hat was he wearing?" Beth asked.

Lindsey gave her an approving nod. Good question.

"Baseball hat," Sam said. "A Mets hat."

"No, it was a Yankees hat," Dennis argued.

"Either way, you should tell Chief Plewicki that the driver was wearing a hat," Lindsey said. "That's the sort of detail she was looking for. Did you see anything else, anything at all?"

"No," they said together.

Lindsey glanced at Beth. She looked as discouraged as Lindsey felt. She supposed this was why eyewitnesses were frequently considered unreliable. Three of them had been watching, and they couldn't agree on the type of car or the type of hat the driver was wearing, none of it, and they had all seen the exact same thing.

"Hey!" Toby Carter, another student from the study group, jogged toward them. "Did I just see Liza climb into an ambulance? Is she okay?"

"She's all right," Meredith said. She turned to face Toby. "But Theresa, her dad's fiancée, was hit by a car. That's who was in the ambulance."

"Oh no." Toby frowned. "Is she going to be all right?"

Zach shrugged. "It looked pretty bad. We saw the crowd gathering from the library window, and Liza recognized Theresa's sweat suit and came running out here. Where were you? You know we were supposed to meet up to study, right?"

"Yeah, sorry, I spaced on the time," Toby said. He glanced away, taking in the calm water of the bay before turning back to his friends. "Did anyone see the driver? I mean, who would drive like that through the middle of town?"

"That's what I want to know. A crazy driver almost took me out in front of the Blue Anchor, and he was coming from this direction." Charlie Peyton, Nancy's nephew who worked for Sully part-time as a boat captain, strode toward them. His shoulder-length black hair hung over his face, and when he pushed it back out of his eyes, Lindsey noticed his fingers were shaking.

"You all right, Charlie?" she asked.

He put his hand on the back of his neck. "Yeah, I'm just a little shook up. I'd just finished my lunch at the

Anchor when I heard a car screech. I stepped out to see what was happening, and the guy almost hit me. I had to dive out of the way."

He gestured to his jeans, and Lindsey noticed one knee was torn and his Doc Martens were scuffed. He was sweating profusely for a day that was on the brisk side of cool, and his eyes were wide, as if he were stuck in a permanent state of surprise.

"White car?" Lindsey asked.

Charlie nodded.

"Theresa Huston was crossing the street and was hit by a car, a white car, just a little while ago," Beth said. "I'm sure it was the same one that almost hit you."

"Oh, that's awful!" one of the women from the beach said as she joined their small group. "We could hear the commotion but couldn't see anything. I was afraid to come up from the beach in case it was some sort of nut-job on the loose."

"What's worse is the driver took off," Sam said.

Dennis looked at Charlie. "You didn't recognize him, did you?"

Charlie shook his head. "No, but I'll remember his hooked nose and beady-eyed stare for the rest of my life. If I did know him, I'd have chased him down."

"Good thing you didn't then," Beth said. "Clearly, the person is disturbed. If they didn't stop when they hit one pedestrian, they weren't going to stop for a second."

Charlie was shockingly pale, and Lindsey could tell he was trying to shake off the adrenaline surge that had left him shaky. She gave him a bracing hug.

"I'm glad you're all right," she said. Charlie hugged her back hard, and Lindsey felt the breath get squeezed out of her lungs. As if realizing he was holding her too tight, Charlie quickly released her and stepped back. "Sorry."

"It's oka—" Lindsey was cut off by an imperious voice coming from the curb.

"Officer Kirkland, you will let me pass, or I will take down your badge number and file a formal complaint."

They turned as one to see Nancy Peyton nose to nose with Officer Kirkland, who was doing his best to cordon off the area with some plastic yellow crime scene tape.

"I'm sorry, ma'am, but I can't have people traipsing through—"

"That is my nephew," Nancy declared. "If you want to keep me from him, you'll have to arrest me."

They stared at each other for several seconds, and then Kirkland grunted. In the battle of wills, Nancy had forty years of sharply honed endurance on him. He didn't stand a chance.

"Fine, but walk around and not through the area where the victim was struck by the car." Officer Kirkland rolled his eyes toward the heavens as if seeking patience.

"Charlie, are you all right?" Nancy cried as she jogged around the crime scene perimeter and reached for her nephew. She wrapped him in a fierce hug, and then leaned back to study him. "You look like you were in a fight."

"I'm all right, Nanners," he said. He hugged her back, and Lindsey noticed he looked less shaky. "I'm in better shape than Theresa Huston, at any rate."

Another squad car arrived, and Kirkland ushered all the bystanders out of the area so that the police could investigate the scene. Lindsey glanced at the dented railing and wondered whether they would call the state police crime scene unit to come and collect paint scrapings or note any tire marks that might help identify the car that was involved.

Her curiosity made her want to linger, but Lindsey knew the most helpful thing she could do was to get out of the way. Besides, it was possible that someone in the library had seen something, and maybe she could get some information for Chief Plewicki.

"Let's head back to the library," she said to Beth. "We should tell the others what happened."

"Right," Beth said. "And maybe if we're lucky, one of our patrons saw something that will help the police out."

Lindsey glanced at her, and Beth shook her head. "Don't even pretend you weren't thinking the same thing."

"Oh, I was thinking it," Lindsey admitted. "I'm just surprised that you were."

"Clearly, I've been spending too much time with you," Beth said. "Being a buttinsky is contagious."

Lindsey laughed. She knew her need for information was usually her downfall. Over the past couple of years, she'd had several harrowing episodes, such as boat chases, being held at gunpoint, and being locked in a storage shed in the dead of winter. All of these things should have nipped her curiosity, but no. Instead, she took comfort in the fact that in each instance, the criminal had been caught because she hadn't been able to ignore pursuing the facts. She felt the same need for answers right now.

It was like an incurable disease. She desperately wanted to know who was driving that car. Why had they sped up when Theresa stepped into the road? Was it an accident or on purpose? Where had they gone? Were they drunk or uninsured? Had they just panicked? It didn't feel like it to Lindsey. From what she had seen, the car had appeared to be aiming for Theresa. Was Theresa the target, or was the driver out to hit anyone who got in their way? The questions spun through Lindsey's mind, ending with the most concerning of all: If Theresa was a target, would the driver come back and try it again? Lindsey knew the events of the day would plague her until she had some answers, and what better place to start asking questions than the library?

CHAPTER

3

BRIAR CREEK
PUBLIC LIBRARY

"Maybe they had pedal confusion—like, they stepped on the gas instead of the brake," Paula said. She was balancing her plate on her knee as she nibbled on Ms. Cole's herbed zucchini-ricotta flatbread.

"How do you figure?" Beth asked. "And even if they did, wouldn't they have figured it out in time to stop before they almost took out Charlie as well?"

"That's a solid point," Mary said. She clutched baby Josie close, and Lindsey knew she was thinking it could have been her crossing the street with the baby.

The thought made Lindsey's heart clutch in her chest. She glanced at her cell phone. It had been less than an hour since the incident, and they were all in the crafternoon room, eating while they discussed the hit-and-run. Both the book and the craft for the day were forgotten.

"I hope they catch the driver and throw the book at him," Ms. Cole said. "There is absolutely no excuse for such reckless behavior in the center of town. What if it had been after school? So many children come here to wait for their parents to pick them up. It could have been devastating."

It was one of the few times Lindsey could remember being in complete agreement with her cantankerous staff person. It was horrible that Theresa had been hit, certainly, but it could have been so much worse. Theresa could have been killed.

Given that the driver had almost taken out Charlie as well, Lindsey didn't think the driver had planned to hit Theresa. She was a popular tennis coach who had lived in Briar Creek for most of her life. There was no reason to think she'd be a target for malice.

In fact, Theresa was well regarded in town. She had recently gotten engaged to Larry Milstein, Liza's father, who owned a franchise of furniture stores up and down the East Coast. Larry had gobs of money, and he was more than happy to spend it on the petite tennis coach who had captured his heart. They were an outgoing couple in the community of Briar Creek, using Larry's wealth to fund loads of programs for schools and seniors and any other philanthropic venture that caught his eye. Considering their background, Lindsey couldn't think of anyone who had a grudge against Theresa or Larry, and neither could any of the crafternooners.

"Maybe the driver was drunk," Violet suggested. "Could be he was passing out at the wheel and had no idea that he hit Theresa and almost took out Charlie."

Everyone glanced at Nancy. Charlie had gone home
when they came back to the library. He was still a little
shook up, and Lindsey noticed as he walked away that
he stayed well away from the edge of the curb. She did
not blame him a bit.

"I'm with Ms. Cole," Nancy said. "I hope they catch
whoever did this and cut his license into tiny little bits.
Poor Theresa, how is she supposed to coach now? And
Charlie, what if—"

She stopped talking and lifted her spoon to her lips,
taking a big mouthful of the gazpacho Ms. Cole had
made for their meeting. Lindsey followed her lead. The
gazpacho was cold and smooth and perfectly seasoned.
She glanced at Ms. Cole and found her staring into her
own bowl, looking forlorn. Lindsey knew that Ms. Cole,
who had lived here most of her life, was likely struggling
with the events of the day.

Lindsey suspected Ms. Cole was thinking what they
all were. That if something as horrible as a hit-and-
run could happen in broad daylight in the center of
town . . . well, was the town they all knew and loved as
safe as they'd once thought? The past several years had
brought several murders to light, one of which had been
over twenty years old, but this sort of aggression in the
middle of the day made the small village lose even more
of its humanity. When a person wasn't even safe crossing
the street, things had changed and not for the better.

"This is excellent, Ms. Cole," Lindsey said. "Really
delicious."

"Thank you." Ms. Cole smoothed one hand over her

teal blue skirt. The compliment seemed to shake her out of her moroseness, which was what Lindsey had intended.

The lemon was known for dressing monochromatically, as if assured that if she wore all blue or green or red, all the pieces of her outfit would match. It made for some interesting wardrobe combinations, such as today's teal blue skirt and periwinkle blue blouse paired with navy blue pumps. It was one of the oddities that made Ms. Cole her own true self, like shushing and badgering patrons for their overdue materials. Still, she was here and she was participating. A year ago, Lindsey never would have believed it.

"Poor Larry," Mary said. "I can't imagine how he felt when he got the call from Liza that Theresa had been hit by a car."

"He suffered so much when his first wife passed away," Nancy said. "We belonged to the same bereavement group for a while."

"He's a widower?" Lindsey asked. "I didn't know that. I don't know why, but I assumed he was divorced."

"That's because of his television ads," Beth said. "They are so obnoxious. On an unconscious level, you probably assumed he was divorced because, really, who could live with a guy like that? He's handsome and all, but he's always yelling about low, lower, lowest prices on sofas, sleepers, recliners, blah, blah, blah. I lunge for the mute button every time one of his ads comes on."

"Don't think too harshly about him—he's a self-made man," Violet said. "I remember reading about him in the

New York Times. He grew up in the projects in the Bronx and worked his way up from furniture deliveryman to owner of the company with no education, just a lot of hustle. He's never had it easy."

"Besides, you can't be judging him when you married a man who dresses up like Thomas the Tank Engine for a living," Mary teased.

"That's different," Beth protested. "Aidan is a children's librarian like me. We pull out all the stops to get kids reading."

"Mary's just joking," Lindsey said. "Although, that one time when Aidan came into the library dressed as the Headless Horseman from *The Legend of Sleepy Hollow*, he scared the bologna out of me."

Beth laughed and nodded. "Headless is not his best look. And yet, still not as scary as when Milstein promoted his furniture store by dressing up as a hot dog and jogging around the bases at Fenway. I heard he paid a hundred thousand dollars to shoot that ad in the ballpark."

"Yeah, and then there's the one where he was posing with the beluga whales at the Mystic Aquarium," Paula said. "I swear it looked like the whale was swim-dancing while Milstein played his ukulele, which in all fairness was not as painful as it could have been."

"Oh, I love those whales," Beth said. "They always look like they're smiling."

"Don't forget the ad where he looks like he is parasailing in New York Harbor," Nancy said. "And still he was yelling about low, lower, lowest prices, and then the phony shark jumps up and swallows him."

"I thought it was pretty funny in a campy sort of way," Paula said. Nancy gave her a look. "Or not."

"You're right. His personality is larger than life," Lindsey said. She had never met Larry Milstein, but she knew the mayor of Briar Creek cleared his calendar whenever Larry called. "Milstein's is the biggest furniture retailer on the East Coast. It seems to me other people in the same business might not be as fond of him as we are. He might have made some enemies along the way."

She felt everyone turn to stare at her, even baby Josie, who puckered her mouth and made a smacking noise. She could feel the concern, the worry, the anxiety pouring off her friends in waves.

"I'm just theorizing," she said. "You know, acknowledging the possibility that if someone had a beef with him, they might have tried to hurt him by going after his fiancée."

"But you're not planning to start investigating something that was probably just a hideous traffic accident, right?" Nancy asked.

"Right, absolutely," Lindsey agreed. They were still staring. "So, what did you all think of *A Tree Grows in Brooklyn*? Did you like the protagonist, Francie Nolan?"

She took a big bite of her herbed ricotta bread and glanced around the room while she chewed. They all continued to stare.

"What?" Lindsey asked. "Do I have something in my teeth?"

Paula shook her head. "You are the worst liar ever.

You know you're not going to let the incident rest until you know for sure that it actually was an accident."

"Which Emma will determine by the end of the day, no doubt," Violet said. She gave Lindsey a stern look as if daring her to argue. Lindsey had no intention of doing so.

Beth glanced from Lindsey to the others and said, "I really enjoyed reading about Francie getting her education in the book. I felt like it sent such a positive message about the value of learning."

Now all the heads in the room swiveled toward her.

"I'm sorry. Are we not discussing the book?" she asked.

"Of course we are," Mary said. "On the off chance that the hit-and-run wasn't an accident, I don't think we need to remind Lindsey that my brother, Sully, would be devastated if anything happened to her, do we?"

Lindsey swallowed the mouthful of bread. It went down hard. "Have you been practicing the guilt-trip thing in anticipation of Josie, or does it just come naturally when you become a mom, like a superpower when you've been zapped by lightning?"

"Pretty sure it just comes," Mary said. "How'd I do? Did it work?"

"Yes," Lindsey said. "I promise I will stay away from the whole rotten mess with the car and Theresa and let the police figure it out."

She noticed half of the room gave her side-eye, while the other half seemed to believe her. Fine. Whatever. She wasn't going to get involved. Really, she wasn't. It's not like the car or the driver had anything to do with her or the library. She was just a concerned citizen. That was all. Really.

Three days after the accident, and there was still no news about the car or who had been driving it. Larry Milstein had been seen in the police station, yelling in his auctioneer's voice about wanting the driver responsible apprehended and locked up. Chief Plewicki had done her best to calm him down, but there was no appeasing him. In an uncharacteristically aggressive move, he threatened to have her job if she didn't arrest someone and soon.

The small town of Briar Creek was agog, with everyone taking sides in the Plewicki versus Milstein debate. Lindsey heard most of the details because Officer Kirkland bought his morning coffee at the bakery at the same time Lindsey did. He was rabid in his defense of his boss, and Lindsey understood that, but she also grasped the fact that Larry Milstein's temper was mostly coming from a place of fear. People behaved badly when they were afraid.

Lindsey was sitting at the reference desk giving Ann Marie, her adult-services library assistant, a break, when Liza Milstein entered the building. The last time Lindsey had seen Liza, she had been climbing into the ambulance to ride to the hospital with her soon-to-be stepmother, so Lindsey was surprised to see her in the library, especially since it was not the usual day for her study group.

"Liza, how are you? How's Theresa?" Lindsey gestured for Liza to take the seat beside her desk.

Liza tucked a hank of light brown hair behind her right ear. She clutched her book bag in front of her and sat down. She was wearing an oversize hooded white sweatshirt, skinny jeans, and white Converse high-tops. Lindsey wasn't sure whether it was the same outfit as a few days ago or whether all of Liza's clothes looked like this. Either way, she'd probably had a rough couple of days, so Lindsey wanted to put her at ease in any way she could.

"I'm fine, Ms. Norris," Liza said. "And Theresa will be fine, eventually. I really just stopped by to thank you for taking care of her. She said you were very comforting right after she was hit."

"Wow, she was in so much pain, I'm surprised she can remember anything about that," Lindsey said. "Does she remember anything from right before she was struck by the car?"

"No." Liza shook her head. "She said she didn't even hear the car coming. She was thinking about some wedding-related detail, her flowers, I think, and the next thing she knew, she was clipped by the car and sent up into the air to land with a crunch. She says she only remembers the crunch. She doesn't remember the car or the driver or anything else."

"Maybe that's a mercy," Lindsey said. "Otherwise she might have nightmares. Although it probably doesn't help the police very much."

"No, Chief Plewicki was pretty disappointed when she talked to her, although she tried to hide it behind an all-that-matters-is-that-you're-okay attitude," Liza said. "I could tell she was struggling."

"Yeah, an eyewitness who actually saw the driver would be a big help," Lindsey said. "Charlie Peyton tried to describe him to a sketch artist, but when he was asked specifics about the driver, he couldn't recall the face well enough to describe him. How's your dad doing?"

"Is that code for 'Has he calmed down any'?" Liza asked.

Lindsey nodded.

"No, not even a little. Theresa is his whole world."

Lindsey considered Liza's words. From what the crafternooners had said, she knew it had been only Liza and her dad since her mother had passed. She wondered how Liza felt about her dad getting married.

"Is that weird for you to have your dad getting married?" she asked.

Liza shrugged. Not being versed in the nuances of twenty-year-old mannerisms, Lindsey wasn't sure whether this meant she didn't care, she did care, or she wasn't sure.

"More weird to have him marrying my tennis coach," she said. "Theresa has been coaching me for six years. She was always there for me, you know, when he was traveling and I needed someone to talk to about school or boys. I thought she was my friend. I didn't realize— never mind."

"Realize what?" Lindsey asked. "It's okay, you can talk to me. We have librarian-patron privilege."

Liza laughed as Lindsey had hoped she would.

"It's dumb, but I guess there's a part of me that

wonders if Theresa was my friend at all—like, maybe she was always kind to me just to get close to my dad."

There was a vulnerability in Liza's eyes that made Lindsey choose her next words carefully. She didn't want to dismiss what Liza was feeling, but she knew Theresa wasn't the sort of person who would manipulate a young woman to get close to her father.

"That doesn't seem like the Theresa I know," Lindsey said.

Liza ducked her head and gave a quick nod. "You're right. And I'd never ever want anything bad to happen to her."

"Of course you wouldn't," Lindsey said. "Don't worry. I'm sure Chief Plewicki will have a lead soon. She's the best."

"Sure," Liza said. She looked doubtful, but then changed the subject and said, "I also stopped by because I was wondering if you could help me pick out some audiobooks for Theresa. She said you two like the same sort of things, and she's too tired to read or watch television."

"I'd be happy to," Lindsey said. "I imagine she'll be stuck in bed for a bit."

"She's in a cast for at least two weeks and then a boot if she's lucky," Liza said. "It's all so crazy. They're supposed to get married in three weeks, and I thought they'd postpone it so Theresa could have the wedding of her dreams, you know, without a cast, but nope."

"They're going ahead with the wedding?"

"Yes, but they've scaled it back so that it's just a small family gathering," Liza said. "They planned a trip around the world, just the two of them, for their honeymoon, and neither one of them wants to give it up."

"I can understand that," Lindsey said. "What an adventure."

"I think they're crazy," Liza said. "What's the big deal with waiting until Theresa is well again? It's so typical of my father. He gets something in his head, and that's it. He's like a big terrier—a lovable terrier, but still a terrier. I hope Theresa goes through with marrying him after all of this. He tried to move her into our house, but she was having none of it. She wants to be in her own home with all of her things, which makes total sense. You know, when you're sick, you want to be home."

Lindsey realized she hadn't been sick in a while, but if she was, she'd be in her new home with Sully. She wondered how that would go, since she was the sort of person who liked to be left alone when she was ill. Like totally alone, in a cave, out in the wilderness somewhere. She realized she'd never seen Sully sick. Oh, he'd been in the hospital over a year ago, when they'd gotten into a boat crash, but she'd never had to be with him twenty-four seven when he was ailing. Her last partner had been horribly needy when he was sick. Sully couldn't be like that, could he? No, he didn't seem the type.

"What do you think?" Liza asked.

"Huh? I'm sorry." Lindsey forced herself back to the conversation. "My mind wandered there. What did you ask me?"

Liza held up an audiobook of the latest Ingrid Thoft title in her Fina Ludlow series.

Lindsey nodded. "A kick-butt Boston PI mystery? That will definitely take Theresa's mind off her troubles."

Together they gathered several more audiobooks, and Lindsey grabbed a volume of poetry by Rudy Francisco called *Helium* that she thought Theresa would enjoy. As she followed Liza to the self-checkout machine they had recently installed, Lindsey was filled with a sense of purpose: connecting people to words, whether listened to or read or watched. Nothing made her feel as if she was contributing to the betterment of the planet more than introducing a reader to an author's work. As always, she was convinced she had the best job in the world.

She glanced at the stack of materials Liza was checking out. "Maybe we should have gotten Theresa some travel books."

"Travel books?" Beth joined the conversation. "Where is she going?"

"Honeymoon trip around the world," Liza said with an eye roll.

"Oh, honeymoons are the best," Beth gushed.

Now Lindsey had to clamp her eyeballs into place to keep them from rolling. Beth was her very best friend in the whole wide world, and she loved her like a sister, truly, but if she had to hear about—

"Paris, tell me they are going to Paris," Beth said.

"Oh, hey, is that the phone in my office ringing?" Lindsey craned her head. "I'd better get that. Liza, please let Theresa know we're thinking about her, and if she needs anything, more books or whatever, be sure to let us know."

"I will," Liza said.

"I just got back from my honeymoon in Europe," Beth continued as Lindsey backed away. Slowly, slowly, she was almost out of there.

Lindsey took another step back and bumped into the person standing behind her. With a small yelp and an apology at the ready, she whipped around to find Emma Plewicki standing there.

"You can't outrun the stories from her honeymoon. I don't know why you're even trying." Emma shook her head as if she couldn't believe Lindsey had attempted to ghost out of the conversation.

"Ugh, Beth's post-wedding honeymoon phase is going to end someday, isn't it?" Lindsey asked.

They both glanced at Beth, who had gotten to the Eiffel Tower portion of her story. "And then he got down on one knee and proposed . . ."

Lindsey and Emma mouthed the words *to me all over again* to each other.

They exchanged grins.

"She will get over it someday," Emma said. "Probably when she gets pregnant, and then it will be all about baby names and decorating the nursery and all that junk."

"Junk?" Lindsey said.

Emma shrugged, and Lindsey had the feeling that Emma was a kindred spirit in the no-desire-for-a-baby club.

"That sounds really romantic," Liza said. She glanced past Beth at Lindsey with a *please help me* sort of look that Lindsey knew she'd had on her face when hearing Beth's wedding stories for the umpteenth time.

"We should save her," she said to Emma.

"Agreed, but first I have some news." Emma straightened her shoulders, looking more official than she had a moment ago.

"Is Theresa all right?" Lindsey asked. She felt her stomach drop in preparation for the worst.

"As far as I know, she's fine," Emma said. She blinked. "Unless you know something I don't?"

"No, I just panicked," Lindsey said. "Sorry. What's up?"

"We think we have a lead on the car," Emma said. "And I wanted to see if you could look at a video clip and verify that it's the same one you saw."

"The car that hit Theresa?"

"Were we looking for a different one?"

Lindsey gave her an exasperated look.

"Sorry," Emma said. "Lack of sleep, I'm grumpy."

"Forgiven." Lindsey dismissed Emma's mood with a wave of her hand. "It was a dumb question. When no one recognized it, I figured the driver was from out of town and we'd never see them again."

"So did I," Emma said. "But luckily the Blue Anchor has a security camera that monitors the outside of the restaurant even when they're open. I had Ian bring up the video from when Charlie was almost hit. We didn't get a license plate, but we did verify that it almost hit Charlie."

Emma took her phone out of her pocket and opened a

video. She handed it to Lindsey and said, "If you can tell me if that's the car you saw, that would be a huge help."

Lindsey squinted at the video on the phone. It was tiny, but she recognized the front door of the Anchor. She watched a man exit the restaurant. At least, she assumed it was a man, judging by his build and the work clothes he was wearing: boots, jeans, a flannel shirt, and a beanie on his head. He looked like Ray Michel, a local fisherman known for being able to drink six pints and six shots, and still be able to recite the entire Greek alphabet in order and in reverse. In the video, he was checking over his shoulder while he wandered over to the edge of the pier. Judging by his pose, it took Lindsey only a second to figure out what he was doing.

"Oh, gross," she said. She shoved the phone at Emma. "I did not need to see Ray Michel peeing off the side of the pier."

Emma cringed and grabbed the phone. "Sorry, sorry, I forgot to queue it up to the pertinent part. I haven't erased the part with Ray, because he and I need to have a chat about indecent exposure. Honestly, just because these guys urinate off their fishing boats, they think anyplace with water near it is a go."

Lindsey waited while Emma looked for the segment of the video that had the car. She glanced at Liza and noted that the young woman looked half asleep as she listened to Beth's description of the best tapas to be had on the Spanish Riviera. Once Beth reached this point, Lindsey knew that she was in the homestretch of her honeymoon stories.

"Here." Emma dragged her finger across the screen and handed it to Lindsey.

Lindsey squinted at the screen. There was no sign of Ray. Now it showed Charlie Peyton leaving the Blue Anchor. The video was low quality and grainy, and even if the date and time were not in the corner of the frame, verifying that it was about the same time Theresa had been hit, Lindsey would have recognized Charlie from the distinctive bop in his walk. A musician at heart, he always moved as if he were listening to a tune no one else could hear.

A few seconds into the video, she watched Charlie whip his head to the left. He visibly jumped, and then a white car appeared on the screen, charging right for Charlie. He threw himself backward, got tangled up in the railing around the restaurant's front door, and landed hard on the ground on his knee. The car lurched back toward the street, denting the railing and missing Charlie by one of the long, straggly hairs on his head. When the screen went dark, Lindsey exhaled. She hadn't realized she was holding her breath until that moment, and she felt a bit light-headed.

"Charlie is lucky he wasn't killed," she said. She cringed. "I didn't realize it was so close. Please don't show this to Nancy. She might stroke out."

Emma nodded. "I know *I* almost did. Do you recognize the car?"

"Yes, that's definitely the car," Lindsey said. "A white, four-door sedan, and the time of the tape verifies that it would have been right down the street at the time Theresa was hit."

Emma nodded. "Thanks, that's what I was hoping you'd say."

"How will you find it now?"

"Actually, we may have a lead on it already," Emma said. "The morning of the incident, we had a report of a stolen car. A white, four-door sedan, in fact."

"That would be a heck of a coincidence," Lindsey said.

"Wouldn't it?" Emma asked. "I don't believe in coincidences. I think whoever hit Theresa Huston stole Kayla Manning's car to do it."

A gasp brought their attention around. Liza Milstein clapped her hand over her mouth as if she could force the gasp back.

"Sorry, I didn't mean to eavesdrop," she said. She dropped her hand. "That's a lie. I was totally trying to hear your conversation."

Beth frowned. "And here I thought you were riveted by my honeymoon stories."

"Sorry, but I was sure Chief Plewicki had some information about the hit-and-run, and you do, don't you?"

"It may not mean anything," Emma said. "But yes, there is a possibility that the car used in the hit-and-run was stolen from Kayla Manning. What can you tell me about your father's relationship to Kayla?"

"I'm not sure I know what you mean," Liza said. She turned away and began stuffing the audiobooks into the tote bag she'd brought with her.

"I know that they dated," Emma said.

"That was ages ago," Liza said.

"It was just before your father met Theresa," Emma said.

Liza gave her a nervous glance but said nothing. Lindsey watched her closely. She couldn't tell whether Liza was rattled because of what Emma was asking or because she actually knew something about Kayla.

"Liza, if you have information that might be important to the case, you need to share it with me," Emma said. Her voice was calm, but Lindsey could tell by the way she rocked up and down on her toes that she was fighting for patience.

"You really should talk to Kayla or my father about it, don't you think?" Liza asked.

"Oh, I intend to," Emma said. "But I'd like to hear what you thought of their relationship, especially after the breakup."

Liza huffed out a breath and hung her head. It was the posture of a person who knew they were defeated.

"It's okay," Lindsey encouraged her. "It's important to share everything you know."

"I know nothing, really," Liza said. "It's just that the breakup was pretty bad, mostly because Kayla was on a date with my dad when he found out Theresa was newly single and pretty much ended things with Kayla right then and there so he could make his move."

"I thought Larry and Theresa met at a garden party," Lindsey said.

"They've known each other for years through me, but Theresa was dating someone," Liza said. "Little did I know, my dad had a thing for her. The garden party was

a picnic with a jazz trio out at the Levinskis' house. I
didn't want Theresa to be alone since she was there without a date, so I asked my father to keep an eye on her.
Well, Dad took one look at her and called an Uber for
Kayla and sent her home. Kayla said it was like he
couldn't get rid of her fast enough."

"Ouch," Emma said.

"I told him he handled it badly, but he was so happy
to have a shot with Theresa that he simply did not care,"
Liza said.

"How did Kayla handle it?"

Liza looked pained. "Not well. I mean, she didn't boil
my pet bunny or anything, but she was very hurt and
angry since everyone soon found out exactly what Dad
had done."

"Did she ever threaten your father or Theresa?"

Liza slung the bag onto her shoulder, looking like she
was desperate to escape.

"Not that I know of, but you'd have to ask them. It was
epically awkward," Liza said. "When Theresa found out
about Kayla, she was so upset with Dad. She tried to talk
to Kayla, but Kayla refused to listen. Then my dad was
mad at Kayla for being rude, and they had a tiff. Really,
the whole thing was just so ridiculously messy and embarrassing and overly dramatic. I mean, these people are
old, and they were acting like teenagers."

Old? Lindsey was pretty sure that Theresa was only a
few years older than she was. She glanced at Emma, who
was also frowning.

"How did it get resolved?" Emma asked.

"Dad apologized, then he produced a huge rock, and Theresa forgave him, and, well, that has to sit pretty badly with Kayla, doesn't it?"

Lindsey glanced at Emma. It was clear that Liza viewed the whole thing with the mortified eyes of an unseasoned adult. She was still close enough to her teen years to think of grown-ups as being too old for relationship drama, and if they did have any, well, it was just embarrassing. Lindsey was sure it was beyond Liza's comprehension to imagine the hit-and-run might be part of the romantic fallout between her dad and Kayla.

A quick glance at Emma, however, and Lindsey realized that was exactly what she was thinking. Could Kayla Manning have reported her car stolen and then used it to try to run down Theresa Huston?

Lindsey didn't know Kayla Manning very well. She wasn't a library user, not that Lindsey held that against her, so while Lindsey had talked to her at happy hour at the Anchor several times, she'd never really gotten to know her as a friend or neighbor. That didn't mean she hadn't heard the locals talk about her, especially after a public breakup with her boyfriend Jason Portland a couple of years ago.

After a tiff over who was picking up the check for their dinner date, Kayla had announced to the entire restaurant Jason's disappointing lack of stamina in the sack before she turned on one very narrow heel and stalked out of the restaurant, leaving Jason to pick up the shattered pieces of his manliness, which lay in shreds on the floor along with the check.

Lindsey's impression of Kayla had been of an intense woman who was dedicated to maintaining her departing youth and fading good looks in any way she could. It was well known in town that Kayla was in her midforties but by all accounts was leaving claw marks on her late twenties.

She had a knockout figure, which she maintained by kayaking in the bay and competing in Ironman competitions. Her blond hair was plumped with extensions, her tan was the sort that came out of a can, and the figure she was so proud of was enhanced by surgical steel and saline combined with rigorous hours spent on the treadmill.

An executive for a bank in nearby New Haven, Kayla was aggressively looking for a partner with the same workaholic-playaholic tendencies she had. The trouble was that Kayla had very high standards, and she kicked any man who didn't meet them to the curb, like Jason.

From what Liza had said, Larry had ditched Kayla before she ditched him. That had to chafe Kayla's ego, not to mention the fact that Larry was very wealthy, which was number one on Kayla's list of criteria. But would it bother her enough for her to run down her competition in her car? If it was her, did she report the car stolen before she hit Theresa or after? If it was before, it was clearly premeditated, but if it was after, she'd obviously been trying to distance herself from the accident. So many questions.

Lindsey glanced at Emma. She was putting away her phone and her face gave nothing away, but Lindsey would have bet all the library fines on record that her next move was going to be a visit with Kayla Manning.

Emma's shoulder radio beeped. *"Chief Plewicki, what's your twenty?"*

Lindsey recognized Officer Kirkland's voice. He sounded highly stressed. She supposed she shouldn't listen to police business, but Emma's radio was so loud she didn't really feel it was her fault.

Emma unhooked her radio and spoke into it. "I'm at the library. Over."

"We have a ten-twenty-seven happening at 1220 Cedar Street," Officer Kirkland said. The sound of a police siren came out of the radio, and Lindsey realized Kirkland was talking while driving.

"What's a ten-twenty-seven?" Liza demanded.

"I'm on my way," Emma said. "I'll meet you there. Over."

"What's a ten-twenty-seven?" Liza asked again. This time her voice was higher, almost shrill.

"It's a burglary," Emma said. "Excuse me, I have to go."

"Wait!" Liza cried. She dropped the tote bag and reached out as if to grab Emma. She thought better of it at the last second. "That's Theresa's address. Are you saying someone called in a burglary from her house?"

Emma blinked. Then her face became stern, and she said, "Do not go over there! I mean it. Let my team handle this. We'll report in as soon as we can."

She grabbed her radio and began issuing commands to her officers as she ran from the building.

Liza waited three seconds, and then she was right behind Emma. Her fallen tote bag was forgotten as she raced
from the building. Beth looked at Lindsey in alarm. "We
have to stop her. She could get shot and killed if she
charges in there when the police are responding to a call."

"You're right," Lindsey said. "I'll see if I can stop her
or at the very least stall her."

Lindsey dashed out of the library. The sky was dark
with thick gray clouds that appeared to be looking for the
perfect location to squeeze out their heavy load of mois-
ture. A brisk wind was whipping in from the bay, and it
tossed Lindsey's long blond curls across her face. She
dragged them back, fastening her hair into a loose knot
as she hurried around the side of the building to the parking lot.

She looked for Liza's white sweatshirt, but she didn't
see it anywhere. A car lurched toward her. It was a Jeep,
the sort used to go off-roading, with a snap-on cloth top
and big wheels. Lindsey peered through the windshield
and saw Liza. She raised her arms and waved her down.
Thankfully, Liza stopped.

"You can't go over there," Lindsey said. "The police
might mistake you for the burglar, and you could get shot."

"How can I not go?" Liza said. "Theresa is the closest
thing to a mother I've had since my mother died. I'll
never forgive myself if something happens to her and I
wasn't there to try and help."

Lindsey understood. She really did. If she were in
Liza's position, she would feel the exact same way, and
she was pretty sure she'd be halfway to wherever she

felt she was needed by now. Unlike Liza, she probably wouldn't have stopped if someone had flagged her down.

Lindsey reached for the door handle and opened the passenger door just as a fat raindrop plopped onto her head. The wind picked up, and the weather the sky had been promising suddenly arrived with a blast of cold air and a deluge of rain.

"All right," Lindsey said. "I understand how you're feeling, but I don't think you should go alone."

"Oh, thank goodness," Liza said. "I was actually hoping I could talk you into going with me. I'm nervous, but I want to be there for Theresa."

Lindsey climbed up into the Jeep and fastened her seat belt. "All right then, let's go."

Liza hit the gas, and Lindsey instinctively reached for the handle built into the door. They wheeled around the corner, and Lindsey was sure they'd gotten up on two wheels. Her stomach lurched, but she didn't cry out or even whimper, and she considered this a small miracle of self-control. She understood that Liza was probably freaking out. If Lindsey remained calm, maybe she could get Liza to be easy, too.

"Listen, we're not going to be much good to Theresa if we get into an accident," Lindsey said. "Do me a favor and take a deep breath and try to relax."

"But—"

"Deep breath."

Liza gave her an impatient side-eye, but she took in a deep, steadying breath and then let it out slowly.

"Do it again, but hold it a bit longer and let it out even slower," Lindsey said. Liza did as she was told.

Lindsey took the moment to study her. Liza was cute in an upturned-nose, long-eyelashes, fresh-faced sort of way. She was twenty going on twelve, as in very young looking, and had a slight, petite build, which only enhanced her youthful appearance.

From the talks they'd had before, Lindsey had learned that even though she was a college student and well on her way to being independent, Liza still lived at home. Lindsey wasn't sure whether it was by choice, as in she liked being at home, or whether it was more that her father wasn't ready for her to leave yet.

Larry Milstein had a personality that was pugnacious but also friendly and exuberant. Lindsey didn't know him well, but she got the feeling he was the sort who always started out by believing the best in everyone and then adjusted his expectations accordingly. Of course, that was likely why his ads were so over the top. His zest for life knew no bounds.

Liza huffed out another breath, and Lindsey asked, "Better?"

"A little," she said. "I just can't help thinking about Theresa stuck in her house in her cast while a stranger breaks in. She's powerless. How is that not terrifying?"

"It is, but I bet the police are already there. Emma won't let anything happen to her."

This time a sob bubbled up from Liza's chest. "I just don't want her to be frightened. She's been so good to me. I can't stand the thought of anything bad happening to her."

"Of course." Lindsey reached across the console and squeezed Liza's hand. "She'll be okay. You'll see."

Liza gave her a small smile as if she believed Lindsey was right. Lindsey returned the smile, hoping she hadn't just told the biggest whopper ever.

Theresa lived in a modest two-story house with a gray wooden-shingle exterior that looked weathered from years of oceanic mood swings. Flowerpots lined the small porch, and they were bursting with early-season petunias with bright pink, purple, and white blossoms. The trim was painted a pretty shade of country blue, and the yard was neat and tidy, with a bird bath and a couple of Adirondack chairs placed for an optimal view of the bay and the Thumb Islands.

Two police cars were parked in front of the house, and Lindsey felt her pulse kick up at the sight of them. There was no sign of Theresa or Chief Plewicki, but she recognized Officer Kirkland's fiery red hair poking out from under the hood of his raincoat. He was standing by the front door with his radio in hand, clearly awaiting instructions.

Liza parked on the street in front of one of the cruisers, and they both turned to study the house through the rain, which was still falling in earnest.

"Do we go up to the house?" Liza asked.

"I don't think that's a good idea," Lindsey said. "The police are here, and they won't want any civilians getting in the way."

"But how do we know what's going on?" Liza asked. "I mean, what if Theresa needs me?"

"I know it's hard," Lindsey said. She sympathized, she really did, but she also knew that they could compromise the situation if they went charging in there.

"I'm calling my dad," Liza said. She glanced at Lindsey as if expecting her to argue, but Lindsey didn't.

"Good idea," she said. "He'll want to know what's happening."

Liza took her phone out of her purse and thumbed open the contact info for her father. She then held the phone up to her ear. Lindsey wasn't trying to listen, but Larry Milstein had a booming voice, and it roared right out of his daughter's phone, filling the small, humid car with its deep rumble.

"Liza, honey, what can I do for you?"

"Hi, Dad," Liza said. She twisted her finger in the handle of her purse. "I have some news."

"Perfect score on your chemistry exam?"

"No, Dad, it's not school. It's Theresa," she said. Her voice had a tremble in it, and Lindsey could have sworn she heard Larry Milstein sit up straighter over the phone.

"Theresa? Is she all right? Are you with her?"

"I'm at her house, because when I was in the library, Chief Plewicki came in, and while we were talking, she got a call on her radio that there was a burglary in progress at Theresa's address," Liza said. "I'm sorry, Dad. I'm so sorry."

A glance at Liza's face, and Lindsey could tell she was close to tears.

HITTING THE BOOKS   59

"A burglary? What the hell? Do not go near the house, baby," Larry barked. "I'm on my way."

"Okay," Liza said.

The call ended, and Liza looked at Lindsey. "I'm going in."

"What? No, you just said—"

"Of course I did." Liza rubbed her fist across her eyes. "I didn't want to worry him. He's getting up there in years. He could have a heart attack or something."

Lindsey was betting that Larry wasn't even fifty yet. She tried not to take the ageism personally, but it was a challenge. Luckily, she didn't have time. Liza was already jumping out of the Jeep and running for the door.

"Damn it." Lindsey looked at the rain, turned up the collar on her shirt, and dashed after Liza.

Officer Kirkland was standing on the porch. He saw them and began to wave his arms, as if signaling that a bridge was out. Liza plowed ahead, not stopping until she was beside him under the porch roof. Lindsey hurriedly tucked herself in beside her.

"You aren't supposed to be here!" Kirkland frowned. He'd been with the force for a couple of years, and Lindsey noted that his frown had become much more formidable.

"How could I not be here?" Liza argued. "Theresa is about to become my stepmother. I'll be wrecked if anything happens to her."

"It's not safe—" Kirkland began to argue. His radio beeped, and Chief Plewicki's voice crackled over his.

"Ten-fifty-two, Kirkland," she ordered. "And then get up here."

"Roger that," Kirkland replied. He glared at Lindsey and Liza. "Don't move."

He banged inside the house, and they heard him using his radio to call dispatch to send for an ambulance. Liza waited a few seconds before she hurried in after him.

"Liza, don't—"

The door slammed shut in her face, leaving Lindsey talking to the storm glass. With a sigh, she pulled it open, knowing that she was in for a tongue lashing from Emma—if she was lucky, that would be all, but it would likely leave the tips of her ears blistered.

Theresa Huston's home was done in shades of cobalt blue and white. It was cheerful, with lots of leafy houseplants, books, and comfortable furniture that looked as if it were waving Lindsey in for a long sit with a book, a pot of tea, and her dog, Heathcliff, at her feet. From what Lindsey knew of Theresa, it was exactly what she'd have expected of the former tennis pro's abode.

She passed through the front room, noting the doorway that led to a kitchen, a dining room, and a huge back deck that offered a superb view of the ocean, which with the current weather was choppy with white caps and the occasional spray that jetted up from the large rocks on the beach.

Lindsey heard the sound of footsteps upstairs walking over her head and figured everyone was up there. She glanced around the downstairs to see if anything had been disturbed, but it all looked to be in order. If this was a burglary, the perpetrator had neglected to grab anything off the wall full of tennis trophies, the laptop sitting on the coffee table, the large flat-screen TV, or the handful of valuable-looking knickknacks that filled the room.

She crossed to the staircase. She'd put her foot on the first step when she heard a resounding *boom*. Thunder? Had the rain turned into a thunderstorm? She leaned over the banister to glance out the window toward the ocean. No lightning. Instead, she saw a person dressed all in black jump up from their crouched position on the deck and begin to run. Lindsey hurried down the hallway. Was that the boom? Had the person jumped onto the deck from above?

She ran through the kitchen, hoping to get a look at them. The rain obscured her view, and the figure remained blurry in the storm. She reached out to open the back door to try to get a description, but a voice behind her made her freeze in her tracks.

"Don't even think it!"

Lindsey turned around, and there was Emma. She was running for the door, and Lindsey jumped out of her way. Emma yanked the door open and ran outside, in hot pursuit of the person who had just fled the house.

The interior door banged open behind Emma, and a gust of wind brought in a torrent of rain. Lindsey had to put her shoulder into it to close it. She glanced through the window, hoping to spot Emma, but the chief had disappeared behind the high grass that separated the house from the beach.

Lindsey tried not to worry. Emma was the best cop she knew. She was tough but fair and as fit as any person in town, running double marathons just for the fun of it. Who did that by choice? Also, she had a gun on her, and she knew how to use it. Lindsey closed her eyes for moment, hoping with all she had that Emma wouldn't need to use it.

She heard footsteps from above and doubled back to the stairs to see whether she could help. She had just turned the corner when she saw Officer Kirkland coming down the steps, carrying Theresa Huston. The pretty brunette was blotchy faced and sniffing as if trying to hold back her tears. She was also pasty, and her lips were pressed into a thin line, as if she was trying to keep from crying out. No matter how gently Officer Kirkland carried her, the hip-to-toe cast was massive and unwieldy, and moving had to hurt Theresa terribly. Liza was right behind them, carrying a pair of crutches.

"Theresa!" cried Lindsey. "Are you all right?"

Theresa nodded. Then she shook her head, and a sob burbled up out of her mouth. "A man broke into my house and tried to suffocate me with a pillow."

Lindsey gasped. This was so much more than a burglary. She glanced at Liza, whose eyes were huge. She looked like she was on the verge of tears, and her hands were shaking as she tucked her hair behind her ears. She looked at Theresa with worry in her eyes and then shook her head as if she just couldn't understand how anyone could do such a thing.

"How did you manage to call the police?" Lindsey asked.

"I didn't," Theresa said. "Larry had a security system installed on the house yesterday. He was worried about me being here alone during the daytime. If a window or door is opened, it sends an alert to my watch with a video feed of the area for verification. When I looked at the alert, I saw the man. I saw him come through the back door. All I had to do was tap my watch, and the police were called."

Theresa's breathing was quick, as if she was reliving the terror she must have felt when the man came into her house.

"I wanted to hide, but I was so panicked I couldn't get off the bed without making noise, not in this thing." She tapped her cast with her knuckles and then winced. "I don't know what I was thinking. I couldn't make it to the closet or hide under the bed. I was just sitting there like a big target with an enormous bull's-eye on me."

She pushed her long dark hair off her face and blew out a breath. She was clearly trying to pull it together. Lindsey was impressed with her inner resolve. Comparatively, Lindsey didn't think she'd bounce back so fast from a possible suffocation. Her skin prickled at the thought of being stuck in a cast in bed with a bad guy skulking around her house, intending to do harm. Terrifying.

"Where do you want me to set you down?" Kirkland asked.

"The couch will be fine," Theresa said. Her voice was thin, as if she was on the last reserves of her energy.

Kirkland carefully navigated all the furniture in the front room and set Theresa down on her brown leather sofa.

"It's a good thing Dad had that system put in," Liza said. "I mean, that probably saved you, right?"

"Yes, I'm sure it did."

Theresa shuddered, and Liza sat on the arm of the couch behind her and awkwardly patted her shoulder. Theresa reached around and hugged Liza. The young woman stiffened and then hugged Theresa back before pulling away and moving to a nearby chair.

Officer Kirkland stepped back and glanced toward the kitchen. Lindsey was betting he knew that Emma had run after the suspect and he was dying to go out there, too.

"We need you here," she said. "In case there is more than one of them or if he loses Emma and comes back."

Kirkland glanced at her and nodded. He then looked back at Theresa. "If it's all right, I'd like to ask you a few questions so you don't forget anything that happened."

Theresa gave him a droll look. "I'm pretty sure I'll never forget. Not for the rest of my life."

"I understand. Still, can you tell me what happened after you alerted the alarm company to call the police?" he asked.

"I tried to get up," she said. "So stupid. I dropped my crutches on the floor, and they made a horrible thud. I'm sure he heard it, because within minutes I heard him coming up the stairs. I suspect he checked the house to make sure I was alone before he attacked me."

A single tear dripped down Theresa's cheek. She brushed it away impatiently, as if irritated with herself for the show of emotion. Liza grabbed a tissue from a nearby box and handed it to her, then she sat back down on the arm of the couch beside Theresa and crossed her arms around her middle as if she could keep the horror out.

"Even without my crutches, I tried to get out of the

bed. I thought I could roll onto the floor and then hide under the bed. I had just scooted to the edge when he burst into my room."

Lindsey hadn't thought it possible, but Theresa went even paler. She put her hand to her throat as if to reassure herself that she was still there, still breathing, still alive.

"Do you remember what he looked like? Could you describe him?" Kirkland asked.

Theresa shook her head. "He seemed large and very muscled, probably because he was standing and I was lying down. I remember he had a black hooded sweatshirt on, and it was tied tight around his face. I couldn't see his eyes, because he had aviator sunglasses on. That was all I saw before he snatched a pillow and pressed it down over my face. At first I tried to flail and fight him, but I couldn't get any leverage with the cast, and my leg hurt so much, I practically passed out with the pain."

This time there was no stopping the sobs that erupted from Theresa's slender frame. Liza slid off the arm and moved to sit facing Theresa. She hugged her and let Theresa cry all over her shoulder. She glanced up at Lindsey and Kirkland, and her expression was fierce.

"We need to catch whoever did this," she said. "Before they strike again."

A door slammed at the back of the house. They all jumped. Theresa let out a startled cry while Officer Kirkland's hand went to his holster. He stepped forward in front of them, using his own body as a shield.

It was unnecessary since the gust of wind that blew into the house when the door opened pushed Emma into the room as it blasted them with a rainy-day temperature drop. Emma was soaked through, and her black hair hung in limp strands over her face. She sneezed, and the sound, so normal in all the chaos, made them all come back to themselves.

"Bless you," Liza said.

"Thanks," Emma replied.

"Liza, go grab a couple of towels for the chief," Theresa said. Her voice was high and tight, as if she was forcing herself to try to sound normal and it was a strain. "She's drenched and shivering and will catch a cold if we don't get her dry and warm."

"No, it's all right. I'm fine," Emma protested.

Theresa wasn't having it. She looked at Liza and said, "Go, please."

"But I want to hear what happened. Why can't Ms. Norris go?" Liza balked.

Theresa frowned at her. She didn't say a word. She didn't have to, as her disapproval was clear.

"Fine," Liza said. She dashed up the stairs to get the towels.

Her feet pounded up the steps, and Emma listened until she heard the door of the linen cupboard being opened before she spoke.

"Theresa, it's clear that you're in danger. I don't want you to stay here alone anymore," Emma said. "It's not safe."

"I don't think—"

"I know you don't want to believe it, but you were the victim of a hit-and-run, and now someone has broken into your house and tried to suffocate you. There is no way these are random incidents. Someone wants you dead."

Theresa glanced at the stairs. It was obvious she didn't want Liza to overhear the conversation.

"But that makes no sense," Theresa said. "I'm nothing, a nobody, a retired tennis pro who coaches now—that's it. Who could possibly have a grudge against me that would warrant killing me?"

"You're not nothing or a nobody. Perhaps your athletic career is over, but you're about to marry one of the richest men on the East Coast," Emma pointed out. "And we all know that at least one person is really unhappy about it."

"Kayla Manning," Theresa said. She didn't sound surprised that Emma had mentioned her. "No, I refuse to believe it. I mean, I know she was upset when Larry and I got together, but it doesn't make sense. What would she gain by harming me? It's not like Larry would go back to her."

"Murdering you—the words you're looking for are *murdering* and *you*, and there's no telling what Kayla is thinking, which is assuming she's the one who's behind this," Emma said. "It could be someone else, someone who is obsessed with you, maybe an old fan or a former boyfriend. Heck, it could even be a neighbor who doesn't like the way you put out your trash."

Theresa looked like she was about to protest, but Liza hurried into the room and handed Emma two big fluffy blue towels.

"Thank you," Emma said. She wrapped one around her shoulders and used the other to dry her hair.

"What happened to the suspect?" Officer Kirkland asked. "Did you get a good look at him?"

Emma's dark brown eyes flashed, her frustration as palpable as the puddle of water slowly forming around her shoes.

"No, he got away," she said. "Somehow he managed to jump from the upper deck to the lower without breaking anything, and then he took off into the marsh. I thought I had him, I really did, but between my utility belt, the weather, and the sand underfoot, I just couldn't get ahead of him."

Despite being the chief of police, Emma wore a uniform and a duty belt just like her officers. Briar Creek was small enough that at times she was the only officer on duty and as such needed to have all her equipment. Lindsey knew for a fact that the belt that had all her gear strapped to it weighed a solid twenty pounds when fully loaded. It'd be like trying to run with twenty hardcover books strapped to her middle. Ugh.

"It's all right, Chief," Officer Kirkland said. "We'll get him."

"You had better. If anything happens to my fiancée because of your incompetence, so help me, I'll have your jobs," a deep voice boomed from the entrance to the house.

As one, they all turned toward the door. Standing in a pricey bespoke suit, with his hair flattened to his head by the rain, was Larry Milstein. His cheeks were ruddy, but Lindsey wasn't sure whether it was from the cold or his temper.

She recognized him from his commercials, and he was as good looking in person as he was on television, with his square jaw, full lips, long nose, and bright blue eyes. He retained his all-American handsomeness even though his brown hair was fading to gray and he had the crinkles in the corners of his eyes that were common on people well into their forties.

"Liza, we're going to need more towels," Theresa said. She didn't seem phased by Larry's hulking presence at all; if anything, his bluster seemed to calm her. "Larry, I'm fine. Chief Plewicki and Officer Kirkland saved my life. I think you owe them a thank-you before you threaten their jobs."

"She's right, Dad," Liza said. "If not for them, well—"

She ran toward her father and stopped to hug him quickly before darting back up the stairs to get more towels.

Larry ran a hand over his face, wiping away the rain, then he came forward and kissed Theresa on the head, as if afraid that if he touched any other part of her, she might break. There was a tenderness in his gesture that surprised Lindsey.

"I'm sorry," Larry said. "I'm just upset. I got here as fast as I could. When Liza called, I about had a heart attack. The thought of you in your cast and someone in the house with you, trying to rob you, and you unable to defend yourself. I think I just aged five years."

Theresa smiled and pulled him down for a hug, disregarding his wet clothes. "It's all right, honey. I'm fine. Perfectly safe."

Larry studied her for a moment as if trying to see past the calm facade to what emotions were beneath the serene smile. Theresa met his gaze and didn't look away. Reassured, he turned to Emma and Kirkland.

"I'm sorry about before. I was an ass," he said. "It's just, this whole thing—"

"It's crazy," Liza finished for her father as she bounced back into the room and handed him two towels as well. His were pink.

"Thanks, Lizzie," he said. He looped one arm around her shoulders and hugged her into his side before he let her go. "And you're right. It is crazy. Why are these things happening? I mean, who could possibly want to harm Theresa?"

"That's what we're trying to figure out," Emma said. She glanced at Liza as if worried about frightening her but then pressed on. "As I was telling Theresa right before you arrived, these were not random events. Between the hit-and- run and the break-in, it is clear that someone has targeted her."

Everyone was silent for a beat as they absorbed the seriousness of Emma's words.

"I just don't understand why," Theresa said. She swallowed and it was audible.

"It doesn't matter. It stops right here, right now," Larry said. "We will find out who is doing this, and we will have them arrested. I just found you. No one has ever made me as happy as you do, and I am not going to lose you. Not now. Not ever."

The intensity of his gaze was so intimate, Lindsey

felt the need to look away. As she did, she saw Liza watching them with a tender look on her face. She wondered how old Liza was when she lost her mother. Given that Theresa had been her tennis coach for years and was now her father's fiancée, she might be the closest thing Liza could remember to a mom. This had to be terrifying for her.

"Oh, Larry, don't you worry," Theresa said. "I am not about to leave you. I love you. You and Liza are my family now, and it's going to take a helluva lot more than a bad driver and a lunatic with a pillow to take me away from you."

"I'm glad you feel that way," he said. "Because you are moving in with Liza and me today, this very minute, in fact, and I won't hear any more arguments about it."

"No, you won't," Theresa said. "I realized when that man held the pillow over my face and I couldn't fight him off—"

"My God!" cried Larry. He staggered a bit. "I thought it was just a break-in! He tried to suffocate you?" He looked at Chief Plewicki, and she gave a small nod. Larry's face became ashen.

"He did and he came close, way too close," Theresa said. "In that moment, I realized I don't want to be alone again. Not until I can defend myself."

Lindsey knew it must be hard for the lifelong athlete to admit that she was afraid. When Theresa's gaze rested on her for a moment, Lindsey gave her an encouraging nod.

"I think that's an excellent idea, Theresa," Emma said.

"I'll feel much better if you have people with you at all times, at least until we catch this guy."

"Did you see him?" Larry asked Theresa. "Did you recognize him? Do you have any idea who he is?"

"No," Theresa said. "I didn't get a good look at him. It all happened too fast."

"But the alarm system worked, and the police arrived in time," Larry said. He took Theresa's hand in his, as if to reassure himself of her presence. "Maybe this will have scared him off for good."

"That would be great," Emma said. "But to be on the safe side, Mr. Milstein, I think we need to assume the worst and operate with the utmost caution."

"What is the worst?" he asked.

Lindsey watched Emma's face grow hard. This was the same expression she used whenever she had to deliver really bad news at the weekly department head staff meeting held in the mayor's office.

"That someone is out to murder your future bride," Emma said. "And they're not going to stop until they get the job done."

Lindsey caught a ride back to the library with Officer Kirkland. The rain hadn't stopped, and when she tried to dash into the library, she had to duck through the steady stream that was pouring over the gutters on the roof of the old stone captain's house that had been remodeled into the local library. Despite her best efforts, she was soaked when she arrived back in the building.

"Didn't catch her in the parking lot, then?" Beth asked. She was standing behind the circulation desk next to Ms. Cole.

"No, I actually made a split-second decision and went with her to Theresa's house," Lindsey said.

Ms. Cole grabbed a fistful of paper towels from under the desk and handed them to Lindsey without saying a word, not even her usual critical remark. Lindsey assumed she must look even worse than she thought.

"Is Theresa all right?" Beth asked.

"Yes," Lindsey said. She didn't mention that the intruder had tried to smother Theresa. She suspected Emma would want to keep that information on a need-to-know basis. "Unfortunately, they didn't catch the person who broke in, but Larry is moving Theresa to his house as we speak, and I am quite sure she will be safe there."

"I would have thought she'd have gone there after she was hit," Beth said.

"I think she was trying not to be a burden," Lindsey said. "Especially before their wedding."

"Huh, if you ask me, she could do a lot better than Larry Milstein," Ms. Cole said. She looked a bit puckered when she said it, and Lindsey was oddly reassured to have the lemon back in fighting form.

Lindsey studied her for a moment. There was knowledge in Ms. Cole's eyes. She knew she shouldn't ask, but darn it, her curiosity wouldn't let it go. "Know something about Larry, do you? I noticed when everyone else was talking about him at our crafternoon the other day, you were awfully quiet."

"I was eating," Ms. Cole said.

"And?" Lindsey prompted her by waving her hand in a circular motion.

"Nothing. He's got some skeletons in his closet, and that's all I'll say about it," she said.

"What sort of skeletons?" Beth asked.

She was too late. Ms. Cole turned and headed into the workroom, cradling a stack of books in her arms, blatantly ignoring the question. Lindsey glanced at Beth as she dabbed her clothes with the wad of paper towels. They were rough industrial towels that felt as if they could alternate as sandpaper in a pinch, but she wasn't complaining, since she was beginning to shiver.

"Robbie's here. Go have some tea and warm up," Beth said. "I'll keep an eye on things out here and see if I can work my magic on Ms. Cole and get her to talk."

Lindsey grunted. If there was anyone who qualified as immovable as a mountain, it was the lemon, but she didn't want to be negative.

"Keep me posted," she said. "I'm going to go sit on the portable heater in my office until I dry out."

Beth nodded.

Lindsey crossed the workroom, which led to her office at the back. Before she reached her door it opened wide, and there stood Robbie Vine, famous British actor and current boyfriend of police chief Emma Plewicki.

"All right, pet?" he asked. Despite the alarm in his voice, his accent curled around Lindsey like a hug. She shrugged it off, knowing that she shouldn't tell him anything that had happened at Theresa's house.

"Not today, Robbie," she said. "I'm stressed and cranky."

"Not to mention leaving a trail of water behind you," he said. "What happened? Did you decide to go for a swim off the pier?"

"No." Lindsey glanced behind her, and sure enough,

there were water spots all along the faux-wooden floor. She sighed. She turned and went to get a mop out of the utility closet, but Robbie beat her to it.

"No, no, I've got this," he said. "I made tea. Why don't you sit and dry off and have a cup? I'll be back in a moment."

Lindsey knew she should argue, but she didn't have the energy. Instead, she let him grab the mop while she sank into her desk chair. She switched on her portable heater and reached for the teapot he had waiting for her on the corner of her desk. Being a celebrity, Robbie traveled quite a bit, but when he was in town, he and Lindsey usually had afternoon tea together. She wasn't sure when the habit had started, but it had never been more welcome than it was today. At least, the tea portion of it was welcome.

She lifted the pot and poured its contents into a delicate china cup. The dark aroma of the oolong tea with soft floral notes drifted up into the air on a curl of steam, relaxing her as she inhaled even before she had her first sip.

A plate of butter cookies sat beside the teapot, and she helped herself to a couple of them. The stress of the afternoon began to recede just as Robbie banged back into the room. He clapped his hands together and rubbed them briskly as if he was warming up for something.

"All right, let's get down to business, shall we?"

"Business?" Lindsey asked. She lowered her cup so that she could stare at him over the lip. "What business could we possibly have?"

"I was listening to my beloved's police scanner—"

"No," she said.

"What?" he asked. "A chap has to have a hobby."

"Listening to a police scanner isn't a hobby. It's you being a big busybody," she said.

"Kettle." Robbie pointed to himself and then to her. "Pot."

"I wasn't listening to a radio," she said. "I was here, trying to help out a patron of my library."

"By jumping in her car and racing to the scene of a burglary?" he asked.

He rolled his eyes and then reached for the teapot. After pouring himself a cup and doctoring it with sugar and milk, he reached for a butter cookie and dunked it into his tea.

"Liza was worried, and I didn't want her to go alone and walk into a situation she was unprepared for," Lindsey said. She sipped her tea, pretending that her reasoning was not as flimsy as it sounded. Robbie wasn't having it.

"Codswallop," he said. "You heard there was a burglary in progress, and you jumped at the chance to be on the scene. Now I suspect it wasn't a robbery at all. Do tell, what really happened out there?"

"I'm sure if Emma wants you to know, she'll tell you herself," Lindsey said.

Robbie ran a hand through his hair, leaving deep finger trails in the thick strawberry blond waves. "She won't. You know she won't."

Lindsey shrugged. She was not going to get in the

middle of Robbie and Emma. Her life was complicated enough without being the cause of any tension between the chief of police and her man.

"Fine, don't tell me anything," Robbie said. His light green eyes latched on to hers, and she could see the formation of an idea swirling in the depths. "Just say yes or no. That's all I ask."

"Like twenty questions?"

"Yeah," he said. "Was it a burglary?"

"This is dumb."

"Have a cookie and answer the question," he said.

Lindsey reached for another cookie and studied him. The thing was, Robbie was really smart about people and their motivations. He studied people tirelessly for his craft, so he picked up on things that most people missed. If someone was trying to kill Theresa as Emma suspected, maybe having Robbie be hypervigilant wasn't such a bad idea.

"No, it wasn't," she said. She bit into the cookie.

"I knew it!" cried Robbie. "It was entirely too coincidental. I mean, who gets hit by a car and then burglarized within a matter of days?"

"The unluckiest person in the world," Lindsey said.

"Which is hardly the case, since Theresa was a tennis star and is about to marry one of the wealthiest men in the country," Robbie said. "That's not what I would call bad luck, so it has to be that someone is out to harm her."

"I'd say they want to do more than harm her," Lindsey said. She cradled the delicate china cup in her hands, letting its warmth seep into her palms and move up her arms.

Robbie sat up straight. "You think they meant to kill her?"

Lindsey hesitated. She didn't want to cause a false alarm. She also didn't want to pretend alarm wasn't warranted when it could have been so easy for the person who broke into Theresa's house to snuff her out with the pillow, or the car that had hit her to have broken her entire body and not just her leg. She decided the situation warranted everyone to be on high alert.

"Yes, I do," Lindsey said. "I think someone is trying to kill her."

"But why?" Robbie asked.

Lindsey shrugged. "The only person that's been mentioned with a possible motive is Kayla Manning, since she was dumped by Larry for Theresa."

"'Heaven has no rage, like love to hatred turned,'" Robbie quoted.

"'Nor hell a fury, like a woman scorned,'" Lindsey finished the line. "*The Mourning Bride* by William Congreve."

"Well done." Robbie grinned. "Most people attribute that to the bard."

"It was published in sixteen ninety-seven," Lindsey said. "About a hundred years too late to be Shakespeare."

Robbie saluted her with his tea, and Lindsey smiled.

"So, what's our plan?" Robbie asked.

"Plan?"

"Yeah, you know, what are we going to do next?" he clarified.

"Um, nothing," she said.

"Nothing?" He looked outraged. "But you just said Theresa Huston was going to be murdered. How can we do nothing?"

"Because we aren't the police, you remember? You're dating the chief. She wears a badge and we don't."

"But Emma won't tell me anything," he said. "She won't let me do anything either."

"You're a civilian—of course she won't. What if you got killed? Besides, what exactly do you think you can do?" Lindsey asked. "Short of staking out the Milsteins' house to keep an eye on Theresa, I'm not sure there's anything we can do that the police aren't already doing."

Robbie smacked his forehead with his palm. "Of course we can do something. We can find out who wants her dead."

"Again, isn't that a task for the police?"

"Sure, but we have access to people that they don't," he said.

"How do you figure?" Lindsey took another cookie and bit it in half. Robbie did the same but paused to dunk his in his tea first.

"Quite simply, I'm a famous actor, and you're everyone's favorite librarian," he said. "If we ask questions, no one will give it a second thought."

"Except you're an actor and I'm a librarian, and why would we be asking questions about who would want Theresa Huston dead? That's just not something you can slide into a conversation as casually as inquiring about the weather."

"Having been the cover story of many a tabloid, trust

me when I tell you people love a good goss," Robbie said. "If we just chat them up, the information will come."

"Suppose that's true," she said. "Where do we start? We'd have to talk to Theresa first, and now that Larry has moved her to his house, it's not as if access to her is going to be easy. We'd need a reason to pop in, a reason that won't make your girlfriend want to arrest you for butting into an ongoing investigation."

Robbie opened his mouth and then closed it. Twice. He cast Lindsey a chagrined look and slumped back in his seat in defeat. She was right and he knew it.

A brisk knock sounded on Lindsey's door before it was pushed open and Ms. Cole strode in.

"What can I do for you, Ms. Cole?" Lindsey asked.

"When Liza Milstein ran out of here." Ms. Cole paused to make a disapproving face—running was never allowed in the library—before she continued. "She left the books she'd been checking out behind. I can either check them back in, or someone can deliver them to her house."

Robbie sat up again. "Ms. Cole, I could kiss you."

"Try it and it'll be your last," she said. She scowled at him and Robbie laughed, which made her blush.

"Thank you, Ms. Cole," Lindsey said. "Since these were for Theresa for use during her convalescence, I'll see that they are delivered to her myself."

Ms. Cole glanced between them. She lifted one eyebrow but didn't say a word. She backed out of the office, closing the door behind her.

"Yes!" Robbie said. He balled his hand into a fist and drew his arm down in front of him in a sign of triumph.

"Don't get so excited," Lindsey said. "You're not going."

"Of course I am," he said. "It's bucketing out there, and you don't own a car, so I'm your ride."

Lindsey looked past him and out the window. He was right—it was still raining. The heavy downpour that was going to make the grass green, the leaves on the trees unfurl, and the flowers bloom was also going to soak her through if she tried to ride her bike all the way to Larry Milstein's house.

When Lindsey had moved to Briar Creek a few years ago, she had decided to be more environmentally friendly and had given up her car. Other than borrowing Sully's pickup truck occasionally, she had only her handy Schwinn cruiser to get herself around. She could easily stuff Theresa's books into the saddlebag baskets in the back, but she didn't want to risk the materials being ruined in the rain, and she didn't think she could stand to be soaked through to the skin again.

She glanced at Robbie with a frown. "Fine, but you wait in the car."

He shot up from his seat as if he'd been launched.

She held up her hand in a *stop* motion. "And we're not leaving now, because I am still on duty. I get off work at five. I can't go before then."

Robbie sank back into his seat and picked up his tea with a sigh. "This civil servant stuff is for the birds."

* * *

Lindsey left the library a little after five with Robbie carrying the tote bag of materials Liza had left behind when she fled the building. It was a short drive to Larry Milstein's house, as he lived on the same street as Nancy Peyton, Lindsey's former landlord. Whereas Nancy had turned her three-story captain's house into three apartments, so she could live on the first floor and rent the two apartments above, Larry's house was still in its original form.

The wide shell-encrusted driveway led them to a huge house that stood on the very end of the cul-de-sac, with a large corner lot and an unparalleled view of the ocean and the Thumb Islands.

Robbie parked right in front of the house, and Lindsey noted that there were several cars in the driveway, none of which were police cars.

"Your girlfriend isn't here," she said.

"Bit of luck there, I'd say," he said.

The rain had finally eased to a light drizzle, but the early evening had a cloak of gloom about it. Everything felt damp and gray, as if the life had been wrung out of it. Lindsey shivered in her raincoat.

"I hope we're not intruding on their dinner," she said.

"We're not intruding," he said.

He climbed out of the car as he spoke, jogging around the front to get Lindsey's door for her. She would have gotten it herself, but she was holding the bag of audiobooks on her lap. Robbie took the bag from her and slung it over his shoulder.

"We're doing them a favor by dropping off the library materials. I'm sure they'll be glad we stopped by. You'll see."

Lindsey didn't share his optimism but followed him up the steps and across the wide front porch to the large double doors. Matching spring wreaths made up of silk daffodils and wrapped with bright green ribbon adorned each door. Robbie lifted his fist to knock, but the door opened before he connected, causing him to awkwardly drop his arm back to his side.

"What do you want?" A tall blond giant with the chiseled good looks of a male model glared down at them.

"Mr. Milstein?" Robbie asked. "Huh. Funny, you appear old—er . . . more mature in your television commercials."

"Stieg, is that you?" Lindsey nudged Robbie aside and squinted at the big Swede.

The man's face cracked into a wide grin, and he said, "Ms. Norris!" Then he swooped down and hugged her close, lifting her off her feet.

"Oh, now, just a moment," Robbie protested. "That's awfully familiar of you."

Lindsey hugged him in return and laughed when he put her back on her feet.

"It was a fifty-fifty shot," she said. "I'm glad I got it right."

"Actually, you didn't," he said. Behind him, his twin brother popped up and said, "He's Stefan. I'm Stieg."

Lindsey glanced between the Swedish Norrgard brothers. She didn't have the heart to tell them that with their long blond hair, handsome masculine features, and bright blue eyes, she didn't really care what their names were, and neither did any other woman with a pulse. Instead, she opened her arms and reached out to hug the real Stieg.

"Well, it's good to see you both," she said.

"Oy, that's enough with the hugging," Robbie said. "I take it you know these lads, Lindsey?"

She stepped back from Stieg and glanced at Robbie. "Yes, they're the Norrgard brothers. Don't you remember? They worked with the salvage company to find Captain Kidd's treasure on Pirate Island."

Robbie blinked. "I think that was before my time."

"Oh, well, let me introduce you. Robbie Vine, these are the Norrgard brothers, Stieg and Stefan," she said. She made sure she put the right twin with the right name.

Robbie shook their hands and looked expectantly at the young men. Neither of them recognized Robbie as the famous actor that he was. Lindsey had to bite her lip to keep from chuckling at the look of chagrin on his face.

"DI Gordon?" Robbie said.

"I thought she said your name was Robbie," Stieg said. He scratched his chin, clearly confused.

"It is," Robbie said. "I was referencing a role I played on television. You've heard of it. The light-up box in your living room with the people in it who talk to you?"

"He's snarky," Stefan said. "I like him."

The brothers exchanged grins.

"Stieg, Stefan." Lindsey brought their attention back to her, hoping to change the subject and keep Robbie from acting out any of his more famous movie roles. "We're here for a reason."

"Oh, sure, what can we do for you, Ms. Norris?" Stefan asked.

"I'm here to see Theresa," she said.

The twins glanced at each other. Stieg lifted one heavily muscled arm and put his hand on the back of his neck. His thermal shirt molded to each curve of his muscled abs, and his jeans sank lower onto his hips. Lindsey kept her gaze on his, refusing to treat him like a piece of man candy, even though, yeah, he totally was.

"Bloody show-off, that's what that is," Robbie muttered from behind her. "Any lad could look like that if he had nothing better to do than pump iron at a gym all day. Blimey, my grandfather could look like that if he felt like it and he's ninety."

"Hush," Lindsey shushed him.

"The thing is, we can't let anyone inside," Stefan said. His voice was full of regret, and his sympathetic gaze made Lindsey willing to forgive him anything.

"We're Ms. Huston's bodyguards," Stieg explained. "We're under strict orders from Mr. Milstein that no one gets through."

"If you're meaning through that thick skull of yours, I'd have to agree," Robbie continued muttering. He stepped up and turned to look at Lindsey. "Does Sully know about these two?"

"Stop."

"Wait, more importantly, does Emma know these two?"

"Chief Plewicki?" Stieg perked up. "Oh, sure, we go way back."

"Way back," Stefan repeated.

"What? How far back? And what does that even mean?" Robbie demanded. He looked ready to brawl. Lindsey could tell the situation was going to spiral swiftly out of control if she didn't step in.

"How about if you let Liza know we're here," Lindsey said. "These are materials she checked out from the library for Theresa, and she'd probably like to give them to her."

The twins exchanged a considering look and then nodded at the exact same time. It was like watching a person looking in the mirror. Eerie.

"Wait right here," Stieg said. Then he closed the door in their faces.

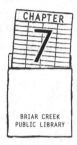

"Two great big lummoxes," Robbie muttered. "I hope they don't get lost on their way out of the foyer."

Lindsey turned to study him in the porch light. "What exactly are you jealous of? Their youth? Good looks? Bulging muscles? Or is it the fact that they have a history that predates your arrival in Briar Creek and that most of the women in town are at least half in love with them?"

"Check, check, and checkmate," he said.

"You are more shallow than that puddle," she said. She pointed to a tiny pool of water on the gravel driveway. "Honestly, you're not even that deep."

"I'm not shallow," he argued. "I'm vain, egocentric, and self-absorbed. There's a difference."

Lindsey shook her head.

The door was pulled open, but instead of the twins, it was Larry Milstein who appeared. He was looking much more composed than he had that afternoon. Lindsey imagined having Theresa safe in his house with the Norrgard brothers as bodyguards had calmed him down considerably. He peered at Robbie as if he couldn't believe it. Then he beamed.

"Robbie Vine, come in," he said. He reached out a hand to Robbie and all but yanked him into the house as if afraid he might get away. "A pleasure to meet you, truly. I'm Larry Milstein and I'm a huge fan. Super huge, in fact. This is amazing. Robbie Vine in my house!"

Robbie's chest puffed up as he shook Larry's hand in return. "No, no, the pleasure's all mine. Always happy to meet a fan."

Lindsey trudged through the door without either of the men acknowledging her. She closed it behind her and stood to the side, waiting for the bromance to subside.

"Say, you don't drink whiskey by any chance, do you?" Larry asked.

"Does a one-legged duck swim in a circle?"

Larry blinked and then barked a laugh. "Excellent, I was just about to pour myself a glass of twenty-five-year-old Macallan."

"And we're still standing here?" Robbie asked. "Lead the way, mate."

"Ahem." Lindsey cleared her throat. Both men ignored her. She reached up and yanked the bag of materials off Robbie's shoulder.

"Excuse me, Mr. Milstein, would it be all right if I popped in and visited with Theresa?" Lindsey asked.

At this, Larry spun around and studied her as if just noticing she was there. "You, how do I know you?"

"She's Lindsey Norris, the town librarian," Liza said as she joined them in the entryway. "She was there this afternoon, Dad. She was with me when I went to check on Theresa. We like her."

"Oh, right, absolutely," Larry said. "Sorry, I never forget a face, usually, but I was a bit undone this afternoon."

"It's fine," Lindsey said. She held up the tote bag. "Liza, you left the books you'd checked out for Theresa at the library. Robbie gave me a ride over so I could deliver them and check on the patient to see how she's doing."

"Oh, thank you. I forgot all about the books on CD." Liza took the bag. "Come on up and say hello. We've got her settled into the guest bedroom next to Dad's."

Larry looked like he was about to object, but Robbie clapped him on the shoulder. "How about that whiskey?"

"Yes, of course," Larry said. "Did I mention it was twenty-five-year-old Macallan?"

"You did," Robbie said. "Might I ask where you acquired such a find?"

Their voices trailed off as they disappeared into the study.

Liza rolled her eyes at Lindsey and led the way to a winding staircase on the opposite side of the foyer. "Dad and his whiskey, I swear it's an obsession."

She led the way up the stairs, and Lindsey tried for a

casual tone when she said, "I'm surprised Chief Plewicki isn't still here."

"She just left a half hour ago," Liza said. "She was headed over to Kayla Manning's to talk to her."

"Have they found her car yet?"

"No, but the one on the video was definitely hers—even my dad said so when Chief Plewicki showed him the clip," Liza said. "Too bad there wasn't a clear shot of the driver. I bet it was her."

"Really?" Lindsey asked. "I have a hard time picturing her doing a hit-and-run."

"People do crazy things for love," Liza said. She paused on the landing and waited for Lindsey to catch up. "Or in her case, they do crazy things for their love of money."

"Do you really think she wanted your father's fortune that much?"

"Yes," Liza said. "I didn't know her very well, as she and Dad only dated for a few months, but she was definitely driven, and I got the feeling she wouldn't put up with anyone standing in between her and her goals."

Given that Lindsey didn't know Kayla as well as Liza did, she couldn't argue the point.

"This way," Liza said. She led Lindsey down the wide hallway to a room at the end. She rapped her knuckles on the door, and when they heard a muffled greeting, she opened the door and entered.

The bedroom was enormous, with vaulted ceilings and plush area rugs tossed over the hardwood floor. A California king–size bed with a canopy commanded the largest portion of the room, but there was also a dressing screen in the corner, an entertainment armoire, and two large dressers. Floor-to-ceiling glass windows looked out over the bay, and a divan and two armchairs were arranged in front of the windows. Theresa reclined on the divan while Stefan stood by the window, scanning the backyard for any sign of a bad guy, no doubt.

"Lindsey, I heard you were here." Theresa smiled. She gave it her best effort, but it was wan, as if she just didn't have the reserves for her usual bright smile.

"I had to check on you," Lindsey said. "It was such a stressful afternoon, plus Liza left some materials for you at the library."

"The library director giving door-to-door service," Liza said as she put the bag down beside Theresa's chair. "You can't beat that, now can you?"

"No, I can't," Theresa agreed. "Stefan, you can take a break while Lindsey is here. She won't let anything happen to me. Liza, Stefan and his brother must be starving. Will you take them down to the kitchen and have Mrs. Armand heat up something for them?"

Stefan looked ready to argue, but Theresa shook her head.

"You may as well give in," Liza said. "Once Theresa starts nagging, she doesn't stop until she gets what she wants."

Lindsey glanced at Theresa, who gave Stefan a tight smile. "She's right."

"All right, since you put it that way," he said. He glanced at Theresa. "Shout if you need me. Better yet, use your radio."

"If she doesn't, I will," Lindsey said. They all looked at her, and she felt her face get warm. "For help—I would shout for help if we needed it."

Stefan grinned, appreciating her fit of the flusters. Lindsey felt her face get even hotter.

Liza laughed and walked to the door, gesturing for Stefan to follow. When the door shut behind them, Lindsey turned to Theresa and gave her a rueful look.

"Well, that was mortifying," she said.

"Please, we've all been there," Theresa said. "I don't know what Larry was thinking, hiring the two of them to watch over me. They cause most of the female staff in the house to be tongue-tied, even Mrs. Armand, the cook, and she hates everyone."

"I suspect he was thinking they both look strong enough to play catch with spare tires and bend steel beams with their bare hands," Lindsey said. "Anyone who comes after you is going to have to get through them. That ought to make you feel safe."

"I suppose," Theresa agreed. "It's certainly better than being home alone."

"Even though Liza seems to be a bit prickly?" Lindsey asked.

"You noticed," Theresa said. She gestured for Lindsey to sit in the chair beside the divan. Lindsey sat on the edge of the seat and patted Theresa's knee.

"She never struck me as being moody before. Do you think it's a bad reaction to everything that's happened?"

"I wish it was, but no, she's been like this since Larry

and I got engaged," Theresa said. "I think because she and I had a relationship—a friendship—around tennis, and obviously she is close to her father, so when her father and I got together, she felt left out. I can't blame her, but I really hoped that in time, she would adjust."

"She will," Lindsey said. "You're right—she likely just needs time to figure out the new dynamic. So, how are you feeling? Really?"

Theresa visibly swallowed, and her eyes grew damp. "I'm fine."

Lindsey nodded. The standard answer for a woman who was trying to be brave or not pissed off. Fine.

"Save the canned answer for the menfolk," Lindsey said. "Fine is never really fine. You can tell me how you really feel."

"No, I can't, because if I do, I'll cry," Theresa said.

"That's okay. Maybe you need a good cry."

"Maybe." Theresa covered her face with her hands. "As long as I live, I don't think I will ever forget the terror of having a pillow held over my face while I was trapped and unable to fight back."

She dropped her hands with a shiver and then swiped at the tears on her cheeks. Lindsey reached out and took Theresa's free hand in hers.

"I can't imagine," she said. "I'm so glad you're here, safe, with bodyguards, until Emma figures this out."

"I suppose," Theresa said. "My only consolation is that if something horrible does happen to me, Larry will be compensated with a huge life insurance policy."

Lindsey sat up straight and tipped her head to the side.

"You've made him the beneficiary of your life insurance?"

"When we got engaged, Larry insisted, although I did specify that it go to Liza, since Larry doesn't need the money and she is like a daughter to me, despite her present attitude—or maybe because of it," she said. "When he hired the Norrgard brothers, he told me it was to ensure that he never had to collect on the policy. Isn't that sweet?"

"Yeah, sweet," Lindsey said. Or was it? Lindsey decided to keep this thought to herself for the moment.

"It just doesn't make any sense," Theresa said. She didn't seem to notice the concern in Lindsey's voice. "Who would want to do me harm? I haven't competed professionally in years. I am no threat to anyone."

"Maybe this isn't about tennis," Lindsey said.

"Kayla? Are you trying to say it's Kayla attacking me in a jealous rage?" Theresa asked. "I can't believe that. "

Lindsey squeezed her fingers and let go. She sat back in her chair and studied her friend. Theresa was a pretty woman with long, dark hair and a heart-shaped face who looked younger and more innocent than her years. She was always happy and smiling and seemed to make the best out of any given situation. It was no wonder that Larry Milstein, who had known such personal tragedy in his life, was drawn to her.

This situation, however, was not the sort of thing in which Theresa could find a sunny side. Someone was out to do her harm at the very least or to kill her at the very worst.

"Larry is one of the richest men in the country," Lindsey said. "Is it really inconceivable that a woman who wants him for his money sees you as a threat? I mean, with you out of the picture, Larry is back on the market."

"No, it isn't inconceivable, but Kayla Manning? I know she can be pushy and abrupt, but I just don't see her as a violent sort."

"Liza said you tried to talk to her before, but she was having none of it," Lindsey said.

"She was hurt and angry. I didn't hold it against her. Larry did treat her very badly. But I never got the feeling that she wanted to do me harm over it—Larry, sure, but not me."

"Is there anyone else that you know of who isn't happy about you marrying Larry?" Lindsey asked. "Any ex-boyfriends? Lovers? Friends with boundary issues?"

Theresa smiled, which was what Lindsey had intended. "No, and if there are, they haven't said it to my face."

"I'm sure Emma already said this, but if you think of anyone—"

"Who is furious enough with me to try and run me over or suffocate me," Theresa said. "Yeah, I'll be sure to mention it. There is one . . . No, that's just me being silly."

"There's no such thing as silly when it comes to your well-being," Lindsey said. "What were you going to say? Do you have someone in mind besides Kayla?"

"No." Theresa's gaze slid away from hers, and Lindsey noticed that it lingered for just a moment on a small framed photograph on the mantel over the fireplace.

"If you do think of someone, anyone—" Lindsey began, but Theresa interrupted her.

"I'll be sure to let the police know—I promise."

It was clear she didn't want to talk about it anymore.

"Excellent," Lindsey said. It was an effort not to press Theresa for more information, but she managed it. "Now let's take your mind off of all of that. Look at what Liza and I picked out for you."

Lindsey opened the bag, and together they looked at the audiobooks they had picked out. Theresa was delighted, and Lindsey put the latest Jill Shalvis novel into the CD player in the entertainment armoire so Theresa could listen and enjoy a few laughs while she rested.

When Theresa looked relaxed and involved in the story, Lindsey slipped from her chair. She crossed the room and pretended to warm her hands by the fire. With her back to Theresa, she took the opportunity to use her phone to snap a picture of the framed photograph on the mantel. Maybe it was nothing, but she wanted to know who it was and why the picture had seemed to disturb Theresa.

She pocketed her phone, and with a wave to her friend, she left the room. She found Stieg waiting outside, and he nodded to her as he entered, letting her know he was on duty. Lindsey was halfway down the hallway when she heard Stieg chuckling at the story along with Theresa, proving Lindsey's personal theory that there really wasn't any funky mood swing in life that a solid romantic comedy couldn't cure.

Robbie and Larry were still in the study. They were

sitting in matching wing chairs in front of a roaring fire, enjoying their whiskey. All they needed were smoking jackets and cigars, and they'd look like two characters out of a BBC *Masterpiece Mystery!* episode.

Liza was seated at the desk in the corner with a stack of textbooks in front of her. One was open, and she was poring over it with her chin resting on her hand, as if forcing herself to stay awake while she read. Stefan appeared right behind Lindsey and exchanged a nod with Larry before moving on.

"Are they constantly surveying the house?" she asked.

Robbie half rose from his seat, indicating that she should take it, but Lindsey declined with a smile. She still felt cold from her drenching that afternoon, so she happily sat on the hearth and let the warmth from the fire wash over her.

"That's what I hired them for," Larry said. "It was really quite lucky. I had ordered some chowder from the Anchor for Theresa after her scare, and there they were at the bar, asking Ian Murphy if he knew of any work in the area. I remembered them from when they were working with that salvage company and hired them on the spot to be Theresa's bodyguards."

"That is lucky," Robbie said. He sent Lindsey a concerned glance.

"I know what you're thinking," she said. "That it's too coincidental, but I know Stieg and Stefan, and I trust them."

"Are you sure that's not just blind loyalty to their good looks talking?" he asked.

Lindsey rolled her eyes. "Mr. Milstein trusts them, too, obviously."

"Call me Larry," he said. "Can I offer you some whiskey or wine?"

"No, thank you," she said.

Larry glanced back at Robbie. "She's right. I do trust the Norrgards. Those two Goliaths are my first line of defense in keeping Theresa safe. She is the greatest thing that's ever happened to me. I will not let anyone harm her—ever."

Lindsey glanced at Liza to see what she made of her father's words. She was still engrossed in her studies, and Lindsey doubted she'd heard him. It was clear that both Liza and her father had fully embraced Theresa into their home. Lindsey wondered whether there was anyone else in the furniture giant's life who might consider Theresa a threat.

"Mr. Milstein, er, Larry, do you have any other family besides your daughter?" she asked. "Parents, siblings, cousins?"

"No," he said. He took a sip of the amber liquid in his glass. "It's just me and Liza. I was an only child, and my parents passed five and seven years ago. Whatever family they had, they never kept in touch with, so it's just me and the kid."

"I'm not a kid," Liza piped up from the desk. "I'm twenty."

"Not legally allowed to drink yet and still living under my roof," Larry said. "That makes you still my kid." He winked at her, and it was full of affection.

"I'm only still under your roof because you won't let me move out." Liza shook her head at him. Lindsey sensed this was an old argument between them.

"You're not moving in with that loser boyfriend of yours," Larry said. "He doesn't even have a job. How would he provide for you?"

"Provide for me?" Liza asked. "What century is this? I have my own money. I don't need anyone to provide for me."

"Yeah, your money, as you call it, is my money," Larry said. "As long as I'm footing your bills, you'll live where I can keep an eye on you and make sure you're safe."

Liza looked at Lindsey and Robbie. "The paranoia runs deep in this one."

"It's not paranoid to accept that having money makes you a target. It does. All sorts of hustlers, crooks, and criminals will come after you, and if they think they can rob you blind, they will. And that includes unemployed boyfriends."

Lindsey noticed that Liza was frowning down at the top of the desk. She wondered how Liza felt about her father having so much say over her life. While Lindsey understood that Larry wanted to protect his daughter, she wondered whether Liza didn't chafe a bit at the digs to her boyfriend and her father's refusal to let her move out on her own.

"Sounds like the voice of experience," Robbie observed.

"I've been bitten a few times," Larry conceded. He drained his glass.

"As have we all," Robbie said. He polished off his whiskey as well.

Lindsey took a moment to study Larry. The firelight highlighted his rugged features, and Lindsey got a glimpse at what he had looked like as a young man. There was an optimism beneath the surface that she hadn't expected. She wondered how he had managed to retain that, given the loss of his wife and the ups and downs of a life spent in retail. She glanced at Liza—perhaps she was the person who kept Larry hopeful.

"Dinner is served, Mr. Milstein," a woman in a chef's coat announced from the door.

She was short but slender, with her gray-streaked hair tied back at the nape of her neck. Lindsey guessed her to be in her fifties.

"Thank you, Mrs. Armand," Larry said. He glanced at Lindsey and Robbie. "Would you care to join us? Mrs. Armand is an amazing chef."

Lindsey glanced at Mrs. Armand to see whether the sudden possibility of two additional people at the dinner table caused her any stress. She didn't bat an eye. Lindsey was impressed.

"You're very kind," Robbie said. "But we are otherwise engaged."

"Too bad," Milstein said. "I have a Rémy Martin XO cognac that I was hoping to share with a discerning palate."

"Another time." Robbie set his glass down on a coaster on the coffee table and rose to his feet. Lindsey followed.

"I'll hold you to that," Larry said.

"Bye, Liza," Lindsey said.

"Good night." Liza waved good-bye from the desk while Larry walked them to the door.

"If Theresa needs anything from the library, please don't hesitate to call me," Lindsey said. "And I'd be happy to come and sit with her if she would like some company."

"Thank you," Larry said. "That's very kind of you. I didn't know the library offered such door-to-door service."

"We don't usually, but I consider Theresa a friend," Lindsey said.

"That's Theresa for you," he said. "She makes friends wherever she goes."

Lindsey followed Robbie to his car. It was now fully dark, and the evening's chill reminded her that spring wasn't here just yet. The occasional April snowstorm did happen, and if today's temperatures had dropped any lower, all the crocuses and daffodils that had just begun to sprout would have been suffering from some frostbite.

Robbie opened her door for her, and Lindsey slid in. She glanced back at the house as Robbie climbed into the driver's seat, and she saw a face watching them from a second-story window. She thought it was Theresa, and she lifted her hand to wave. But how could Theresa be in the window? Her cast made standing difficult at best, and Lindsey was sure her room had been on the other side of the house, overlooking the water.

Lindsey squinted, trying to get a better look at the dark-haired woman. Her face was pale, and she was too far away for Lindsey to make out her features clearly, but she looked an awful lot like an older version of Liza. Lindsey felt her heart beat hard in her chest while the hair on the back of her neck prickled. The woman also bore a striking resemblance to the woman in the photograph in Theresa's room.

"Robbie." Lindsey reached over and grabbed his arm. "Look at the second-story window all the way on the left side of the house. Do you see what I see?"

Robbie had to lean across the console to be able to see. Before he could get there, the woman with the closed-lip smile stared hard at Lindsey and then disappeared with a twitch of a thick lace curtain.

"Um, am I supposed to see something?" he asked.

"There was a woman standing in the window," Lindsey said. "I thought it was Theresa, but how could she be standing there when her room is on the other side of the house?"

"There's no one there now," Robbie said. "Maybe it was just a reflection."

Lindsey turned to glare at him, and he backed up into his own seat. "Just throwing out theories."

"Well, you can throw that one all the way out," Lindsey said. "There was a woman standing there. I saw her. She was as real as you or me."

"All right, don't have a wobbler on me," he said. He started the car and proceeded down the driveway a bit slower than Lindsey would have liked. She was ready to put some distance between her and the Milstein house. "Maybe it was Liza. From a distance, she could appear to be a grown-up."

"It wasn't Liza," she said.

"They have staff," he replied. "Could it have been a cook or a maid? Or maybe Theresa has a private nurse staying with her."

"A nurse," Lindsey said. She hadn't considered that. "That makes sense, I suppose."

"Of course it does," Robbie said. "I mean, who did you think it was? The ghost of the late Mrs. Milstein?"

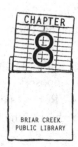

CHAPTER

8

BRIAR CREEK
PUBLIC LIBRARY

66 No," she said. It was a lame effort. Even she could
hear how defensive she sounded.

"Oh my God, you did," he accused. He chortled as he
turned onto the neighborhood road that would lead them
back to town. "Someone has been reading too many
gothic novels."

"I have not," she said. This was also a fib, as she'd
recently dug up all her old Victoria Holt novels and
delved into what she considered her *Rebecca*-light reading. Maybe it had gotten into her head, or maybe there
really was something creepy and wrong about the Milstein house.

"Specters or whatever aside," Robbie said, "I'm going
to mention my talk with Larry to Emma. The man has a
fine taste in whiskey, I'll give him that, but I felt like he

wasn't telling me something. I was studying him, and he paused quite a bit while we were talking, as if he was considering every word he said. That's odd, don't you think?"

"Weirder than seeing a face in the window? No," she said. "It could be that as a public figure he's very careful, but, yes, you should tell her anyway. Listen, Theresa told me something that I also find odd. Larry has taken a hefty life insurance policy out on her as the future Mrs. Milstein."

"Really?" Robbie frowned.

"That's what she said. I feel like it's strange that he did it before they were married."

"Agreed."

"How are you going to explain that you were enjoying whiskey with Larry Milstein while she was questioning Kayla Manning, the only suspect in the case so far?"

"I am simply going to tell her the truth," he said. "I saw you struggling with a big bag of books that needed delivering to the Milstein's, and I offered you a ride."

"That's a slight variation on the truth."

"And yet, still true," he said.

"Only by the narrowest margin," she agreed.

"And I'll mention the life insurance policy and see if that gets me out of hot water," he said.

"Good move."

They drove silently through town. Robbie was dropping her off at home, and while Lindsey was happy to be going home, where she'd be with her dog, Heathcliff, and Sully, she was also a teeny bit reluctant. Being in the

Milstein's house, so like her former residence, with its three stories and ocean view, before she moved in with Sully, had made her a bit homesick for her old apartment.

As Robbie pulled into the driveway and waited for her to climb out, he said, "Tell the soggy sailor I said hello."

"I will," Lindsey said. She didn't move.

"Something wrong?" Robbie asked.

"No, not really. Does Emma whistle?"

"Huh?"

"Sorry, that was a random thought. Never mind, forget I said anything," she said. She reached for the door handle and popped open the passenger door, letting the cold night air into the warm car.

"No, no, no," Robbie said. He took her arm and held her in her seat. "You don't get to ask a weird question and then just climb out of the car with no explanation. Why do you want to know if Emma whistles?"

"No reason," she said. "Really, it's stupid."

"Good, then it shouldn't be a problem to tell me."

"It's nothing," she insisted. Robbie stared at her, waiting, clearly prepared to wait for however long it took. Lindsey shut her door to keep the heat pouring out of the floor vents from escaping. "Oh, all right, it's just that Sully whistles every morning when he wakes up. Every morning, whistling, it could make a girl mental—that's all."

Robbie blinked at her, and then he laughed. "He's driving you crazy."

"No, *he* isn't," she clarified. "The whistling is."

Robbie nodded, his grin showing every bit of his gleaming white Hollywood teeth.

"You're laughing at me," she said.

"Only a smidgeon," he admitted. "It's nice to know the buoy boy isn't perfect."

"No one's perfect."

"No, but I come pretty close," he said.

Lindsey laughed and rolled her eyes. Leave it to Robbie to make her grateful she had to deal only with whistling and not an ego the size of the Atlantic.

"And with that, I will talk to you later," she said. Again, she reached for the door handle, but Robbie didn't let go of her arm. Instead, he gave it a quick squeeze to bring her attention back to him before he let go.

"Can I make an observation from one friend to another?" he asked.

"Sure."

"Listen, I know this might be weird coming from me, but have you considered that the little things Sully does aren't really what's bothering you?"

"No, I'm pretty sure the sunrise serenade is exactly what's bugging me."

"Humor me," he said. "You and the water boy have been on and off a couple of times, and it could be that you're trying to protect yourself from a future hurt by using some of his idiosyncrasies as a buffer for your feelings."

Lindsey blinked at him.

"Oh my God, you have been watching entirely too much *Dr. Phil*," she said.

Robbie raised his hands in the air in a gesture of innocence. "I'm just saying you should consider the possibility. Maybe it's not his annoying habit that's got you on edge so much as your own vulnerability now that you live together."

Lindsey gave him side-eye. "I'm telling Emma that you are entirely too in touch with your feminine side."

"She's the chief of police," he said. "One of us has to be."

Lindsey laughed at his pointed look and said, "Women can have any job they want and still be feminine." Then she held up a hand to stop his retort. "And, yes, men can be in touch with their feminine side, too. I'll think about what you said."

"That's my girl," he said. "But do not under any circumstances let Captain Knuckle Dragger know that I have his back. It would ruin our adversarial rapport."

"I promise."

She climbed out of the car and headed toward the house, determined not to let a little whistling get on her nerves.

L indsey unlocked the front door and strode inside. Out of habit she braced herself. Sure enough, Heathcliff, her hairy black rescue dog, came at her at a run. He barked and wagged his tail at the same time, and when he got to Lindsey, he stood on his back legs and hugged her about the knees.

"Oh, who's a good dog? Who's mommy's handsome fella?" Lindsey asked as she scratched him behind the ears.

Heathcliff promptly dropped to the floor and offered

up his belly for rubs. Lindsey bent over him and rubbed his tummy until his tongue lolled out of his mouth.

Sully's head popped out of the kitchen. "Dinner in five minutes."

"You cooked?" she asked. She toed off her shoes, happy to be home.

Sully's head popped back out. He watched her kick her shoes to the side of the foyer. He frowned.

"I didn't cook exactly," he said. "The deli in the grocery store had a special on their beef stew, so I bought a quart of it along with some fresh bread."

"It smells amazing."

"Thanks."

Sully walked toward her, and Lindsey lifted her face for a hello kiss, but he ducked around her and grabbed her shoes, putting them in the wicker basket to the side of the door, where they kept all their shoes. Then he turned around, kissed her quickly, and went back to the kitchen.

Lindsey looked down at Heathcliff. "Huh, what do you make of that?"

Heathcliff barked, and Lindsey was pretty sure he was telling her that Sully was not down with her not putting her shoes in the basket.

With Heathcliff at her side, Lindsey slid onto a stool at the kitchen counter. Sully was just pulling the bread out of the oven. He had already put two steaming bowls of stew on the counter, and now he put the bread in a basket between them.

"Are you mad at me?" Lindsey asked.

"No, why would you think that?"

"Um, perfunctory kiss hello," she said. "No 'How was your day?' In fact, I've seen none of the usual I-haven't-seen-you-all-day-gosh-I-missed-you niceties coming from you, which makes me think you're irritated."

"Not irritated," he said. He poured her a glass of wine and got himself a beer. Then he took the seat beside hers. "Was that Robbie who brought you home? I ask because when I swung by the library to give you a ride home so you wouldn't get soaked in the rain, Beth let me know that you'd taken off with him."

"Ah." Lindsey smacked her forehead with her palm. "I forgot to text you, didn't I? I am so sorry. That was unforgivably rude. I have no excuse except that Liza Milstein was in and then Emma came by and then there was a break-in at Theresa's house—"

"Which, of course, you had to help with," Sully said. "Being the head librarian and all."

Lindsey studied the severe line of his mouth. He looked annoyed, but Sully was never annoyed, so was he annoyed or . . . ?

"Are you laughing at me?" she asked.

He lifted one eyebrow as he studied her. "Me?"

Lindsey grinned. "You are, aren't you?"

She closed the space between their chairs and looped her arms about his neck, pulling him close. When they were just inches apart, he smiled.

"No one warned me that a librarian for a girlfriend

would be such a handful," he said. "I think I was woe-fully unprepared."

"Sorry," she said. "It's that whole rage-for-order thing. It makes us troublesome."

"Good thing I like trouble," he said. Then he kissed her, and Lindsey knew everything was all right. Still, the shoes. She needed to ask about the shoes. He kissed her again and she forgot.

When they broke apart, Sully's smile was wide, and he pushed her stew toward her and said, "Eat and talk."

"In that order?"

"Yes."

Lindsey didn't need to be told twice. She tucked in and recounted the events of the day while she did.

Sully's eyebrows went up when he heard about The-resa's attacker, but he didn't interrupt, letting Lindsey tell all of it before he asked questions. It occurred to her that this was a rare and wondrous quality in a man. It made her want to hug him again and more than made up for the morning whistling.

When she paused to eat, Sully broke off a chunk of bread and used it to swab up the stew in his bowl. He chewed while he considered what she'd told him, and then he asked, "How did Theresa seem tonight when you stopped by?"

"She seemed to be making the best of a very scary situation," Lindsey said. "But I could tell she was tired and wary."

"Wary," he said. He picked up his beer and took a long

sip. "That's an interesting word choice, given that she is in her fiancé's house with bodyguards. Why wary?"

Lindsey blew out a breath. Here it was. The end of her story. Did she tell him about the photograph and the face in the window or not?

"Okay, so I don't want you to think I'm crazy or overly imaginative or weird," she said.

Sully slowly lowered his beer. "Now you have my full attention. Tell me, why would I think any of those things?"

"I think I saw a ghost," Lindsey said. The words came out in a rush, as if they were tripping over each other to get out.

"A what, who, huh?"

"Ghost. *G-h-o-s-t.* Ghost."

He stared at her and then drained his beer before plunking the empty glass onto the counter. He ran a hand over his face.

"Okay, I'm ready. Explain."

"I know—I know I sound crazy," she said.

"Not crazy, exactly," he said. "Tell me what happened. I bet we can figure it out."

Lindsey told him about Theresa's pensive glance at the picture on the mantel and then how she saw a face in the window that resembled the picture when she and Robbie were leaving.

"You had a really stressful day," he said.

"No, don't," she said. "Don't dismiss it as me being overwrought. You know me—I am never overwrought."

"True," he said. "Even when you've had to do things you're afraid of, like jump into deep water in the dark."

"Yes, that's much more terrifying. I will take a room full of ghosts over that any day," she said. Then she shivered.

"Do you really think it was a ghost?" he asked. "I never thought you were the ghost-believing sort."

"I'm not saying I believe in ghosts." She paused. "But I'm not *not* saying it either."

"What did Robbie say when he saw it?"

"He didn't," she said. "He missed it, but he theorized that it was staff in the house or a nurse for Theresa."

"That makes sense," Sully said. "A house that size with the money Milstein has. They are bound to have a full staff."

"I suppose," Lindsey said. "Did you know Larry's first wife?"

"Sarah Milstein?" he asked. "Yes, she was a Creeker, born and raised in the village like Mary and me. She was seven years ahead of me in school, and her maiden name was Sarah Hubbard. I didn't know her very well. In fact, I was in the navy when she married Milstein, which by all accounts was the wedding of the century in Briar Creek."

Lindsey took her phone out of her bag. She opened up her pictures and chose the one she took at the Milstein house. She gave the phone to Sully.

"Is that her?" she asked. She held her breath while Sully enlarged the picture. He blinked and then glanced up at her. His face was grim.

"Yes, that's her."

"Sully, that's the woman I saw in the window. I know it is."

He ran a hand over his face as if he didn't like anything about this.

Lindsey put her hand on his arm. "Sully, how did Sarah Milstein die?"

"You don't know?"

"No."

"Oh, I thought Liza or Theresa or one of the crafternooners would have told you."

"Told me what?" Lindsey forced herself to be still and not kick her feet with impatience. "I thought she died of a disease or an aneurysm or something."

"No, in fact, no one knows the truth. She disappeared from town one day just like that." He snapped his fingers. "Since there's been no sign of her, it's believed she was murdered, but her body was never found."

Lindsey slumped back against the counter. "Body? Her body? Is there a reason to believe she was murdered?"

Sully shrugged. "When a person vanishes without a trace, foul play is usually involved."

"Who was the main suspect?"

"Larry, initially, but when it was discovered that he was out of town on business, it seemed highly unlikely. Plus, he adored her."

Lindsey thought about the man who doted on Theresa. Maybe she was misjudging him, but she just didn't see him as a murderer.

"And she just vanished?"

"Yup," Sully said. "Larry tried everything. He hired detectives, he ran commercials begging anyone who might have seen her to call, but even with a hefty reward being offered, there was no sign of her. She vanished without a trace."

Lindsey's eyes went wide, and she reached for her glass of wine. The tart beverage gave her taste buds a slap of wakefulness, and she put her glass down, focusing on Sully.

"Tell me everything you remember," she said.

He frowned. "I'm afraid it's not much. Like I said, I was away in the navy when all of this was happening."

Lindsey felt something press against her leg. She looked down, and Heathcliff was giving her his *I'm starving to death* expression. Lindsey hopped off her stool and grabbed his bowl from his mat in the corner. He followed her as if to offer his assistance as a sous chef.

Lindsey prepped his food, keeping an eye on Sully while she did. He looked to be trying to remember the details of what had happened. Lindsey let him gather his thoughts, patting Heathcliff on the head as she put his food down. She resumed her seat and stared at Sully expectantly, much like Heathcliff had watched her with the food.

"If I remember right, and that's a big if," Sully said, "Liza was five years old and attending kindergarten at Briar Creek Elementary. I remember because my mother was teaching there at the time, and it was quite the

scandal. School ended, and Sarah didn't show up to re-
trieve Liza. When they called her, she didn't answer her
phone."

Lindsey didn't say a word. She waited quietly and let
him sift through what he remembered. It was excruciating to resist the urge to pepper him with questions, but
she knew he would have an easier time if she didn't
heckle him.

"One of the teachers stayed with Liza while the prin-
cipal called Larry," Sully said. "He was opening a new
store down in Virginia, so it wasn't like he could race
home. Liza ended up being collected by the housekeeper,
who had not seen Sarah all day. In fact, no one had seen
her that day. She dropped off Liza at school that morning
and vanished."

"Oh, poor Liza," Lindsey said. "She was just a kid.
That had to have been devastating."

Sully nodded. "I could call my mom for more specifics if you want."

Lindsey appreciated the gesture, but she suspected
from his reluctant tone that he really didn't want her to
dig into the disappearance of Sarah Milstein any more
than she already had. Still, she had to wonder out loud.

"Do you think Theresa knows about this, and if so, do
you suppose she's worried that whatever happened to
Sarah Milstein is about to happen to her, too?"

"Maybe, but she's not even married to Larry yet,"
Sully said. "If it was foul play that got Sarah, wouldn't
the person—assuming it's the same person—who made
Sarah vanish wait until Theresa was Mrs. Milstein?"

"I suppose that depends upon what the gains would be to have Theresa gone—say, a life insurance policy taken out on her, for instance."

Sully's eyebrows went up, and Lindsey nodded.

"Theresa told me Larry hired the Norrgard brothers as bodyguards to keep her safe because he said he had no interest in collecting on the life insurance policy he'd taken out on her when they got engaged."

"Weird. Does she believe him?"

"She seems to."

"Are you going to tell Emma?" he asked.

"Robbie is," she said. "I wonder if there was an insurance policy on Sarah Milstein."

"I'm sure there must have been, but I doubt he collected it, since her body has never been found," Sully said. "I'm not even sure he's had her declared dead yet."

"Wouldn't he have to if he's planning to remarry?"

They exchanged a look. This was one more thing to mention to Emma.

"So, from what you know of the two situations, do you think they're connected?" Lindsey asked.

Sully shrugged. "I think it's an awful coincidence that both Larry's wife and now his intended have had suspicious things happen to them. But given that we don't know what happened to Sarah Milstein for sure, how can we determine if there's a connection, especially when Sarah went missing but Theresa seems to be blatantly under attack?"

"True, that is different, but we also don't know whether Sarah Milstein had weird things happening to her before she vanished. So what you're saying is we need to find out what happened to Sarah Milstein," she said.

Sully shook his head and waved his hands in a *no no no* gesture, but it was too late. Lindsey knew that this was exactly what they needed to do.

CHAPTER

9

BRIAR CREEK
PUBLIC LIBRARY

Sifting through old issues of the *Briar Creek Gazette*, Lindsey found the articles written after Sarah Milstein's disappearance. The stories were fast and furious at first, speculating on everything from kidnapping to murder to the possibility that she had orchestrated her own disappearance. Sadly, there was no evidence to prove any of the theories, and as the months went by, the articles appeared less and less, until the community seemed to accept that it was a mystery that would never be solved.

Larry Milstein was never considered a suspect, as he was proven to be in Virginia at the time of her disappearance and also because he seemed utterly distraught at losing his wife. It was observed that he was tireless in his search for her, following any lead, pursuing every avenue available to locate a missing person, from hiring a private detective to offering a reward. There was nothing. Sarah Milstein had vanished without a trace.

Lindsey leaned back from the microfilm machine. The last article written about Sarah Milstein was ten years after she vanished. After that, there was nothing. No mention of her or her disappearance. The police chief at the time Sarah disappeared was not a name Lindsey recognized, and the ones who followed afterward had even less to say about the case.

Lindsey knew that the only people who might be able to tell her more were people who had been around at the time, who knew Sarah and Larry. Given that a housekeeper had collected Liza from school that day, she seemed like a good person with whom to start. Unfortunately, there was no mention of the housekeeper in any of the papers. Lindsey didn't know her name and couldn't figure out how she could ask Larry. She didn't want to ask Liza, because she had no wish to make the young woman revisit what must have been a very painful and confusing time in her life.

Lindsey rewound the final reel of film while she mulled over the possibilities. She could talk to Ms. Cole. She had lived in town her whole life and might know something, but she wasn't one to gossip, which was one of the things Lindsey liked about her—except in this case. She could ask Milton Duffy, her newly reinstated library-board president, as he was also the town historian. The only problem was that he was dating Ms. Cole, and she wouldn't like it if Lindsey dragged Milton into her quest for information. Bad things had happened before when Milton had helped her out, and now that she and Ms. Cole were getting on somewhat, she didn't want to jeopardize the relationship.

Larry wouldn't be inclined to talk to her, since he hardly knew her, but he might talk to Robbie. Maybe the new drinking buddies could share another glass of the good stuff, and Robbie could slyly interrogate his new friend and get the name of the housekeeper and, with any luck, her address and phone number.

Lindsey put the film from the machine back in its box. She'd always liked the microfilm machine; if she hit just the right speed when she was spooling the film, she could give herself a nice case of vertigo. But as the *Gazette* got archived digitally, she knew the microfilm was going to be weeded out of existence, taking with it it's grainy photos of the actual paper from days gone by. Sometimes progress was hard.

She left the reference area of the library and did a sweep of the facility. It was late afternoon, and the chess club had taken over the glassed-in study rooms as they practiced for a tournament this weekend. The computers were all in use by a mix of town residents. The children's area had two large families in it, running roughshod around the room. Beth was there, corralling the kids by bringing them to the puzzle table in the center of the room. It looked like she was herding cats. She'd get all of the kids at the table, and then two would take off for the puppet theater, which was fine, although there were kids already using it. Thankfully, the kids already dressed in garb from the costume box were more than happy to have more players in their puppet production.

Lindsey turned away with a smile, admiring not for the first time her friend's ability to manage chaos. She saw Ann Marie Martin helping one of their regular patrons with the copy machine by the front door. Ann Marie had the toner cartridge out and was giving it a good smack. To get more prints out of it, no doubt. Working at a small-town public library with a limited budget, Lindsey and her coworkers had refined the art of stretching their spending like squeezing pennies into copper wire.

In the two soft chairs by the new magazine display, Leo O'Donnell and Chester Jones, two of Lindsey's favorite patrons, were asleep with their heads tipped back, and Leo—yep, it was Leo—was snoring. She had no idea what shenanigans the two men had gotten into the night before, but if she were a betting woman, she'd place money on CJ doing his stand-up comedy routine (he was always good for a laugh) and Leo breaking out his rendition of "Mack the Knife" (he had an amazing singing voice) at the amateur talent night held weekly at the Blue Anchor.

She decided to let them nap. Life moved pretty fast; sometimes a body needed some shut-eye. She wouldn't kick them awake until someone complained or the snoring got too loud. Knowing them, they'd wake up unassisted as soon as happy hour started.

She circled back toward her office, thinking about the articles she'd read. How had Sarah just disappeared without a trace? With the world under surveillance at all times by phones, cameras, security checkpoints, and so forth, it didn't seem possible. True, her disappearance had been fifteen years ago, but surely if she was alive, someone must have picked up a trace of her somewhere. Unless she didn't disappear. Lindsey thought about the face she'd seen in the window; could it have been . . . ? No. That was crazy. Still, the air suddenly seemed colder, and she shivered, pulling the sleeves of her sweater down over her wrists.

Lindsey thought about her colleagues from library school. She considered them and their various fields and knew that Susie McAllister had taken a position as a genealogy librarian. She was an expert with vital records and had databases at her fingertips that Lindsey could only dream about. She decided to send her an email asking her about Sarah Milstein. If only she had Sarah's social security number—but that was going too far.

She was standing by the front doors when they whooshed open.

"Lindsey, your office, now," Emma Plewicki said as she strode into the building, not slowing down or stopping but cruising right past Lindsey.

Lindsey could tell by the tight set of her shoulders that something was bothering the police chief. She scanned her brain. Other than her visit to the Milstein house, she had steered clear of Theresa Huston and whatever was happening—well, other than looking up old articles of the *Gazette*, but that was just being a librarian. It wasn't as if she'd expected to find anything, not really.

Lindsey followed Emma into her office. Emma sat in the chair opposite her desk, and Lindsey closed the door and sat down.

"Can I get you anything?" she asked. "Water or coffee?"

"No, thanks, I don't have time," Emma said.

She stared at Lindsey for a moment. Lindsey got the feeling she was considering her words very carefully. Lindsey waited, not wanting to rush her. Whatever Emma had to say, it was clearly important to her.

"I can trust you, can't I?" Emma asked.

"Do you really have to ask?" Lindsey responded. "I mean, I know we don't always see eye to eye on things, but I like to think you feel I'm trustworthy."

"I do, but you have a knack for getting into trouble, and I really don't want any trouble right now," Emma said.

"Trouble? Me?" Lindsey asked. She blinked, as if she were the picture of innocence, but Emma wasn't playing.

"Save it," Emma said. She tossed her long dark hair over her shoulder and leaned her elbows on the edge of Lindsey's desk. "We found the car."

"The car that hit Theresa?" Lindsey leaned in.

"Yes, and the driver was still in it," Emma said.

"So you caught him? This is great! Did he say why he did it? Was it an accident, or was he aiming for her?"

"Let me be more specific: we found the *dead* driver in the car," Emma said. "Charlie Peyton has confirmed that he was the man who tried to run him down outside the Blue Anchor."

"Oh." Lindsey slumped back in her seat. She could feel her heart beating hard in her chest in a rush of anxiety. "Did he have any tie to Kayla?"

Emma shrugged. "He's not local, and we're still working on identifying him. Kayla says she's never seen him before."

"Do you believe her?" Lindsey asked.

"In my line of work, you never believe anyone," Emma said.

They were both silent, and Lindsey wondered how far she could press Emma for information. She decided to go for it, knowing Emma would stop talking whenever she felt like it.

"I don't suppose there's any chance he died of natural causes," she said.

"Not judging by the bullet hole in his head, no," Emma said.

"Do you think it was Kayla?" Lindsey asked. She tried to picture Kayla as a killer. She couldn't do it, not that that signified anything.

"I'm not sure yet," Emma said. "Kayla says she doesn't own or know how to operate a gun, and I have no evidence to the contrary, so . . ."

Her voice trailed off, and Emma leaned back and clasped her hands in front of her. While Lindsey was pleased that Emma had decided to trust her, she couldn't help but wonder why. A murder victim found in a car that had been involved in a hit-and-run really had nothing to do with the library—or her, for that matter.

"Was there something I can do to help you in regard to this?" she asked.

"Maybe." Emma didn't say any more.

Lindsey waited. Emma didn't elaborate. Lindsey could hear the ticking of her big, round battery-operated office clock in the silence.

"Can you give me a hint?" Lindsey asked. "Or at least tell me if we're dealing with animal, mineral, or vegetable?"

"Twenty questions? Robbie loves to play that game." Emma's lips tipped up on one side. Lindsey shrugged. She didn't think it was prudent to mention that's where she got the idea.

"All right, I'll tell you why I'm here, but this is in the strictest confidence," Emma said. "And I mean that. You can't tell Sully or Robbie or any of the crafternooners, no one. Do you understand?"

"Absolutely, I won't say a word to anyone." Lindsey sat up straighter. She had no doubt that Emma was as serious as a heart attack.

"The state police are helping in the investigation," Emma said. "Both the body and the car have been turned over to their crime scene investigators and medical examiner."

Lindsey nodded. Briar Creek was too small of a town to support a crime lab, so things were frequently turned over to the state.

"This includes everything that was in the car," Emma said.

Lindsey felt her tension ratchet up. This was what Emma wanted to share; she was certain of it. She waited while Emma pulled a small notebook out of her pocket. She flipped through the pages and then ripped one out and handed it to Lindsey.

Lindsey glanced at the list. Being a librarian, she caught on right away that it was a list of music and audiobook CDs.

"I don't have the discs, because the crime scene unit took them," Emma said. "But every one of those titles came from your library."

Lindsey recognized a few and nodded as the pieces fell into place. "These were found in the car."

"Yes," Emma said. "And I need to know if they were checked out to Kayla Manning. If they were, then they signify nothing except that she used the library."

"Which would be odd," Lindsey said. "As far as I know, Kayla has never been in the library, never mind checked anything out."

Emma's brown eyes glowed like a predator spotting prey. "Excellent. Then I'll need to know who checked those CDs out."

Lindsey felt her stomach twist. "It's not that simple."

"What do you mean?" Emma asked. "All you have to do is look up the title and tell me who checked it out. Surely, in this day of technology, you can do that."

"Well, yes, if I had the library barcode from the CDs, but you've only given me the title. These are all popular artists, and we own multiple copies, so I'll have to track them all down and then cross-check them to see who borrowed them."

"I'm not seeing the problem. I'll call the crime scene investigator and have them send me the barcodes."

"Even with that, I won't be able to help you."

"Why not? What's the issue?"

"You're going to need a subpoena," Lindsey said. "From a judge or a court of competent jurisdiction."

Emma threw her hands up in the air. "What? How can you stonewall me like this?"

"I'm not. I'm merely following the library code of

ethics put forth by the ALA and adopted by the Briar Creek Public Library."

"Screw procedure—I have a dead body in a stolen car and a citizen holed up in her house who has barely escaped with her life—twice. Do you want her death on your hands?" Emma popped up on her feet and leaned across the desk as if she could intimidate Lindsey.

"Don't!" Lindsey said. She rose, too, and met the chief of police halfway. "Don't simplify privacy laws like that. You know why we protect our patrons' right to privacy."

"That's not the point," Emma argued.

"Yes, it is," Lindsey snapped. "You were there last year when Tammy Moore was sneaking into the library, checking out books on how to leave an abusive partner. Her husband tried to bully me into turning over her circulation records, and what would have happened if I did? It would have gone really badly for her, and you know it. Tammy got away from him because we were able to give her the privacy and resources she needed, so don't you diminish it."

"I am not Steve Moore," Emma said.

"No, you're not," Lindsey agreed. "But the privacy laws remain. Get a subpoena."

Emma stomped toward the office door.

"And, Emma," Lindsey said before the door shut. "By the time you have the appropriate paperwork, I should have a name for you."

Emma met her gaze, gave her a curt nod, and slammed the door behind her. So, still mad.

Lindsey glanced at the list of titles. It was an eclectic

list, and she couldn't help wondering what a man who was about to commit a hit-and-run had been doing with everything from show tunes to Metallica in a stolen car. Weird. She set to work.

Lindsey had just brought up the holdings records for the first CD, which had seven copies in the system, when there was a polite knock on her door. She glanced up, surprised to see Sully leaning against her doorjamb. He had a small smile that tipped the corner of his lips, and she got the feeling he'd been watching her for a moment before he knocked.

"Are you ready, darlin'?" he asked.

It was then that she noticed he wasn't in his usual captain's attire of jeans and a flannel shirt but was spiffed up in khaki pants and a waffle-knit pale blue Henley. She blinked at him.

"You forgot, didn't you?" he asked. "We have a dinner date with Beth and Aidan tonight."

"No, or not completely," she said. It was a fib. She had absolutely spaced that they had dinner plans.

Sully gave her a dubious look, and she sagged in her seat. "Oh, all right, I admit it. I'm working on a project, and I was so engrossed I forgot."

"That's all right," he said. "If we leave in five minutes, we won't even be late."

Lindsey bit her bottom lip. She didn't want to go. She wanted to stay here and work on tracking down who had checked the CDs out. So far, she had a complete list for only one of the CDs, and Kayla Manning's name was not on it. Not a big surprise, since when Lindsey had checked the patron records, she'd noted that Kayla Manning didn't have a library card.

"Oh no," Sully said. "You are not thinking of canceling."

"Well." She drew out the word while she studied his face. He did not look like he was going to be swayed. She decided she needed to tell him what was up. "Emma stopped by and asked me to look something up for her. I don't think I should put off the chief of police, do you?"

"Does it involve Theresa or the car that was found with the dead man in it?"

"Heard about that, did you?"

"Yup," he said. He pushed off the doorjamb and walked into her office, closing the door behind him. He sat in the seat across from her desk and bent forward with his elbows resting on his knees. "So, which is it?"

"The dead man," she said. "This is between us, but they found some library materials in his car, and Emma wanted me to see if I could figure out who checked them out."

"Aren't there privacy laws protecting patrons' records?" he asked.

Lindsey nodded. "She's going to need a subpoena."

"Think she'll be able to get it tonight?"

"No," Lindsey said. "She has to prove her cause to a judge. It might take a while."

"So, dinner is a go." He rocked back up to his feet. "Come on—they're probably waiting for us."

"I don't want to. Beth is driving me crazy with her post-wedding talk," Lindsey said. Then she clapped a hand over her mouth. "Did I say that out loud?"

Sully dropped back into his chair with a laugh. "Yes, you did."

"Bad form," Lindsey said. "I mean, I was her maid of honor. I should be more supportive of her post-wedding glow."

"She has been talking about it pretty much nonstop for weeks," Sully said. "Even I know that the filling in her cake was wrong, but it tasted good so she was okay with it, oh, and that the organist played the march down the aisle so perfectly that she was standing in front of Aidan on the last note just as she had always imagined."

He clasped his hands over his chest and made an earnest face that was such a spot-on impersonation of Beth that Lindsey laughed out loud.

"So, it's not just me?" Lindsey asked. "I mean, I've tried to be patient, but good grief. I'm beginning to feel like it's Groundhog Day and I am reliving the wedding again and again and again. I honestly don't think I can go through with dinner tonight."

Sully considered her for a moment. He squinted one eye and then said, "Why do I get the feeling there's more to it than that?"

"What do you mean?"

"Be straight with me," he said. "I've sensed that things are off between us, so I have to ask, are you regretting moving in together?"

CHAPTER

10

BRIAR CREEK
PUBLIC LIBRARY

"What?" she asked. Then she shook her head. "No!"
"Are you sure? Cohabiting is a big adjust-
ment."

"No, I'm happy, really," she said. "I just—"

Lindsey's voice trailed off. She wasn't sure how to
tell him that every time they were with Beth and Aidan
and the wedding thing came up, she felt like it was
hanging over them. Were they headed toward marriage,
did she want to be, and more specifically, did he want
to be?

"Just what?"

"You know what? You're right," she said. She turned
and began to close down her computer, saving her Excel
file before she logged out. "We promised to meet them,

and we should go. Talking about the wedding isn't that bad. I'm sure we'll have a great time."

"Why do I get the feeling you're not telling me everything?" he asked.

"Me?" She put her hands over her heart in a pose of innocence.

"Yes, you," he said. "I'm onto you, Lindsey Norris. You're keeping something from me, and I'm going to figure out what it is."

"Is that so?" she asked.

"Count on it," he said. "In the meantime, come here."

He stepped around the desk and opened his arms. Lindsey moved toward him without hesitation. On a day that had been stressful and crazy, this felt right. She leaned against him and absorbed his strength and his warmth. When she stepped back to study his handsome face, he kissed her, and everything was right with her world.

"Hey, you two." Beth appeared in the doorway. "No canoodling now. We're late for dinner, and look what I brought—my wedding album. I just got it from the photographer." She held up a navy blue leather album and did a jig. "This is going to be so great!"

Sully put his arm around Lindsey and leaned in close and asked, "Should I call ahead and tell Ian to have our drinks waiting for us?"

"He might want to make them doubles," Lindsey replied out of the corner of her mouth. Then she forced a big smile and followed her friend out of the library to the restaurant across the street.

* * *

There were some perks to not having to talk during dinner. Lindsey was able to enjoy every bite of her broiled fillet of sole while Beth did a sort of story time with her wedding album. Each page was presented with the recounting of the events by both Beth and Aidan, while Sully and Lindsey smiled and nodded. A few times, Lindsey caught Sully's speculative gaze on her, and she gave him a quick wink to let him know she was all right.

They were just finishing dessert when Sully's sister, Mary, who owned the Blue Anchor with her husband, Ian, strode across the restaurant to their table. She held the baby out to Sully and said, "Uncle Sully, I need you. I've got an emergency in the kitchen. Can you hold Josie for a bit?"

"Absolutely," he said.

Sully dropped his fork and reached for the baby. Lindsey watched as his big man hands gently cradled the wee one, bringing her right to his shoulder for a snuggle. It hit her, not for the first time, that he was really good with babies. He should be a father. How could she stay with him, knowing that she wasn't really mom material but he'd be amazing dad material? How could she deny a child that?

"Thanks, bro," Mary said. She adjusted a spit rag on his shoulder and ran her hand lovingly over Josie's head. "I'll be right back."

Then she turned around and dashed toward the

kitchen doors, looking like she was about to open a can of whoop ass.

"I feel sorry for whoever is on the other side of that door," Aidan said.

Sully grinned. "Me, too—Mary is not one to tolerate nonsense." He lifted the baby up so they were nose to nose. "Did you hear that? When you get into trouble with your mama, you come find me. Uncle Sully has your back, Josie-girl."

Lindsey smiled and then glanced across the table. Beth looked like hearts were going to start pouring out of her eyes. Without taking her eyes off Josie, Beth reached out for Aidan's hand and slid her fingers into his. Aidan cast his wife an indulgent look, and it hit Lindsey that they would likely be next. In fact, they were probably trying already. She reached for her wine and took a healthy swig.

Marriage. Babies. She had been engaged before. Why did it all seem as if it was coming at her so fast? She put her glass down. She had to get out of here. She needed to be somewhere quiet and contained, where she knew who she was and what she was doing. A place like the library, where everything was under her control and the emotional risk was minimal.

Lindsey pulled her phone out of her bag and glanced at the screen, willing anyone anywhere to need something from her at this moment. There was a message from Emma Plewicki. She had the barcodes. Excellent.

"Duty calls," she said. She pushed back her chair and rose to her feet. "I am so sorry, but I have to go."

"What? Why?" Beth asked.

"I have a request for information from Emma that can't wait," she said.

Sully rocked forward to rise to his feet, as did Aidan, but Lindsey waved her hand to indicate they should stay seated.

She leaned around the baby and kissed Sully on the cheek, taking in Josie's fresh baby scent as she did. Okay, so she could see the appeal there. She leaned back and studied the tiny girl making time with her man. She put her hand on Josie's head, marveling at the downy soft feel of her hair.

The baby squinched up her little face, turned bright red, and let out an ear-piercing wail. Lindsey dropped her hand as if the baby had suddenly sprouted fangs. Sully rose and began to rock the baby, gently patting her back.

Lindsey glanced at Beth and Aidan to see whether they'd registered how much the baby disliked her. Clearly, she was not kid friendly. She glanced at Sully and found his bright blue gaze watching her. He tipped his head to the side and gave her a small smile.

"It's not personal, you know," he said. "She's probably just gassy."

"I know," she said. She returned his small smile with a rueful look. "I'm just more used to Heathcliff, who likes to share when he's feeling air bloated."

Sully laughed. "Go, but call me later."

"I will," she said. She glanced at Aidan and Beth, who were watching intently as Sully unleashed his baby magic and began to calm Josie down. She waved at them. "Bye!"

Lindsey was halfway across the restaurant when a toss of bright blond hair caught her eye. She turned, and there was Kayla Manning sitting at the bar. Although she had no idea what she was going to say, the opportunity to talk to the other woman was too good to pass up.

Lindsey maneuvered herself next to Kayla's stool and leaned in so that it looked as if she were ordering a drink. Kayla gave her a cursory glance but then turned to the man on her other side. Lindsey pursed her lips. Since Kayla wasn't a library user, Lindsey's usual conversation opener of mentioning a favorite author was useless. She racked her brain. She had nothing.

Ian Murphy, Mary's husband and owner of the Blue Anchor, saw her and hustled down the bar toward her.

"Lindsey, what can I get for you?" he asked.

"Um," Lindsey stalled. She glanced at Kayla, hoping to get her attention. The woman was oblivious. "Did I tell you my car was stolen?"

"What?" Ian shook his head like a dog shaking off water. "But you don't own—"

"I know!" Lindsey said. She raised her voice to drown him out. "I parked it in front of my place, and then it was gone. Can you imagine that? My car—stolen!"

Kayla swiveled on her stool toward Lindsey. "Excuse me, did you say your car had been stolen?"

"Yes," Lindsey said. She glanced at Ian, who was looking at her as if he thought she was having a mental breakdown. "Water, please."

"Sure," Ian said. "Because clearly alcohol is not a good plan for you right now."

Lindsey gave him a blank smile and made a shooing gesture with her hand.

"I can't believe your car was stolen," Kayla said.

"I couldn't believe it either," Lindsey said.

Okay, so technically her car had been stolen five years ago, when she lived in New Haven, so it wasn't a total lie. Besides, how else could she get Kayla to talk to her?

"Hi, I'm Kayla."

"Lindsey."

"My car was stolen, too," Kayla said.

"No way," Lindsey said.

"Way, and the police found it with a dead guy in it. Can you believe that?"

"No. Oh, man, I don't want my car back with a dead man in it." Lindsey hoped she looked more surprised than she felt.

"Right?" Kayla said. She shook her head. "This has been one hell of a week."

Lindsey noticed that the small pitcher of margaritas in front of Kayla was mostly empty and she was swaying on her seat. While Kayla wasn't out-and-out slurring, she was definitely well lubricated by the tequila coursing through her system.

"And it gets worse. I had just made the final payment on it," Kayla said. "Can you believe it? What are the odds?"

Lindsey blinked at her. So finding the dead guy in it wasn't the worst part? Interesting.

"Yeah, that's a tough break," Lindsey said. "I had a pair of very expensive shoes in my car." This was true. "Designer black patent pumps with bows on the toes. So cute, and they took those, too."

"No!" Kayla said. "That's just rude. I mean a car is one thing, but taking a girl's kicks? That's low."

Even five years later, Lindsey still mourned the shoes. Kayla's feminine outrage was a balm on the old hurt.

"How about you? Was anything stolen out of your car?" Lindsey asked.

"No," Kayla said. "I don't keep anything in my car."

"That's smart," Lindsey said. "I had shoes, makeup, workout equipment." She glanced at Kayla to see whether this was jogging anything in her memory. "Books, oh, and my favorite CDs."

Kayla took a sip of her margarita and gave her a pitying look. "Maybe if they find your car, you'll get it all back."

"Especially the CDs," Lindsey said. She studied the other woman. "They didn't belong to me, you know—I checked them out from the library."

Kayla blinked at her. Suddenly, Lindsey felt like she was on a one-woman mission to get this woman to check out her local library.

"You use the library, don't you?" Lindsey asked.

"I can't say that I do, no," Kayla said. "I'm not much of a reader. I think books are a big yawn."

It was like a knife to the chest, and Lindsey would have staggered, but she didn't want to let Kayla know how much her feelings about the library hurt. Lindsey had met book-resistant people before, and she tried not to judge, but really, the library offered so much more.

"Well, how about movies?" she asked. "They have loads of movies."

"I download movies," Kayla said. "It's so much easier than having to load a DVD into a player—know what I'm saying?"

Lindsey felt desperate to find something at the library for this woman to be excited about. "How about programs? Did you know there are all sorts of clubs that meet at the library?"

"No."

"There's a craft club, chess club, cooking club, a travel club." Lindsey ticked off the different clubs on her fingers.

Kayla frowned. She looked Lindsey up and down and said, "No offense, but you're boring me."

She turned away, adjusting herself on her seat and tossing her blond hair in a clear dismissal of Lindsey and her advocacy of the library.

Ian pushed a glass of ice water at Lindsey. The look he gave her was one of pure pity.

"Well," he said.

"Don't say it," she said.

"Say what?" he asked. His innocent look didn't fool her one bit.

"Good boy," she said. She downed the water and pushed the glass of ice back at him. The brain freeze when it hit almost took her out at the knees, but she refused to let it show. Instead, she turned and exited the restaurant, tucking what was left of her dignity into her purse as she went.

L indsey hurried back to her office. The library was still open. Paula was manning the front desk while Ann Marie oversaw the reference area. They both glanced at Lindsey as she came dashing into the building.

"Silly me, forgot something," she said.

Paula smiled and nodded, but Ann Marie gave Lindsey a speculative look. Having two young boys who were notorious mischief makers, Ann Marie had a sixth sense for malarkey. Lindsey didn't linger for questioning but closed her office door and fired up her desktop.

She logged into the circulation module and then opened her phone to see the list of barcode numbers Emma had forwarded to her. Since each item in the library had its own barcode, this should be a simple matter of looking up the item by barcode and seeing who had it checked out. Then they would know who had left materials in Kayla Manning's car. Of course, there was still the question of why their items were in her car, but that would have to wait until they had a name. The bigger concern was whether they had anything to do with the hit-and-run driver. Could they identify him? It was a big leap, but Lindsey was hopeful.

She yawned and glanced at the clock on the wall. It was seven o'clock, and the big meal she had just consumed was making her sleepy. She felt her head bob as the weight of sleep pulled it down while she waited for the circulation database to open. Her desktop computer was getting pretty old, and while the slowness usually didn't bother her, right now she was feeling tired and impatient.

Coffee would help. Coffee always helped. She left her computer to continue its process and went to the break room to see whether there was any coffee in the community pot. There was but it was cold. Lindsey didn't care. She didn't care how old it was either. The only thing she cared about was that she could have some right now.

She found her *I Like Big Books* mug sitting rim-side down in the drying rack by the sink. She poured the remainder of the cold coffee in and popped it into the microwave. While she waited, she scrubbed out the coffee pot and left it to dry in the rack. Ann Marie had taped up a sign that read, WASH YOUR OWN DISHES. YOUR MOM DOESN'T WORK HERE. There were water spots on the sign and it had started to fade, but it was effective, as no dishes were ever left in the sink.

She was just leaving the break room with her reheated beverage when she heard an earsplitting squeal of tires coming from outside the library. Several patrons glanced toward the large windows that looked out onto the street, and Lindsey joined them. She saw a red muscle car, possibly a Camaro, roaring down the street.

She didn't recognize the car and wondered whether a teen from a nearby town had gotten hold of their parents' car keys and decided to rip up the pavement in a town where they wouldn't be recognized. It was now fully dark, and the headlights of the car sliced through the night with a menace that made the hair on the back of Lindsey's neck stand on end.

"What's going on?" she asked her staff as she left the window and hurried to the front desk.

"No idea," Paula said. "But it looks like someone decided to go for a joyride through the center of town."

Pop pop pop.

Lindsey jumped, and hot coffee spilled over her fingers and dripped onto the carpet. She and Paula exchanged shocked expressions.

"Were those gunshots?" Paula asked.

"Everyone get down!" Sully ordered as he dashed into the building with his shoulders hunched as if bracing for a hit.

CHAPTER

11

BRIAR CREEK
PUBLIC LIBRARY

No one needed to be told twice. Patrons dropped to the floor as one, shielding themselves with tables and chairs. Lindsey put her coffee on the counter and did a visual sweep of the room, making certain everyone was down, as she crouched low and hurried to Sully. She glanced over her shoulder and watched Ann Marie as she ducked behind the main desk with Paula.

Sully was hunkered low against the wall beside the open doors. He craned his head around the doorjamb, trying to assess what was happening outside.

Lindsey reached into her pocket for her phone. *Darn it!* She'd left it on her desk. The sound of an engine revving and the squeal of tires ripped through the quiet. Lindsey could feel her heart pounding in her chest. Sully pulled her down beside him, and Lindsey pressed herself against his solid warmth.

"What do we do?" hissed Paula. She was peeking around the side of the circulation desk. "Last time I checked, random gunfire wasn't covered in the staff manual."

Lindsey had just opened her mouth to answer when Sully, using the voice of command that she suspected he had perfected during his years in the navy, said, "Stay down. I've called the police. They're on their way."

As if he had cued it, the faint sound of a siren could be heard in the distance. It sounded far away. Lindsey wondered whether Emma had stationed her officers to watch over Theresa Huston and now they had to hustle back to the center of town to deal with whoever was shooting up Main Street.

Pop pop pop!

Sully pushed her up against the wall even while he moved to get a better look. Lindsey fought against his hold, trying to see for herself what was happening. She leaned against his back and peered over his shoulder.

The red sports car had spun around and was now charging down the center of the road, right on the back bumper of another vehicle. A tricked-out, high-end SUV was swerving and dodging, trying to lose the smaller sports car like a big dog shaking off a playful puppy.

As they watched, the SUV jumped the curb and sped through the park, tearing up the new spring grass in its race to get away. The driver's-side window of the sports car was down, and Lindsey saw the barrel of a gun pointed at the SUV. A shot was fired, and the SUV swerved again, bouncing back onto the street with a bang and a thud. Amazingly, the tires didn't blow, and the vehicle sped past the library.

As it moved under a streetlight, Lindsey gasped. The distinctive bright blond hair of the Norrgard brothers was visible, as was the pale and terrified face of Theresa Huston, who was wedged between them in the front of the vehicle.

The SUV executed a tight right turn at top speed, turning onto a side street. The muscle car missed it and sped past. Lindsey watched with wide eyes as the sports car pulled a U-turn in the center of Main Street to go after the Norrgard brothers. Just as it reached the side street and turned onto the road, the Norrgards came roaring out of the side street, passing the muscle car, which was now headed in the wrong direction.

The SUV raced through town while the sports car was left trying to turn around on a narrow side street full of parked cars. The sound of one bumper crunching another and of one car scraping up the side of another shredded the night air. There was a beat of silence, and then with another squeal of tires, the muscle car was in pursuit of the SUV once again.

Sully was up and moving toward the door as soon as the taillights disappeared. Lindsey was right behind him. She thought it spoke well of their relationship that he didn't ask her to stay behind. Perhaps she had worn him down after their years together, or maybe he just didn't want to take the time to argue. Either way, they were out of the building and running at top speed for his truck, which was parked on a side street beside the library.

They jumped in, and Sully jammed the truck into drive and rocketed out of the parking space. He shot out onto Main Street with a teeth-jarring thump, and Lindsey grabbed the handle that was built into the door, trying to steady herself as she bounced in her seat.

The road ahead was empty; the faint sound of the police siren still wailed in the distance.

"How are we going to find them?" she asked. "We have no idea where they might have gone."

"True, but I don't think whoever is after them is going to give up," Sully said. "The Norrgard twins are better sailors than they are drivers. I am betting that they're looking for a way out of town where the car won't be able to follow."

"They're going to take a boat," she said.

"That's my hunch."

"But the town marina is in the other direction."

"Where there are an awful lot of boats to choose from. My guess is that Stieg and Stefan are planning to use a private vessel so whoever is chasing them will be stranded."

"But they have to get to the boat first and have time to load Theresa and get out of there."

"Exactly."

"So your plan is to help stall whoever is chasing them, the person with the gun?" Lindsey clarified.

"I was really just thinking about getting the license

plate to the sports car on the chance that they disappear before the police arrive," he said. "But if stalling is required, I think we can manage that, too. Assuming, of course, that you're in?"

"Oh, I'm in," Lindsey said. "Do you really have to ask?"

"No," he said. He cast her a quick grin as they shot down the road. "Which is why I didn't."

For some reason this charmed Lindsey silly. She liked that Sully knew her so well and had no desire to change her. She thought about his morning whistling and kicked around the idea that maybe Robbie was right. Maybe she was letting all of Sully's quirks annoy her simply to keep him at a distance.

The deeper she got into this relationship, the more powerful the hurt would be if it didn't work out. She didn't enjoy it much the last time they'd taken a break. Now that they were cohabiting, it would be devastating and complicated. And what about Heathcliff? He was so attached to Sully; his little doggy heart would be crushed if he lost his best buddy.

She thought about Sully's exuberant greeting of each day with whistling and a mug of coffee appearing on her nightstand just before she needed to rise and get in the shower. It hit her then that if he wasn't there to whistle in the morning, she would miss it. She would miss him.

She glanced at his profile. His jaw was clenched, and his eyes were on the road in front of him. His hands gripped the wheel with total control while he navigated the turns of a road that had no streetlights, making it

difficult to know what was around each curve. Lindsey
knew that she should be afraid. She should be worried
about what they might find on the road ahead, but she
wasn't. She trusted him completely.

"Hang on," he said. He yanked the wheel to the right,
and Lindsey gripped the handle on the door as she
fought to keep her seat even while being belted in place.
The dirt road, which was barely visible from the street,
cut a narrow swath through the trees. The branches were
reflected off Sully's headlights and looked menacing
with their nearly naked branches stretched out across the
path, scratching the side of the truck if Sully veered too
close.

They hit a patch of bumps, and her teeth clacked together. One rut sent her bouncing out of her seat. Sully
reached across the console to steady her even as he continued to steer through the thick trees, turning the wheel
with the palm of his free hand. Abruptly, they landed in
a clearing. Sully's headlights flashed on the SUV and the
muscle car. He had to stand on his brakes to avoid ram-
ming into them. As his truck lurched to an abrupt stop,
he snapped off the lights just as Lindsey noted that both
cars looked abandoned, with the doors hanging open and
the headlights of the SUV still on.

The Norrgard brothers and Theresa had obviously
made a run for it, and whoever was following them in the
sports car had followed.

Sully put the truck in park and switched off the engine. The night surrounding them seemed to pulse outside their windows with the heartbeat of a predator just

waiting, biding its time as it watched its prey, waiting for them to make one false move. Lindsey shivered.

"I'll go first and do a sweep of the area," Sully said. "When I signal, open your door slowly and carefully and slip down to the ground, or you could just stay here and wait."

"All right," Lindsey said. Then she dashed the hope that flickered in his eyes by adding, "I'll wait for your signal."

With a sigh, Sully carefully opened his door and crept out, closing it softly behind him. Lindsey held her breath, waiting for him to scout the scene and give her the all clear. It was dark in the woods, but as her eyes adjusted, she could make out Sully stealthily walking across the ground toward the cars.

He stopped at the SUV first and checked inside. He didn't linger but moved to the muscle car. He disappeared from sight for a moment, and Lindsey could feel her heart beating in her chest as she waited for him to reappear. He popped up a few moments later and waved for Lindsey to join him.

She carefully opened her door and slid to the ground. It was hard beneath her feet. The few leaves from last season were damp and didn't crunch underfoot. It was quiet here, surrounded by trees that towered overhead. No breeze rustled through the budding leaves; no birds chirped; even the insects were quiet. The night air was chilly, and she regretted not having brought her jacket.

She crouched down beside the truck and then hurried to join Sully by the sports car. Up close, she could see that it was a newer Camaro. The doors were open, as if the occupants had left in a hurry. She glanced inside. They had taken the keys, so obviously they were planning to come back. There wasn't anything else in the car except for a bright yellow hooded sweatshirt tossed onto the back seat and some fast-food bags. The interior of the car had a lingering smell of a burger with onions.

The thought that the shooter could be on their way at any moment made the dark woods surrounding them seem even more ominous. Lindsey glanced into the trees as if she had the ability to pick out anyone hiding amid the thick trunks in the dark. It was a futile effort.

Sully was shining the flashlight app on his phone at the corner of the windshield on the driver's side. He was snapping pictures of the VIN, and Lindsey knew he would be sending them to Emma. He hurried around the back of the car and snapped a picture of the license plate as well. He sent off a rapid-fire text and tucked his phone back into his pocket.

"Come on," he said. "We need to get out of here."

"Do you think they're on their way back?"

Sully scanned the area. He gave her a somber look.

"Probably. There's only one reason the Norrgards would take Theresa here. The hiking path through these trees gives back access to Milstein's private dock, where he keeps his yacht."

"Do you think they made it?"

"There's only one way to know for sure," he said. "Let's go see if the boat is there."

Lindsey raised her eyebrows in surprise. Now that

they had the VIN and the license plate number, she had thought Sully would hustle them out of here. He must have been concerned that the Norrgards hadn't made it.

He held out his hand, and Lindsey slipped her fingers into his calloused palm, letting him pull her into the woods surrounding the clearing. The undergrowth was thick, as they stayed off the path, opting to walk parallel to it on the chance they ran into whoever was chasing Theresa and her bodyguards. It was difficult not to make noise, as twigs snapped beneath their feet and gravel shifted. Branches impeded their progress, catching at their clothes. Still, they pressed on with Sully in the lead, taking the worst of the beating.

Lindsey knew he was hoping to avoid running into whoever had been driving the sports car; obviously they had a gun and were not afraid to use it. But like Lindsey, he must have felt they had no choice. They simply couldn't leave without knowing whether Theresa and the twins were in trouble or not.

The trees became sparser, and the going was easier. The salty sea air of the ocean grew stronger as the ground became sandier, sporting tufts of tall grass and cattails. Lindsey knew they were getting closer, and she felt her heart hammer in her chest. Sully stopped abruptly, and she slammed into his back.

"Sorry," she grunted.

"Shh," Sully said. His big hands steadied her. "Listen."

Lindsey stood utterly still, straining her ears for any sound of movement coming from the trees around them.

There was nothing. And then she heard it in the distance: the sound of shouts just over the purr of an engine.

"This way." Sully breathed the words in Lindsey's ear.

He turned and led her back through the undergrowth and up a small hill. Lindsey followed him, eager to see what was happening. Did the twins get to the boat? Was Theresa safe? Who was chasing them and why?

Sully crouched down behind a thick patch of mountain laurel. Lindsey dropped down beside him. With his free hand, Sully parted the branches, and they glanced down the hill over the small inlet, where a large yacht was chugging its way out toward the sea.

Pop pop pop!

Shots were fired at the vessel, and Sully pushed Lindsey down, shielding her with his body. She would have struggled, but she knew it was just who he was, protecting anyone around him even at the risk of his own life. It was in his DNA, right next to the gene that made him a morning person who whistled.

His face was pressed against hers as he scanned the area, looking for the shooter. The smell of dirt filled Lindsey's nose, and she was afraid she might sneeze, so she took small breaths through her mouth while Sully crouched over her. The bullets hadn't struck the yacht, or if they had, they hadn't hindered its progress at all.

Instead, the lights on the ship were shut off, making it a much more difficult target, and its engines revved as it churned up a wake and headed out into the deeper water of Long Island Sound. There were some shouts and a final popping noise, as if someone had fired their gun in a temper.

Lindsey hardly dared to breathe, as she could hear whoever had been shooting at the vessel off to the right, standing closer to the water's edge, near the large wooden dock where Milstein kept his boat moored.

This was a deep inlet, one of the few in the area, and it allowed Milstein to keep his boat close to home. Lindsey glanced at the house beyond the dock. It was lit up as if expecting company. She wondered whether the shooter would go to the house, looking for another victim, or whether they'd leave since their prey had escaped. The waiting was excruciating.

Sully was as still as she was, as if he, too, was trying to track the shooter's movements. Lindsey felt her pulse flutter with nerves when she clearly heard someone walking on the path just below where she and Sully hid.

"Don't move." Sully breathed the words into her ear, and Lindsey gave a tiny nod. She had no intention of taking on some bad guy with a gun, and she definitely didn't want to put Sully at risk, given that he was on top of her and would likely be shot first.

They waited. Lindsey could feel Sully's heat all along her back and was grateful for it, as it kept her from shivering. She could hear someone muttering as they stomped through the tall grass to get back on the hiking trail. They certainly didn't care if they were making any noise, probably because they had no idea that they weren't alone.

What would happen when they saw Sully's truck?

Would they come back and try to shoot them? Lindsey felt her heart pound in her chest and knew her flight response was kicking in. She desperately wanted to get out of here, but given that Sully didn't move, she figured he thought their best bet was to stay put. Hopefully, the shooter would choose to run.

They waited, and then they waited a little bit longer. When Sully finally rolled off her and pulled her into a sitting positon, Lindsey knew they were safe, and she sucked in a deep breath, letting her lungs fill up with the sweet, cool air.

Sully motioned for her to stay down as he rose to his knees, checking to see that the shooter hadn't doubled back. In the distance the sound of a car engine revving broke the silence, and Sully rose to his feet, pulling Lindsey up after him.

"I think that's them," he said. "Let's get out of here."

They jogged through the trees on the same uneven terrain that had brought them into the woods. Branches swung at them, and trees popped up in the darkness, forcing them to slow down and work their way around the big trunks and long branches. By the time they got to the clearing, the muscle car was long gone, leaving only the faint smell of a puff of exhaust in its wake.

The doors to the SUV were still wide open, but Sully and Lindsey didn't go near it. If the shooter had touched the bigger vehicle, they may have left fingerprints behind.

Lindsey leaned against the side of the truck, catching her breath, while Sully called Emma.

"Emma, it's Sul—"

His words were interrupted by an irate Emma. Lindsey couldn't hear the exact words, but she knew the tone, as she had been on the receiving end of that voice before. She gave Sully a sympathetic smile, and he shrugged.

"Emma, the suspect who shot at Theresa and the twins is headed your way. Now listen," Sully said. His voice was firm, and Lindsey noted that she could no longer hear Emma yelling from his phone.

Sully told the police chief what had happened, that they believed that the twins and Theresa had gotten away, but there was a red Camaro headed toward town that was likely the shooter and that he suspected they could still be armed. Suddenly the sound of sirens came out of Sully's phone, and his eyebrows went up right before the call abruptly ended.

"So, I'm thinking she caught sight of them," he said.

"So it would seem," Lindsey said. She glanced around the clearing, which seemed awfully dark and creepy. Not that she thought the bad guy would come back, but still. "Should we close the doors and lock the SUV?"

"I'll get it," Sully said. "You can start the truck."

He handed her the keys, and Lindsey climbed into the cab of the truck and switched on the engine. She watched through the windshield as Sully used the hem of his shirt to hit the door lock and then his elbow to shut the doors of the vehicle. As he walked back to the truck, his eyes scanned the clearing as if he, too, were wondering whether Theresa's pursuer would reappear.

He climbed in beside her and blew out a breath. "That was intense."

Lindsey moved across her seat so she could lean against him. When he slipped his arm around her shoulders and pulled her close, she couldn't resist. She planted a swift kiss on his cheek. When he turned to glance at her, they were nose to nose and Lindsey smiled.

"I'm having the best time," she said.

She felt him shake as a laugh bubbled up out of him.

"Of course you are," he said. "I have to admit; it does feel like old times."

"Maybe we needed this," she said.

"What? Chasing crazy hit men through the woods on a dark spring night, hoping we don't get shot while we snap a picture of their license plate for the police?" he asked. "That's your idea of a solid date night?"

Lindsey laughed. "Well, it beats bowling."

Sully kissed her. It was swift and sweet, but it let her know that he understood what she was saying. It gave her courage.

The words, when they came, tumbled out of her mouth in a waterfall of insecurity and doubt that rushed out of her in an almost deafening roar, at least to her. Out in the air, they were more like a storm of whispers that took on substance when she said what she'd been dreading admitting for weeks.

"I need to tell you something. I've been freaking out for a while because I don't know how you feel about marriage and children," she said. She took a breath and continued. "I like children. I do. But I don't want to have any.

I know we should have talked about this more in depth before we moved in, but I didn't know for sure until recently, and I know now that as adorable as a baby is, say, asleep across the room, that's about as close as I like to get to them. I'm pretty sure I don't want to have kids, and if you do, well, then . . ."

Her voice stalled from lack of oxygen. She blinked at Sully, awaiting his response while she tried not to pass out.

"So, that's what's been on your mind?" he asked. "Kids?"

Lindsey nodded. She'd seen him with Josie. He was the perfect doting uncle with endless patience, and he adored her. He must want children of his own, and he'd be such a great dad. How could she deny him that?

Plus, she'd seen the way he'd looked at her shoes when she'd dropped them on the floor. She wasn't so sure he loved having her and Heathcliff in his house, so that was another concern. It was time that they were honest about it.

"Also, it occurs to me that you may not love having me and Heathcliff in your house as much as you thought you would. You probably feel as if we've invaded your space, and that has to be off-putting."

"What?" He dropped his arm from around her shoulders and turned so they were facing each other. "No. Never." He laughed and shook his head. "And all this time, I thought you were missing your old apartment and your own space and were reconsidering living together."

"No, I love your house," she said. "Heathcliff loves your house. We're very happy there."

"Except?" he asked.

"The whistling," she said. She hid her face behind her hands and peeked at him from between her fingers. "You whistle very early in the morning."

He looked confused. Then he ran his fingers through his hair. "I had no idea."

"Now admit it—my shoes drive you crazy," she said.

He blinked at her.

"No, don't deny it. I've seen the look. I kick my shoes off wherever I happen to be, and it drives you crazy."

"It does boggle me that you can't seem to get them into the shoe basket," he said. "But it's so not a big deal."

"I knew it!" she cried. "I will try to be better."

"Me, too. No more early morning whistling," he said. "So, are we good?"

Lindsey shook her head. "I'm afraid not."

Sully tipped his head to the side as if he didn't understand.

"Marriage and kids," she said. "I wasn't just saying all that. I don't think I'm mom material."

"What makes you think I'm dad material?" he asked.

"Josie—you're so good with her," she said.

"Well, yeah," he said. "She's my niece and I love her."

"Imagine if she were yours, a child of your own," she said.

Sully gave her a horrified look. "I'd never sleep again. Never ever. Not a wink."

He turned and pushed open his door. Lindsey watched

as he circled the truck and opened her door. He took her hand and tugged her out of the cab until they were standing face to face. The glow of the dome light in the truck cab shone on his face, and Lindsey was caught by the bright light in his blue eyes, which glittered with affection and nerves.

"Now as for marriage," he said. "That is absolutely happening."

CHAPTER

12

BRIAR CREEK
PUBLIC LIBRARY

"I —" Lindsey began, but he cut her off.

"Lindsey Norris, I have been in love with you from the very first time I saw you ride your bike through town with a smile as wide as the sky." Sully glanced down at the ground and then slowly lowered himself to one knee. "I can't imagine spending a minute, an hour, or a day without you in my life. You're my best friend and the person I want to spend all of my tomorrows with."

Lindsey felt like she ought to stop him, but her throat was tight and she couldn't pull the words together to say anything, much less tell him to stand.

"This wasn't how I thought to propose, but since we're here and I feel the need to make my feelings on this matter perfectly clear, I am going to ask you right now. Lindsey, will you marry me?"

"Yes." The answer flew out without hesitation or a second thought, and Lindsey knew it was the correct one, because it felt right all the way to the marrow of her bones.

She cupped his face in her hands and stared into his eyes. "Yes. Yes. Yes."

Then she pulled him back up to his feet and kissed him. It was a promise. That she loved him as much as he loved her and that there was no amount of morning whistling that could ever change that.

Sully broke the kiss and leaned back to study her face. Whatever he saw there made him smile. He opened his mouth to speak, but his phone rang, interrupting him.

"It might be Emma," Lindsey said.

With a sigh, Sully let her go and took his phone out of his pocket. He tapped the screen and put it on speakerphone. "What's the good word, Emma?"

Clearly, it wasn't a good word. In fact, it was a string of outrage so loud that Sully had to hold the phone away from them while Emma let loose. Apparently, the suspect had led them into New Haven, where he or she had ditched the car and fled on foot into a crowd at the train station. There were several trains about to depart, so there was no way of knowing which train they might be on, if they'd jumped on a train at all. Emma's frustration was palpable.

"Are Theresa and the Norrgard brothers okay?" Sully asked.

"Yes, they called in from Milstein's boat," she said. "The Norrgards were bringing Theresa home from a doctor's appointment when they were shot at while stopped at an intersection on the edge of town."

"Was Milstein with them?" Lindsey asked.

"He was at a business meeting," Emma said. "And Liza was in class. It was just the three of them."

"I wasn't accusing—" Lindsey began, but Emma interrupted her.

"I know, but they are the principals in the case, so it stands to reason that their whereabouts must be accounted for, since we have no idea who is trying to harm Theresa and it's clear that she is still very much a target," Emma said. "Hey, Sully?"

"Yeah," he said.

"Nice work on getting the VIN and the plate," she said. "They confirmed the car we found at the station is the same one as on the scene."

"No problem," he said.

"Speaking of the station, can you kids get there and give me an official statement?" Emma asked. "I'm on my way there now."

"Sure thing," Lindsey said.

"We'll be right there," Sully confirmed. He ended the call and pocketed his phone. Then he reached for Lindsey, pulling her close and whispering in her ear. "We'll be there as soon as I finish making out with my fiancée."

Lindsey laughed. She put her arms around his neck and held him tight. She supposed it was crazy to feel this happy after chasing a gun-wielding nutjob through the woods, but she couldn't help it. She was going to marry this man!

* * *

Their visit to the station was brief. Emma took their statements, but given that they'd never gotten a good look at the person who was after Theresa and the twins, they didn't have much more to offer other than the fact that someone had definitely been shooting at the yacht.

Emma gave them a brief lecture on how they could have been killed and how she didn't want to have to do the massive amount of paperwork involved in that, but she didn't belabor the point, so Lindsey figured she knew it was a lost cause.

"Any luck tracking those barcodes?" Emma asked.

"Not yet," Lindsey said. "I was just opening the database when the shooting in the center of town started, but I should have a name for you soon."

"The sooner, the better," Emma said.

Her face was grim, and Lindsey knew that the chief was worried that whoever was after Theresa would get to her first. Knowing that she might have the record of the potential killer was all the motivation Lindsey needed.

As Sully helped her into the truck, she said, "Can you drop me off at the library?"

"It's closed now, isn't it?" he asked.

"Yes, but I can get in with my security code. Besides, all of my things are in there, since I ran off without my phone or anything," she said.

Sully nodded and climbed into the driver's seat. The library was just down the street from the police station, so they were there in no time. It was locked up tight for the night, so Lindsey had Sully park in the employee lot in the back of the building.

When he got out of the truck, Lindsey shook her head at him.

"You don't have to see me in," she said.

"See you in?" He gave her a wide-eyed stare. "I'm staying with you. Until we know who is running amok in town, trying to kill Theresa Huston, I think we need to play it safe, and being alone in the library at night is not safe."

Lindsey knew there would be no talking him out of it, and if she was honest with herself, that was totally fine. She hated to admit it, because her library was one of her favorite places in the world to be, but the thought of sitting there alone did unnerve her a bit, which was just one more reason to be furious with whoever was gunning for Theresa Huston. They were stripping away the simple joys of small-town life, like feeling safe and secure, and that was intolerable.

"Coffee?" Sully asked.

"Yes, please," Lindsey said.

He left her at the door to her office and went to the break room to make coffee. Lindsey waited for her computer to reboot. She'd gotten a text from Ann Marie saying that they'd shut the library down per usual but that she'd also shut down the computer in Lindsey's office. Lindsey took a moment to appreciate her staff and sent Ann Marie a quick text thanking her.

The sound of a fist banging on glass brought her attention

to the front of the library. The security light was on outside, and standing under its glow were Nancy Peyton and Violet La Rue. Nancy was carrying something that looked suspiciously like a cookie tin. Lindsey's stomach growled. It would be horribly rude not to see what her two friends wanted so late at night.

She left her office and crossed the library. When they saw her coming, Violet waved, and Nancy held up the tin of cookies as if she knew a bribe was required to get the library open after hours.

Lindsey crouched and unlocked the door. Once the latch clicked, she pushed the door open, and the two women filed in. Just as the door was sliding shut, a hand shot out and stopped it. Lindsey glanced up to see Robbie standing there, looking quite pleased with himself as he stepped into the library.

"All right, I'll bite—what are the three of you doing here?" Lindsey asked.

"The two of us just happened to be in the neighborhood and thought we'd bring you some cookies," Nancy said.

"Exactly right," Violet said. "They're snickerdoodles, your favorites."

Lindsey gave them a suspicious glance as she took the tin. "Thank you."

"Well, I don't have cookies," Robbie said. "But I heard from a reliable source that you took off after the car that was chasing down Theresa Huston, and I want to know what happened. My girlfriend is being annoyingly hush-hush about all of it."

"Well, she is the chief of police," Violet said. "She can't talk about these things."

"Even with her fella?" Robbie asked. "That doesn't seem right."

"No matter," Nancy said. "Lindsey will tell us what's happening, won't you?"

Lindsey blinked at them. "Do I really look like I can be bribed with snickerdoodles?"

"Yes," all three of them answered as one.

Sully came from the back room and took in the group at a glance. He turned on his heel and said over his shoulder, "I'll go make more coffee. And if you want details, Nancy, those had better be snickerdoodles."

Distracted by the cookies, Lindsey hadn't relocked the door. In seconds it was yanked open, and Emma Plewicki charged into the room. She stared at them all and then looked Robbie over and plopped her hands on her hips.

"I thought the library was closed."

"It is," Lindsey said. She shoved the tin at Emma and crouched to relock the door. When she rose, she took the tin back and marched toward her office, knowing that the group would follow her. "Was there something I can help you with, Emma?"

"I was hoping you already had," Emma said.

Lindsey waved the tin in the air. "Haven't really had a chance."

"That's just as well," Emma said. She cut ahead of the others and followed Lindsey into her office, shutting the door behind her.

Through the glass, Lindsey saw Robbie throw his hands in the air while Nancy crossed her arms over her chest and Violet tipped her chin up at a defiant angle. She hoped Sully could soothe them with some coffee, because there was no way she was opening the door without Emma's okay, and she wasn't giving up the cookies without a fight.

"So, what's up?" she asked Emma.

"Right after you left, I had a visit from Detective Trimble of the state police," Emma said.

"Have they identified the man who was killed?" Lindsey asked.

"Possibly. We think his name was Chad Bauman," Emma said.

Lindsey frowned. She didn't know any patrons by that name.

"I don't know the name either, but there was a receipt for a nearby motel found in the car, and the desk clerk identified a man fitting his description as having stayed there," Emma said, accurately interpreting Lindsey's expression. "We suspect he's from out of state, since the only Chad Bauman in Connecticut is a twelve-year-old who lives up in Kent. Our Chad Bauman also had a woman with him, but the desk clerk didn't get a good look at her. The crime unit did, however, find this in the CD player of the car." She reached into her jacket pocket and withdrew a clear plastic evidence bag that contained a single CD. The Briar Creek Public Library sticker was placed prominently around the middle, with an item barcode visible just below it. She handed it to Lindsey.

Lindsey stared at the CD. It was an audiobook, the third CD in a set for Albert Camus's *The Stranger*. This was it. The key to whoever the dead man in the car was. This would likely identify him and give them their first clue as to who wanted to kill Theresa Huston.

Her fingers shook a little bit as she turned to her desk, sank into her seat, and double-clicked on the icon that would open her circulation module.

She peered at the numbers and then input them in the search-by-barcode option on the module. As soon as she hit enter, a record appeared on the screen. She saw the name that popped up, and a wave of confusion swamped her. How could that be? It didn't even make sense.

She felt Emma press closer, and she minimized the window and turned the monitor away from the chief of police. She didn't want to be a hard-ass, but she would be, especially now, because a patron's right to privacy was not negotiable.

"Lindsey—" Emma said.

"You know I can't tell you who it is without—" Lindsey began.

Emma stopped her by pulling a piece of paper out of the same pocket she'd had the CD in.

"Your subpoena," she said. "It was issued this evening, right after I sent you the barcodes."

"You could have led with that," Lindsey said. She held out her hand and took the paper. She trusted Emma, but she glanced at the paper just to be a stickler.

"I could have, but I like watching you flex your librarian muscle," Emma said. Her teasing grin grew serious.

"It's good that you look out for your patrons like that, and I'm sorry I gave you a hard time about it."

"Thanks," Lindsey said. She folded up the paper, which looked legit, and spun the monitor back. Then she maximized the window. "The person who checked out the CD found in the car stereo was Toby Carter."

CHAPTER

13

BRIAR CREEK
PUBLIC LIBRARY

"Toby Carter? But he's a twenty-year-old Eagle Scout," Emma protested. "I mean, he's so clean, he practically squeaks when he enters a room."

"Let me check the other barcodes from the items found in Kayla's car," Lindsey said. "Maybe there's a mistake."

"Do it," Emma said. "I mean, I thought this would ID our dead guy, not point us in the direction of some earnest college student who spends his free time bringing meals to the elderly."

A knock sounded on the door, and Robbie poked his head in.

"Get out," Emma said. It was her police chief voice. It didn't allow for argument.

Robbie held up two steaming mugs of coffee. "I

thought you might like some coffee to go with the cookies you're hoarding in here."

Emma paused. Her coffee addiction was legendary in the small community. It took all of one innocent blink from Robbie for her to make up her mind. She waved him in. He handed them each a steaming mug. Lindsey noted that he had them prepped just the way they liked them.

"So, do we know who the dead man is?" Robbie asked.

"How did you know—?" Lindsey began, but Emma shook her head.

"He doesn't," she said. "He's fishing for information."

Robbie blew out a breath. "Blast! Thwarted again."

Emma sipped her coffee and said, "Don't take it too hard. There is nothing to confirm yet."

She kissed his cheek and then pushed him back out the door, closing it behind him.

Lindsey turned back to her computer. She opened the email with the barcodes that Emma had sent her, and then she copied and pasted them one by one into the circulation module. The patron name attached to each record was Toby Carter.

Lindsey sent the sheet to the printer. A whir sounded as the machine kicked in, and Emma glanced at her.

"That was quick."

"Every CD was checked out to the same patron. Toby Carter."

Emma frowned. She didn't like this any more than Lindsey did. It just didn't fit. How could Toby have any connection to a man who had stolen Kayla Manning's car and who was now dead from a bullet in his head? These were not people whose paths should ever have crossed.

"Maybe Toby checked out the CDs for Kayla," Lindsey offered.

"Then Kayla lied about having any CDs in her car when I interviewed her," Emma said. "Besides, how would they even know each other? She's a banker in New Haven, and he's a bag boy at the grocery store."

They stared at each other.

Emma put down her coffee and pulled the top off the tin of cookies. She took a snickerdoodle and bit it in half. Then she washed it down with a swallow of coffee. Lindsey followed her lead and reached into the tin, too. No one made snickerdoodles as good as Nancy's. Light and fluffy with just the right amount of cinnamon, the cookie melted in her mouth, making her want more and more. She drank her coffee instead.

"Despite the improbability, could Kayla and Toby know each other? Does he compete in the Ironman or kayak like she does?" Lindsey asked.

Emma made a face. "She's a little old to be pals with him, don't you think?"

Lindsey thought of the Toby Carter she knew. An honor student, he was involved in a hiking club, and was always in the library, studying with his study group. It did seem unlikely that the tall, skinny teen she'd watched grow up, a former member of the chess club who loved epic books that included dragons, would know the hardworking, hard-playing, hard-drinking, forty-something Kayla, but Briar Creek was a small town.

But even if he did know Kayla, maybe they were neighbors or perhaps she was friends with his parents, Lindsey still couldn't wrap her head around Toby having anything to do with a hit-and-run or a shooting, but the CDs put him right in the middle of it. It was just bizarre.

"What are you going to do now?" Lindsey asked.

Emma stuffed another cookie in her mouth and held up a finger in a *wait a second* gesture. Lindsey took another cookie while Emma chewed. After a big swallow, Emma sighed.

"I'm going to go have a chat with Toby and find out why the CDs he checked out were in Kayla Manning's car. There could be a valid reason we haven't thought of," she said. "Then, depending upon his answer, I'm going to go back to Kayla's and find out why she had items Toby had checked out in her car. I am really hoping their stories mesh."

"I don't envy you having to talk to either of them," Lindsey said. "Awkward."

"To put it mildly," Emma agreed.

She finished her coffee and headed for the door. Robbie stood on the other side of it, and she plopped her empty mug into his hand. Then she kissed his cheek and said, "Thanks. I'll be home late. Don't wait up."

Robbie turned and followed her. "Wait! Where are you going?"

"I have questions that need answers," Emma said.

"Let me help you," Robbie offered. "I am brilliant at getting answers."

"No," Emma said.

"But—" Robbie dropped the coffee mug onto the circulation desk as he followed her to the doors.

Lindsey rose from her desk and found Sully, Violet, and Nancy all watching Emma and Robbie as if they were the entertainment portion of the evening. Robbie crouched down to turn the knob that would unlock the doors. As soon as the doors slid open, Emma strode out with Robbie right on her heels.

"Ten dollars says she leaves the drama queen in the parking lot," Sully said.

"That's a sucker bet." Nancy snorted. "We all know who wears the badge in that relationship."

Lindsey wasn't so sure. Emma talked a good game, but Lindsey suspected she was very much in love with Robbie, and while she clearly enjoyed sparring with him, Lindsey didn't think she'd intentionally try to hurt him.

"I'll take that bet," Lindsey said.

"Oh," Violet cooed. "What do you know?"

"Nothing, but I think Emma enjoys Robbie, and I doubt she'd ditch him," Lindsey said.

Emma's squad car passed by, and they all turned to the window to stare. Robbie was in the back seat.

"Ha!" Lindsey said to Sully. "You owe me ten bucks."

"Agreed, but given that he's sitting in the back, I'm not convinced she didn't arrest him for being a public nuisance," he said.

Lindsey laughed. She couldn't argue the point.

"Is your work here done?" he asked.

"Yes," she said.

"That's it?" Nancy protested. "We come here with cookies and we get no information?"

"There's really nothing to tell," Lindsey said. She debated mentioning her engagement, but she wasn't sure how Sully felt about going public with it just yet. For now, she wanted to keep their new status between them. "Emma had some item records for me to look up, and they may point her in a direction, but it certainly doesn't answer all of the questions."

"Like who hit Theresa?" Violet asked. "Or who stole Kayla's car?"

"If someone actually stole it," Nancy said.

"Was it the dead man they found in the car? And who is he, anyway?" Sully asked.

"Is he the same person who tried to suffocate her?" Nancy asked.

"And if so, who shot him?" Violet asked.

"More importantly, who was shooting at her this evening?" Sully said. "Did they shoot the man in Kayla's car, too, and if so, why?"

Lindsey shivered. She glanced at the others, knowing she looked as perplexed and worried as they did. "One thing is certain: whoever is after Theresa, they are certainly determined to finish the job."

Lindsey awoke early the next morning. Sully had a crack-of-dawn pickup in his water taxi. It was so early, the sun wasn't even up. Lindsey stayed burrowed under her covers as he moved about their room, not whistling. When he went out to the kitchen, the whistle crept out of him while he made coffee. Lindsey smiled into her pillow. She was going to marry that whistling fool.

When he returned with her coffee, he planted a kiss on her head, whispered that he loved her, and turned to leave. Lindsey grabbed his hand and tugged him back so that he had to catch himself from falling on top of her by planting his other hand on the edge of the bed.

He grimaced and looked at her from beneath his lashes. "I really did try not to whistle."

Lindsey smiled. She gestured to the floor, where her shoes sat in a heap. "And I really meant to put my shoes away."

His grin was like the sun bursting up from the horizon. "So, we're good?"

"Never better."

Sully scooped her up close and squeezed her tight. "And now I'm going to be late."

Neither one of them cared.

The memory of her morning made Lindsey smile. When she walked Heathcliff to Nancy's, since she liked to pet-sit him, Nancy remarked that she looked especially cheerful. Lindsey shrugged it off. She knew her new status with Sully was the reason for the bubble of joy floating around inside her, but still, she wanted to wait to share the news.

This was, of course, assuming that Sully still felt the same way. It had occurred to her after he'd left that morning that he'd asked her to marry him after a close encounter with a bullet, and maybe it had just been his relief at still being alive. She tried not to overthink it, but she didn't want to get too excited if he'd been impulsive in his proposing.

It was a beautiful spring day, so she decided to ride her bike to work, the same Schwinn cruiser she'd been riding since she'd moved to town. She stuffed her book bag in the back basket and kicked off from her house. The ride from Sully's wasn't much farther than the one from her old apartment, but it was a bit more scenic, as it wound through the older neighborhoods. Even so, she was just going to make it to work on time.

Lindsey was pedaling past the bakery, feeling regret that she didn't have enough time to get a good cup of coffee and a muffin, when she saw Toby Carter come out a side door of the small store, carrying a sack of groceries. While she watched, he ducked behind the hedge that circled the small parking lot in back. Lindsey hit her brakes.

Emma had said she was going to talk to Toby last night. He was wearing the green apron he always wore while working his shift at Briar Creek's only grocery store, so it was clear that whatever conversation they'd had, it hadn't culminated in Toby getting arrested. Hmm.

She knew she should pedal on to work. She knew it, and yet she turned the handlebars of her bike toward the grocery store, parking the bike in the rack in front. She then started up the wooden steps that led to the side entrance of the small shop, inhaling the delicious smell of muffins and pastries as she went. If Toby was delivering someone's groceries, she could wait for him here and then engage him in conversation when he came back.

She took the steps slowly, knowing that once she was at the top, she'd be high enough to see over the hedge and into the parking lot. She could hear muffled voices as she approached, and she paused, inching closer until she could hear what was being said.

"I don't care what's at stake," a voice snapped. "You can't tell anyone. Ever."

"But—" a male voice protested. She was certain it was Toby.

"No, no buts." It was a woman's voice. It sounded familiar, but Lindsey couldn't place it.

"So, you'd rather go to jail than tell the truth, that we're in lo—"

"Don't say it!" the woman shrieked.

Lindsey paused with her hand on the rail. The voices were just beyond the hedge. She was so close. If she just leaned a little bit to her right—say, in an effort to use the banister to tie her shoe—she might be able to get a glimpse of whom Toby was speaking to.

She propped her foot up and yanked her shoelace loose, then she made a big show of tying it while she leaned down and glanced over the hedge into the small parking lot beyond. Sure enough, there was Toby talking to Kayla Manning. She ducked down, hoping that if she stayed still, she could listen to what was being said.

Her opportunity was lost when the door to the bakery opened and Dennis Greaves and Sam Holloway came out.

"Good morning, Lindsey!" Dennis called out as if she were fifty feet away instead of five.

"Morning, Lindsey," Sam echoed.

"Hi, Dennis, Sam." Lindsey finished tying her shoe and rose to her full height. She glanced to her right and noticed that the conversation on the other side of the hedge had stopped.

Kayla's head snapped up in her direction, and her eyes narrowed into slits. Then she snatched a bag of groceries out of Toby's hands and dropped them unceremoniously into the trunk of what appeared to be a rental car.

"Thanks for the help, Toby," Kayla said. She reached up and ruffled his hair. "Such a darling boy. See you around."

Toby frowned at her as if he had no idea what she was saying and was offended that she was treating him as if he were twelve instead of twenty. Lindsey knew the whole thing was for her benefit. Kayla must have suspected that she had overheard their conversation.

Kayla squeezed past Toby, climbed into her car, and sped off as if the long arm of the law was chasing her. Lindsey wondered whether perhaps it was.

Sam and Dennis squeezed past her on the steps with a wave good-bye, but Lindsey lingered, waiting for Toby. He stood forlornly in the parking lot, watching Kayla drive off, looking like he wanted to race after her, his expression a mix of frustration and infatuation.

Lindsey didn't envy him that. When she had speculated about Toby and Kayla knowing each other, she hadn't considered the possibility that they were romantically involved. From what she had overheard, it was clear they were in a relationship, and, oh boy, what a mess that was going to be when Emma found out. And she would find out, because if Toby and Kayla hadn't told her already, Lindsey would.

Toby stared after Kayla's car before turning back to the store. His back was rigid, and his posture was tense. In all the years Lindsey had seen him at the library during his study group, she'd never seen him upset. One of the things she liked most about him was his easy smile and can-do attitude. She wondered whether that was one of the things Kayla liked about him, too.

When Kayla's car disappeared, Toby stomped around the hedge, heading back into the grocery store. When he moved around her, Lindsey reached out and touched his arm.

"Hey, Toby, are you all right?" she asked.

The young man stared at her with a blank expression, then he shook his head as if trying to get his head in the moment.

"Ms. Norris, um, hi," he said. "I'm sorry—I didn't see you there."

"I figured," she said. "You look as if you have something on your mind. Is there anything I can help you with?"

He swallowed, as if he was thinking about talking to her. Then he looked down and studied his shoes. "Nah, I'm good—really, totally good."

Lindsey put on her library-director face. It was the look she gave her staff when she was waiting for them to tell her about something that was going to require paper-work. She had learned pretty early on when she became the director that the less she talked when engaging her staff, the more they spoke to fill in the silence. She noticed they shared more if she didn't interrupt with her own opinion.

"If you're sure," she said.

Toby paused. He glanced at her face, and Lindsey made it as blank as possible.

"I just, you know, there's this girl—well, no, she's a woman," he stammered.

Lindsey waited.

"You know, because I'm a man," he said.

Since Lindsey was in her midthirties, twenty did not seem like a man to her, but she said nothing. She just nodded.

"Anyway, she's got some stuff happening and she doesn't want me involved, but I'm already involved, because I love her."

His voice cracked when he said he loved her, and it was all Lindsey could do not to say, *Aw.* Instead, she nodded.

"The thing is—well, actually, this concerns you," he said.

"It does?" Lindsey blinked. How did he know she was fishing for information? She felt a moment of panic.

"Yeah, because I lost my library card," he said.

"Oh?" she said.

"And it looks like someone checked out some materials on my card," he said. "So, I should probably report it."

"Right, you don't want to be liable for what someone else checked out."

"All right, I'll do that," he said.

Lindsey looked at him. He was a conversational Ping-Pong ball. She needed to get him back on track.

"I'm not really following how your missing library card has anything to do with the woman you love not wanting to get you involved in something," Lindsey said. She hoped he would explain. He didn't.

"It's complicated," he said with a sigh.

"Toby, is there any chance the woman that you love has something to do with your card being missing?" she asked. "Did she borrow it or something?"

"No," he said. "She's not a reader."

"Ah, well, do you know when or where you lost your card?" she asked.

"No," he said. "The last time I used it was over a week ago, to check out some research books for my Japanese class, and I hadn't thought about it until last night, when—"

He stopped talking and looked embarrassed. Clearly, he didn't want to admit that the chief of police had been to see him. Toby was a bright young man. Lindsey knew he would figure out in a few seconds who had told Emma that the materials found in Kayla's car had been checked out on his card. She decided to help him out.

"When Chief Plewicki stopped by your house," she said.

"You know." He looked excruciatingly uncomfortable.

Lindsey crossed her arms over her chest and leaned against the railing. "I'm the one who told her that the materials were checked out on your card. I hope you know I wasn't betraying your patron confidentiality. She had a subpoena."

"Oh, yeah, I can see where you had no choice." His face paled, and he glanced at her from beneath his lashes. "The thing is, I didn't check out any of those things, I didn't have anything to do with the hit-and-run, and I definitely did not shoot the dead guy. I don't even own a gun."

"Did you lend your card to anyone?"

"No, no one," he said. "I always keep it in the front pocket of my backpack, but when the chief stopped by last night and I went to look for it again, because I haven't seen it in over a week, it wasn't there."

Lindsey decided it was time to push. She studied his face when she asked, "Did you tell Chief Plewicki about your relationship with Kayla?"

"I'm not . . . we're not . . ." he protested.

Lindsey shook her head, letting him know he needn't bother. She knew.

He blew out a breath, ran a hand over his face, and dropped his chin to his chest.

"No, I didn't tell the chief. No one knows about us," he said. "I don't care who knows, but Kayla freaked out. She said her reputation was bad enough without adding cradle robber to it. I really do love her. I don't want to get her in trouble."

"I can appreciate that, but you need to tell the chief about your relationship," Lindsey said. "If you don't, the chief is going to consider you a suspect."

"But if I do, Chief Plewicki is going to consider Kayla a suspect," he said. "When we found out my library card was used by the dead guy, she freaked. She thinks someone is trying to make it look like she hired a hit man to kill Ms. Huston or that she had me hire a hit man for her. Why would we do that? We're in love."

"There have been some cases in the media where an older woman has a relationship with a younger man and gets him to kill for her," Lindsey said. "It's a sad cliché, but it does happen."

"But that's crazy. Even though I love her, I would never do that!" Toby's voice went high, and Lindsey glanced around to make certain no one could hear them. "Besides, she would never ask me to do something like that. Kayla is a warm and wonderful woman."

"Even so, I'm sure you can see where people might read it wrong," Lindsey said. "If you are Kayla's alibi, then telling the truth is the best thing you can do for her."

"She'll never go for it."

"Try to get her to agree," she said. "If there's anything I can do to help you, let me know."

"Thanks," Toby said. He jerked his thumb in the direction of the store. "I'd better get back."

"Sure."

Toby held the door for her when Lindsey went into the bakery and ordered a poppy seed lemon muffin with her extra-large high-octane coffee. Given the start to her day, she had a feeling she was going to need it.

She arrived at the library in time to help with setup. The book drop needed to be emptied, the computers turned on, and the phones taken off their nightly call forwarding. Lindsey stowed her purse and her food in her office and joined her morning staff as they hustled around the building.

She set up the reference desk, switching on the computer and the public terminals nearby. She went to help with circulation when she noticed that Ms. Cole wasn't there. Ms. Cole was always there. She was like a commander in battle: the front desk was her front line, and she never abandoned her post. Ever.

"Stupid, ridiculous, idiotic waste of money, bucket of bolts . . . grrr."

The muttering sounded familiar. Lindsey followed the grumbling until she found Ms. Cole holding a roll of receipt paper while glaring at the self-checkout machine.

"Problem, Ms. Cole?" she asked.

"I'll say." Ms. Cole gestured at the machine with the roll of paper. "It won't print. I have loaded the paper three times, in every conceivable direction, and all I get is this." She lifted up a strip of the paper that looked as if it had been neatly folded into accordion pleats.

"Paper jam," Lindsey said. "Not helpful."

"No, it isn't," Ms. Cole said. "We're supposed to open in a matter of minutes, and I do not have time for this."

Lindsey held out her hand. "I'll take a look, and if I can't get it working, I'll call it in."

Ms. Cole stared at her for a moment. "Thank you."

She dropped the roll of paper into Lindsey's hand and walked away. Given how much Ms. Cole hated technology and how resistant she had been to the dreaded self-checkout machine, Lindsey had to take this as a win, even if it meant she was the one wrestling with the stupid paper-receipt printer—and before coffee, too.

She decided to go with a full-on troubleshooting approach and shut the machine down for a few moments before starting it up and trying to get the printer portion of it to work. The machine was resistant. Much like Ms. Cole, she ended up with pleated paper and no receipt, and the printer made a lovely beeping noise like a truck backing up just to let her know there was an error. Lindsey could feel her temples compressing as a headache loomed. She refused to look over at Ms. Cole. She did not want to see any smirking.

She spooled in the paper and hit the feed button. It bunched up. She opened the latch and fed the spool of paper the other way. She hit the feed button again. Again it jammed.

Lindsey switched the machine off. First, she needed coffee. Second, she would call someone from the company to try to troubleshoot the machine over the phone. She made a quick OUT OF ORDER sign and slapped it on the machine. Then she headed back to her office.

She called out to Ms. Cole as she passed, "I'm still working on it."

"Uh-huh," Ms. Cole replied. Lindsey was certain there was a smirk in her tone.

When Lindsey entered her office, she found Robbie sitting there. She jumped and put her hand on her chest.

"Robbie, we're not even open yet," she said. "What are you doing here?"

"I came in the back with Beth," he said. "We have to talk."

"About what?"

"The case," he said. "We have an unidentified dead body—"

"*We* don't," she corrected him. She heard her phone *ping* in her purse and pulled it out of the side pocket. "The police do, and he's no longer unidentified. They have his name. This is their investigation."

She glanced down at the screen in case it was something related to work. The text message was from Susie McAllister at the genealogical library. Lindsey read it and then read it again. She had no idea what to make of this information, but she knew it was huge.

"Fine, you're right. It's police business, but that doesn't mean we can't help gather information," he said. "We have a hit-and-run, an unsuccessful suffocation, not to mention the Norrgard twins barely got Theresa out of the line of fire last night. So, what did you say the dead man's name was?"

"I didn't. And don't ask, because I'm not sharing," Lindsey said.

"Why not?" he asked.

"Because this is dangerous," she said. "There are people driving through the middle of town, shooting guns. It's incredible that only one person has been killed—tragic, but still remarkable."

"See, it's our duty to help the town in any way we can. I mean, who better to find out who is trying to kill Theresa Huston than us?"

"Your girlfriend, the chief of police," Lindsey said.

"She's hampered by the law," he said. "Whilst we are free to question whoever we want whenever we want."

Lindsey shook her head at him, knowing full well she was being a hypocrite, given her conversation with Toby. And with the text sitting in the palm of her hand writhing in her grasp like a living thing. How could she just ignore it? She couldn't. She closed her office door and took her seat behind her desk. Robbie, as if sensing he had her full attention, put aside the newspaper he was holding and leaned forward.

"What if I told you I had looked into the disappearance of Larry Milstein's first wife, Sarah?" she asked. "And that I think I may have found her."

CHAPTER

14

BRIAR CREEK
PUBLIC LIBRARY

Robbie tipped his head to the side. "She vanished fifteen years ago."

"Yes, and there's never been any trace of her, except—" Lindsey paused. She wasn't sure what to make of the text she'd just received, but if anyone could charm the information out of Larry to confirm it, it was Robbie.

"Except? Come on, pet, out with it. You're killing me," he said.

"Okay, I had a librarian friend who works at a genealogy library do a vital records check for Sarah Milstein, thinking maybe she would find something somewhere that would lead to her, since they never found a body. And it did. My friend found a divorce decree for Lawrence and Sarah Milstein in Virginia," she said. She glanced down at the phone and enlarged the document that her friend had attached. "Here's the thing: the petition for divorce was filed five years after she went missing."

"How do the police not know this?" Robbie asked.

"I don't know," Lindsey said. "It could be another Lawrence and Sarah Milstein; it could be because it was in Virginia; it could be because no one went looking for any documents."

"Wasn't Larry in Virginia at the time she went missing?"

"He has stores all down the Eastern Seaboard," Lindsey said. "And I believe he has houses in several states, including Virginia and Florida."

"So he could file for divorce from virtually anywhere," Robbie said. "Especially if Sarah is alive and living in that state."

They stared at each other.

"This means she never went missing," Robbie said.

"But Larry wanted everyone to think she did," she said. "Why? And for that matter, who was the woman I saw in the window? Was it Sarah? Is she still alive?"

"And skulking around the Milstein mansion? That makes no sense," he said. "There's a taint about Larry because his wife went missing—wouldn't he want to clear that up?"

"You'd think," she agreed. "You can ask him that over whiskey."

"Oh, right, that won't be awkward."

"He likes you."

"Enough to admit that he divorced his wife, who went

missing fifteen years ago? And then what happened to her? Did she remarry? Did she become an expat on some Caribbean island?" Robbie asked. "I don't think our mutual love of ridiculously expensive whiskey will get him to open up to me that much."

"Probably, you'll have the best luck after the whiskey," she said.

Robbie tipped his head back and stared at the ceiling. Lindsey knew him well enough to know he was trying to play out the scene in his mind. What he could say that would get Larry to talk to him about his wife, or ex-wife. He blew out a breath and tapped the arms of his chair with his fingers.

"Pissed," Robbie said. He lowered his head and directed his stare at Lindsey. "That's about the only way I can imagine that man will tell me anything. I will have to get him good and truly sozzled."

"I feel like you're up to the task," she said.

Robbie grinned. "There are worse jobs."

"Right, and in the meantime, I am going to get this vital-record information to Emma," Lindsey said. "That should get me out of some hot water with her, don't you think?"

"Eh." Robbie shrugged. "Are any of us ever truly out of trouble with her?"

Lindsey nodded in agreement. Emma could be exacting, which made her an excellent chief of police.

Robbie departed for his mission, and Lindsey forwarded the divorce record to Emma with a text explaining what she had requested of her friend. Emma could get annoyed with her, but Lindsey seriously doubted that she would. Even if it turned out to be another Lawrence and Sarah Milstein, it was something in a case that was seriously lacking any direction.

She glanced at her computer and realized that she needed to tell Ms. Cole to suspend Toby's card. If he really had lost it, then whoever had found it had checked out the CDs that were discovered in Kayla's car. Of course, if it had been the suspect, then it stood to reason that if he had no problem stealing a car, he certainly wouldn't blink at stealing a library card.

A glance out her office window and Lindsey saw Ms. Cole talking to Milton Duffy. The two of them had been an item ever since performing in *A Midsummer Night's Dream*, and while some considered them an odd couple, Lindsey took comfort in the fact that two such opposite personalities had found each other.

She decided to take care of Toby's record herself. She opened the circulation module on her computer and typed in Toby's name. It took only a moment for his record to appear on the screen. She looked to see whether he had any overdue books she should warn him about, but there weren't any listed.

She scanned the list of items, seeing that the CDs found in Kayla's car were still there. She frowned. When she had checked the barcodes for Emma, and Toby had been listed as the person who'd borrowed the items, she hadn't thought to look at his full record. Now that she was looking at it, there were more items than the CDs checked out, but that made no sense.

Toby had said he'd lost his card before the CDs were checked out. If that was true, then whoever had taken his card had checked out more materials, and they'd done it recently.

Lindsey looked at the list of titles. There were some books and some audiobooks. The titles looked familiar, but why? And then it hit her. The audiobooks listed were perfect for listening to when you were dosed on pain medication and didn't have the energy to read—say, for someone who had just been hit by a car and was stuck in an enormous cast. As she recognized the list of titles, her heart lurched in her chest.

The list matched the items she had helped Liza gather for Theresa. In fact, it matched exactly. There was no way this was a coincidence. Liza Milstein had used Toby's card to check out the audiobooks for Theresa, but did that mean she was also the one who had checked out the CDs that were found in the car? Either way, it was not something Lindsey could ignore.

She quickly brought up the circulation records for Theresa Huston and Liza Milstein. Neither of them had any books checked out, so Liza hadn't used either of their cards. She switched back to Toby's record. She tapped her lips with her index finger while she considered the ramifications of what she was looking at.

How had Liza gotten Toby's card? It could have been during their study group. Maybe their cards had just gotten mixed up. But that only proved that Toby wasn't involved and that Liza was, unless, of course, Toby was lying.

Lindsey hated the thought that either one of them could be involved in something this awful. It looked bad for Liza right now, but Lindsey remembered that Toby had come running up to his study group after Theresa had been hit. He hadn't been with them in the library, so he had no alibi as far as Lindsey knew, and he had only his word as proof that he had lost his card—maybe he hadn't. Maybe Liza had gotten her card mixed up with his after the hit-and-run. There was no way to be sure. The only thing that was certain was that someone was lying. The question was, Who?

She picked up the phone on her desk and dialed the police chief's direct number.

"Chief Plewicki," Emma answered.

"Emma, it's Lindsey," she said. "I think I found something that you might want to look at."

"What's that?" Emma asked. Her voice was muffled. It sounded as if she was chewing while she spoke.

"It'll be easier to explain if I show you," Lindsey said.

"I'm kind of busy," Emma said. "I'm trying to trace this Chad Bauman, figure out who was shooting at Theresa Huston last night, and verify that the vital record you texted me is for our Larry and Sarah Milstein. Thanks for that, by the way."

"You're welcome," Lindsey said. "Here's the thing. I think I know who *really* checked out those CDs that the state crime lab has in evidence."

"I'm listening," Emma said.

"Liza Milstein," Lindsey said.

"I'll be right over."

The phone went dead, and Lindsey hung up her receiver. She glanced back at the computer and hoped she was correct. She scanned the titles again. She squinted at the list. It was shorter. A couple of them were missing. She refreshed the page. Another one went missing. What the hell? Had someone hacked the system?

She glanced out at the circulation desk and saw Stieg Norrgard chatting with Ms. Cole, who was checking in a stack of items that was piled between them. Oh no! Stieg had returned the materials!

"Stop!" Lindsey yelled. She jumped to her feet and sprinted out of her office, calling, "Stop, Ms. Cole. Stop!"

"What on earth?" Ms. Cole turned to look at her as if she thought Lindsey was a few volumes short of a set.

"Don't check in any more materials," Lindsey said.

"I . . . but . . . that's . . ." Ms. Cole stuttered. Since she was the head of circulation, checking in and out materials was her thing, and being told not to do so clearly did not compute.

"Just until Chief Plewicki gets here," Lindsey said. "Stieg, hi," she added as she turned to face him.

"Hi, Lindsey, everything okay?"

"No." She shook her head. "Did you bring these materials back?"

"Yes, I'm returning them for Theresa," he said. "She said to say thank you and asked if you had time to find more books and audiobooks for her. She would be ever grateful."

Lindsey nodded and then turned to Ms. Cole. "Where are the books you just checked in, Ms. Cole?"

"On the cart to be sorted for shelving," she said. "Exactly where I always put the returned items."

"Of course," Lindsey said. She shook her head, feeling panicked at the thought of what she'd discovered being erased by Ms. Cole's efficiency. She turned to the cart. It was empty. She glanced back at Ms. Cole. "Where are the books?"

"The cart was full," she said. "Heather took it into the workroom to sort."

"No!" Lindsey turned to go to the workroom but then turned back and said, "Do not check in anything!"

Both Stieg and Ms. Cole looked at her as if she were possessed, and she realized her voice had come out a tad demonic, so she added, "Please."

Once in the workroom, Lindsey found Heather sitting on a stool, organizing a cart of books.

"Heather, where is the cart you just wheeled in here?" Lindsey asked.

The part-time teen worker looked at her with a worried expression and pointed to the end of the row of carts. "I put it right there. Did I do something wrong, Ms. Norris?"

"No, you're fine—I'm just looking for some materials that were just checked in."

"Oh." Heather nodded. She watched Lindsey as she hurried for the cart, grabbing the audiobooks she remembered helping Liza choose.

Lindsey saw only five audiobooks that she remembered. She hoped she got them all. She hurried back to the front desk, where Ms. Cole and Stieg Norrgard stood talking in low voices. She knew they were talking about her, and they probably thought she was having a librarian episode, but she didn't have time to worry about that. It was critical that she gather these audiobooks before Emma—

"All right, Lindsey, I'm here," Chief Plewicki said as she strode into the library. "What do you have to show me?"

"It was better about five minutes ago," Lindsey said. She moved to stand beside Ms. Cole and gestured to her computer. "May I?"

Ms. Cole stepped back as if she thought the craziness might be catching, then she waved for Lindsey to continue.

"I ran into Toby Carter this morning," Lindsey said as she opened up the patron-record option in the circulation system. "He was helping Kayla Manning load groceries into her rental car." She paused to look at Emma and see whether this had any significance for her. It didn't appear to, and Lindsey figured she'd better mention that Toby and Kayla were a thing. If she was sharing, she was going to share everything.

"And?" Emma asked.

"He told me that he lost his library card before the hit-and-run," Lindsey said.

"Yeah, that's his story," Emma said. "He told me the same thing last night."

"He said he didn't check out those CDs," Lindsey said. She finished opening his record and swiveled the computer so that Emma could see the monitor.

Emma glanced at the screen and then at Lindsey. "These are the CDs. I recognize the titles."

"Yes, they are," Lindsey said. "And here, checked out after the CDs, are the poetry book and audiobooks that Liza brought to Theresa on the day someone tried to smother her."

"I'm not following," Emma said.

"I was with Liza when she checked out those materials. The fact that they are on Toby's record means Liza used Toby's card to check them out, using the self-checkout machine, meaning that if she'd had Toby's card for a while, she also could have been the one to check out the CDs that were found in Kayla Manning's car."

"What?" Stieg stood up straight.

Lindsey ignored him, keeping her focus on Emma.

"I had the record with all of the titles, but Stieg returned the items, and Ms. Cole started checking them in, so while I have the materials, I no longer have the record that is an exact match," Lindsey said. "Sorry."

"That's okay," Emma said. "You helped her get the books and check them out and saw the record while it was still active. That makes you an eyewitness."

"To what, exactly?" Stieg asked. He looked tense. "Are you saying that Liza is responsible for the attempts on Theresa's life?"

"Maybe," Lindsey said. She liked the young woman. She hated saying it, but she couldn't deny the possibility. "The other thing I found out this morning is that Toby and Kayla are involved."

Emma tipped her head to the side and said, "Explain."

"I interrupted them when they were having a heated discussion outside the grocery store," Lindsey said. "According to Toby, Kayla wants to keep their relationship quiet because her reputation is already bad, and she's afraid people will think she's using Toby as a boy toy to get back at Larry."

"Or by having him kill Theresa for her?" Emma asked. Her body went rigid.

"He didn't say that," Lindsey said. "Just that her taking up with him might make her reputation worse than it already is."

"Well, there's some self-awareness I wouldn't have credited her with," Ms. Cole said.

"I need to talk to them both again," Emma said. "I swear ninety percent of my job is ferreting out people's lies. But first, I need to talk to Liza about using Toby's card. I don't like what that could mean. Liza has easy access to Theresa."

"More than you know," Stieg said. He shoved his hand into his pocket, pulled out his phone, opened the display window, swiped, and then held the phone to his ear. "Stefan, we have a problem. Theresa cannot be alone with Liza."

Lindsey could hear Stefan's voice on the other end. He sounded upset.

Stieg looked at Emma Plewicki. "Do you have your car here?"

"Yes, why?"

"Stefan dropped off Liza and Theresa at the Thistle Inn and Resort not far from here," he said. "Liza told him not to wait around, since no one knew they were going there. The place is so high end it has its own security, so he figured they'd be fine. Theresa said they were going to have a quiet spa day and not to worry."

Emma started to run, shouting over her shoulder, "Hold those books!"

Stieg jogged after her. The automatic doors whooshed closed behind them, and Lindsey blew out a breath and leaned against the counter. "I hope they get there in time."

Lindsey printed out the records for Toby, Liza, and Theresa. She then put the records and the materials that Stieg had brought back in a cupboard in her office. As far as she was concerned, it was evidence, and she would treat it as such until further notice from Emma.

The wait for news was painfully slow. She found she couldn't focus on any tasks and roamed the library, looking out the window with her phone in her pocket.

An hour went by, and there was still no word. She was straightening the new magazine rack when the doors slid open and Robbie entered the building, scanning the room until he saw her.

"Lindsey, you may want to take a little break, um, now," he said. He was walk-running at her, and Lindsey looked at him in bewilderment.

"What do you mean?" she asked. "What's going on?"

"You!" Larry Milstein came in right behind Robbie. His face was a mottled shade of red, and he looked like he was barely keeping a lid on his temper.

Lindsey knew there was only one reason Larry would be furious with her. He must have found out that she told Emma that Liza might be responsible for the attempts on Theresa's life. She was swamped with a sudden wave of guilt but then remembered she had found documentation that Larry had divorced his wife ten years ago and had never told anyone that she was still alive. She was not the bad guy here.

She put her hands on her hips and thrust out her chin. "What?"

Milstein came to a full stop in front of her. "How could you? You know Liza. She considers you her friend. How could you tell the police that she was the one behind the attempts on Theresa's life?"

"I didn't say that," Lindsey said. Milstein gave her an incredulous look. "I said she might be."

He threw his hands up in the air.

Robbie stepped up beside Lindsey as if to protect her. She appreciated the gesture, but she could handle this.

"Listen, if what Toby said was true, and he did lose his library card before Kayla Manning's car was stolen, then the person who had his card, Liza, is the person the police need to speak with," she said.

"It's all circumstantial," he protested. "Not to mention ridiculous. Liza loves Theresa. Why would she hurt her?"

"Maybe because she found out that her mother is alive," Robbie said.

Milstein gaped at him. "Who told you that?"

Lindsey didn't say anything. She knew Robbie had said what he had to pull Milstein's ire off her, but she had a feeling Emma was going to be unhappy. Too late now.

"I told him," Lindsey said.

"Wasn't really planning to share that part, pet," Robbie whispered to her.

"That is personal information," Larry said. "No one has any right to invade my privacy."

"They do if your wife is alive," Emma Plewicki said. She strolled into the library, looking as if she'd expected to find Larry here. "I had the divorce record that Lindsey found checked out. It is yours. You've known all along your wife was alive, haven't you?"

"I . . ." Larry swallowed. He glanced at each of them, and then his face crumpled from outrage to grief. "Yes, of course I knew." He glanced at Emma with a fierce light in his eye. "Theresa, is she . . . ?"

"She's fine," Emma said. "Stefan found her at the spa and got her out of there. Luckily, she was waiting in the lounge with several other ladies. Stieg searched for Liza, but there was no sign of her. She appears to have run."

"She didn't!" Larry protested. "She wouldn't. She loves Theresa. She considers her more of a mother than her own mother. If anyone is after Theresa, it's that Toby kid. He's sleeping with Kayla Manning, who has never gotten over being dumped by me, and I'm sure she used her sexual favors to manipulate him into doing what she wanted."

Lindsey glanced at Robbie. His eyebrows were up high on his forehead as he took in this torrent of accusation.

"Which is why I asked them both to meet us here, since I knew you were here as well," Emma said. "I'd like to hear what they have to say about that."

"Who cares what they have to say?" Larry shouted. "Wait. How did you know I was here? Are you following me?"

Emma shrugged.

Lindsey glanced around the room and noted that the library had gone still as everyone watched the drama unfold. Clearly, everyone cared.

"Maybe we should take this into another room," she said.

"Chief Plewicki." Andrea Carter entered the library with her son Toby by her side. "You asked us to meet you here?"

"Oh, boy, and now Mom is involved," Robbie said. He folded his arms across his chest, obviously settling in to watch what happened next.

"Yes, thank you," Emma said. She turned to Lindsey. "I think I'll take you up on the offer of a meeting room."

Lindsey nodded. She glanced at the three glass-walled study rooms on the far side of the library. Only one was occupied. "This way."

They were halfway across the room when Kayla Manning arrived. And right behind her was Chief Plewicki's right-hand man, Officer Kirkland. Lindsey watched him exchange a nod with Emma and suspected that the two of them had been keeping tabs on all the persons of interest.

"You!" Larry shouted. He pointed at Kayla as if there were any doubt as to whom he was shouting at. "You're the reason for all of this, aren't you?"

"What are you talking about?" Kayla asked. She was dressed in workout clothes, and the neon green and pink spandex hugged her muscle-hardened thighs, while her taut abs were showcased below the sports bra that framed her bosom to its best advantage.

Toby was riveted, but his mother seemed oblivious, clearly not getting that her baby boy was a man now and a woman like Kayla was making his head not only turn but swivel in an anatomically impossible three-sixty.

"You sent him"—Larry pointed at Toby—"to harm Theresa, didn't you?"

Kayla blinked. "Are you insane?"

"You were mad that I dumped you, so you worked your feminine wiles on this boy so that you could get him to exact revenge for you."

"Toby?" Andrea Carter glanced from her son to Kayla and back. Her eyes were huge. "Is this true? Are you in a relationship with Ms. Manning?"

"I'm in love with her, Mom," Toby said. His look was so earnest, it actually caused a pang in Lindsey's chest.

"Oh, the poor sod," Robbie whispered to Lindsey. "I don't think this is going to end well for him."

Emma leaned around Lindsey to look at Robbie. "Why are you here?"

"I'm being helpful," he said.

"No, you're not," Emma said. She glanced from him to Larry. "In fact, neither of you are."

"I'm not trying to be helpful," Larry ground out. "I'm trying to defend my daughter."

"Well, I can only deal with one problem college kid at a time," Emma said. She crossed to the study-room door and pushed it open. "You two stay out!"

"This is an outrage!" Larry cried.

"Yeah, yeah, call my supervisor," Emma said. "Oh, wait, that's me. Now git."

Larry stomped across the library, and Robbie watched him.

"I'll keep an eye on him, shall I?" he asked Emma.

"Do, but don't get into trouble."

"I promise, love," he said. He kissed her cheek and hurried after Larry, who was charging across the room.

After another nod from Emma, Officer Kirkland followed the two men.

Lindsey moved to hold the door open while they all squeezed into the study room.

"Toby, I don't think you realize—" his mother began, but he interrupted her.

"I love her," Toby insisted. "It's that simple."

"But she's so much—" Andrea began, but Kayla cut her off.

"So much what?" Kayla snapped.

"More mature," Andrea said. "I was just going to say mature."

"You mean I'm too old for him," Kayla said. She

planted her hands on her hips and bent one knee, show-ing off her knock-'em-to-their-knees figure to perfection.

"Well, yeah," Andrea said. "Good grief, you're my age!"

Obviously, Kayla's figure meant nothing to Andrea as she stood in her khaki capris and floral blouse with a sweater tied around her shoulders. Her hair was more gray than brown, and the lines around her mouth and eyes were faint, but they were definitely the signs of a woman solidly in middle age.

"Mom!" Toby protested.

"What? She is."

"So?" he asked. "I don't care. I love her."

"Really?" Andrea asked. She raised her hands in the air in complete exasperation. "Because you know so much about love. How about I throw over your dad and pick up with your best friend, Alec?"

"Mom, ew, gross," Toby said.

"Uh-huh," Andrea agreed.

"It's not the same," Toby protested.

"People, can we get back to the matter at hand?" Emma broke in.

"Yes, let's discuss how Kayla's not over me and is the mastermind behind the hit-and-run and everything else that has happened to Theresa," Larry said as he barged into the room. He glared at Kayla while Robbie stood behind him, shrugging.

"Oh, please," Kayla snapped. "Look at him and look at you." She waved her hand between Toby and Larry. "He's got youth, good looks, and stamina. What do you have?"

"Money."

"Money can't buy you love," Kayla retorted, then she clapped a hand over her mouth.

Andrea closed her eyes and put a hand over her face. Toby grinned.

"So, you admit that you care about me?" he asked Kayla.

"I didn't say that," she said.

"Yes, you did," Toby argued. He crossed the room until he was standing in front of Kayla. "Admit it. You care about me."

"Only as a distraction," Kayla said. She tried to wave him off, but he wasn't having it.

"You are all my witnesses," Toby said. "Kayla Manning is smitten with me."

Kayla blushed a shade of hot pink, while Andrea looked a bit ill. Larry was fuming, and Emma had a speculative look on her face while she watched what was going on around her.

"Toby, we have the little matter of your library card being used to check out the materials that were found in Kayla's car to discuss," Emma said.

"There weren't any CDs in my car when it was stolen," Kayla said. "I'm a satellite radio type of gal. Classic rock is my jam, as it's a workout motivator."

"It's true," Toby said. "That's all she listens to."

"How do you know this?" Andrea asked. "And how do I not know that you know this? I thought we were close."

Toby gave his mom a sympathetic look. "Sorry. It just sort of happened when I ran that marathon last fall." He threw his arm around Kayla and pulled her close. "We just clicked."

Andrea sank into a seat at the small conference table. "My son is dating a woman the same age as me. My brain is shutting down. I can't process this."

"Is there any way to prove that your card was stolen?" Emma asked Toby. "Did you report it to the library?"

"No." Toby shook his head. "I just figured it would turn up."

Emma's mouth twisted. Lindsey suspected she wanted to clear Toby off her suspect list so that she could focus on Liza.

"You lost your card?" Andrea stared at her son. "Is that why you've been using my card? By the way, I just got an overdue notice for a book on biomedical engineering, which I am not paying. You promised me if I loaned you my card, you would be responsible."

"I'll pay the fine," Toby said.

His mother fumed and waved a hand at Kayla. "Why not have your girlfriend pay it? At least she has a job."

"Mom." Toby gasped. "I have a job."

"That's right, you're a bag boy at the grocery store," she said, looking at Kayla. Then she turned toward her son. "And don't you 'Mom' me." She rose from her seat and adjusted the strap of her purse on her forearm. "You don't get to have it both ways, young man, and yes, you are a young man. You don't get to have the older girlfriend while you live in my home, eat my food, and have overdue books on my library card—"

"Are you getting this?" Emma asked Lindsey.

"Oh yeah," Lindsey said. "Give me one minute with our database, and I can verify that he's been using his mother's card and therefore not likely checking out materials on his own."

"Excellent," Emma said. "Go."

Lindsey backed out of the room slowly, so as not to interrupt the discussion between mother and son.

"You want that?" Andrea waved a hand at Kayla. "Then you need to grow up, get a real job, start paying rent, and show me that you're responsible enough to be treated like an adult and not just some old lady's boy toy."

Kayla sucked in a gasp that Lindsey thought might have taken all the oxygen out of the room. Oh boy. She turned on her heel and hurried to her office. She could hear the women yelling at each other, and as she passed Ms. Cole, she felt her curious gaze over the rim of her reading glasses.

"You know, back when Mr. Tupper was the library director—" Ms. Cole began.

Lindsey turned to look at her and figured she must have had her scary-librarian face on, because Ms. Cole's eyes went wide.

"Just kidding," she said.

Lindsey nodded and continued on her way to her office. For privacy, she opened up the circulation database on her computer. When she checked Andrea Carter's library record, she had books about biomedical engineering, the subject Toby happened to be majoring in, checked out and overdue. Lindsey sent the page to the printer.

By the time Lindsey got back to the study room, Emma was standing in between Kayla and Andrea with Toby nearby, hopping from foot to foot as if uncertain whom he should be calming down.

"Listen, cougar," Andrea snarled. "You are to stay away from my boy."

"Mom!" Toby was pleading.

"What if I don't want to?" Kayla snapped back. "Maybe Toby and I are more serious than you realize. Maybe he's going to move in with me."

"I am?" Toby asked.

"Yes," Kayla said. "Why not?"

"Toby, you're not ready for this." Andrea's voice was sharp with warning.

"I'm sorry, Mom," he said. He looked truly wrecked. "But I love her."

Lindsey handed Emma the printout. She looked at it and then at Toby. "Well, it looks like you were telling the truth about using your mother's card, so I'm not going to arrest you . . . right now."

Toby sagged with relief. He dropped his arm around Kayla's shoulders and pulled her close. "Come on—let's go."

Kayla allowed him to guide her to the door. Toby paused to look back at his mom. "I really am sorry you found out this way, Mom. I hope you can accept Kayla and me as a couple."

Andrea looked at Kayla and then at Toby. She studied them as if she were in a poker game, trying to call another player's bluff. "Come to dinner tonight at our house."

"What?" Kayla and Toby asked together.

"About six o'clock? We can sit down and have a nice family dinner with your dad and sister, too," she said. She glanced at Toby. "If this is seriously what your life plan is, then your family will be a part of it, too."

Kayla paled. Andrea was making it very clear that Toby came with his own familial entourage. Lindsey had to give Andrea props. This was well played.

"We'll be there," Toby said. He looked relieved and nervous at the same time, but he nodded at his mother as they left.

The door shut behind them, and Andrea turned away, facing the wall as if she couldn't bear to watch them leave together. The room was shrouded in awkward silence.

Because it was her library, Lindsey was the first to step forward. "Hey, Andrea, it's going to be all right. If you look on the bright side, at least he's been pushed down on the suspect list."

Andrea didn't say anything. She continued staring down at the floor with her hand over her mouth. Lindsey exchanged a glance with Emma, who raised her hands in the universal sign for *I have no idea what to do*.

"Is he gone yet?" Andrea asked.

Lindsey glanced out of the room at the library. Toby and Kayla were just approaching the doors. The automatic doors whooshed open, and they stepped out into the warm spring sunshine as a happy couple, with their arms around each other for all the world to see.

"They just left," Lindsey said.

Andrea turned back around. Her eyes were shining, and a broad grin parted her lips.

"Whoa," Emma said. "Wait. You're happy?"

"About them? No, but I have a plan," Andrea said.

"Did I miss something?" Lindsey asked. "'Cause you looked like you were upset. Not a little upset, big upset—like crying for days, lying on the floor in a fetal position upset."

"I might have been," Andrea conceded. "But they are coming to dinner."

"And?" Emma asked. She cast a concerned look at Lindsey. "You're not planning on hurting Kayla, are you? Because I'm telling you, as a police chief and your friend, that's a bad idea."

"What?" Andrea asked. She put a hand on her chest in a protestation of innocence. "I would never. Besides, I won't have to."

"No?" Lindsey asked.

"I am going to make sure that Kayla gets a good long look at his room," Andrea said. "That boy is the single most disgusting human being who ever lived. I used to do a daily sweep, but two weeks ago, I gave up. The dirty laundry, food wrappers, plates, all of it—if she gets one look at the filth that boy chooses to live in, she will one hundred percent change her mind about having him move in with her."

"Genius," Emma said.

"So you didn't invite them over to make peace," Lindsey said.

"No," Andrea said. "Kayla Manning might think she

has a man in the making, but when she gets a load of his room, she's going to realize she has a boy. I expect she'll be dumping him, oh, at about eight o'clock tonight."

Emma put one hand on her hip, leaned back, and studied Andrea from top to bottom. "Color me impressed."

"Me, too," Lindsey said. "One question: you didn't seem all that surprised by Kayla. Did you know about her and Toby before today?"

"Of course," Andrea said. "I still do that boy's laundry, and when I found the evidence of birth control in use, I had Mike tail him until we knew who he was shacking up with. I wasn't thrilled, but I figured it would burn out before now. Looks like we'll just have to help it."

"You had them completely fooled," Lindsey said.

"Yeah, well, survival of the fittest," Andrea said. She pulled out her cell phone. "Excuse me, I have to call Mike. He needs to have his game face on for tonight." She paused and looked at Emma. "Aside from all of the family drama, you know Toby had nothing to do with the attacks on Theresa Huston, right?"

Her voice was firm, leaving no room for argument. Emma gave her a slow and thoughtful nod, and said, "It certainly appears that way."

Andrea nodded in return. That was good enough for her.

Lindsey and Emma left the room, shutting the door behind them.

"I didn't see that coming," Lindsey said.

"Agreed," Emma said. "Of course, now we only have one direction to look."

"Liza," Lindsey said. "Unless—"

She paused, and Emma stared at her and then motioned for her to continue. "Come on, out with it."

"Unless the person who hired Chad Bauman and whoever tried to shoot Theresa last night isn't Liza but rather is the missing Sarah Milstein, divorced and not dead," Lindsey said.

CHAPTER

16

BRIAR CREEK
PUBLIC LIBRARY

"How do you figure?" Emma asked.

Lindsey hesitated but then admitted what she'd seen. "I thought I saw Sarah Milstein in the house the night that Robbie and I took the library materials that Liza had left behind to the Milstein house."

"And you didn't think this was relevant information?" Emma asked.

"Well, I saw the face from the driveway, but Robbie didn't, and we figured it had to be household staff or maybe the nurse taking care of Theresa," Lindsey said. "Besides, at the time, Sarah Milstein was presumed deceased."

"Fair enough, but now that we know Milstein faked his wife's disappearance and then divorced her, it could be very relevant," Emma said.

"Which is why I'm telling you," Lindsey said.

Emma strode across the library toward Robbie and Larry. Both men must have sensed she was coming, because they stood taller and looked as if they were bracing themselves.

"You." Emma pointed at Larry. "To the police station for questioning, now."

"I demand to have a lawyer present," he said.

"That's up to you, but the longer this takes, the longer you spend in a jail cell," Emma said.

"Jail cell?" Larry squawked.

"That's right," Emma said. "I'm done waiting for answers. I want to know what the story is with your missing wife, whether she's alive or dead, if you're divorced, and what, if anything, this has to do with your daughter and someone going after Theresa Huston, a woman you have a hefty life insurance policy on." Emma glared at him. "So, tell me, how is business, Larry?"

Larry's mouth dropped open. "You can't think that I have anything to do with the attacks on Theresa?"

Emma's brows lifted.

"I love her. I would never ever harm her," he protested. "Would I have hired bodyguards if I didn't?"

Robbie patted Larry on the shoulder. "I think it's time you tell her, mate."

"But it could mean . . ." Larry's voice trailed off, and Lindsey got the feeling he was in anguish.

"It does mean that," Robbie said. "I know you don't like it, but you can't change it by wishing. Now tell the chief what you just told me."

Larry looked at Emma as if he'd give up a kidney not to have to tell her what he was about to say.

"I took out a multimillion-dollar life insurance policy on Theresa," he said. "It's the same one I have for myself, and we agreed that like mine, Liza would be the beneficiary should anything happen to Theresa."

Emma blinked at him. "You mean if something happens to you or Theresa, Liza inherits several million dollars?"

"Yes, twenty million to be exact," Larry said.

"Why didn't you tell me this before?" she cried.

"Because it doesn't matter," Larry said. "Liza would never—"

"Come on, mate, out with the rest of it," Robbie said.

Lindsey looked at him, and he said, "I didn't even need the whiskey."

"What?" Emma glanced between them.

"Nothing," Lindsey said. "Really, it's nothing."

"What else do you have to tell me?" Emma asked.

"I did fake Sarah's disappearance," Larry said. He ran his hands through his hair, as if he'd rather rip it out by the roots than admit what he'd done.

He was becoming overwrought, and Lindsey wished she could offer him some comfort. Emma stepped up, however, and led him to a plush wing chair in one of the many reading nooks in the library. Emma took the chair near his while Lindsey and Robbie sat on a low table facing them.

"I did it to keep Liza safe. I never meant for it to come back and bite me like this," he said.

"Lies have a way of doing that," Emma said. She sounded weary.

"Liza's mother, Sarah, is unwell," Larry said. "I didn't know when I married her or before she had Liza. It came on after Liza was born. The doctor told me she suffered from a postnatal psychosis. They medicated her, but she refused to take her meds and then she started to harm herself, which was horrifying, but then I caught her—" He closed his mouth, as if he couldn't bear to say it. "Certain circumstances led me to believe that she would harm Liza, so one day, when I couldn't figure out any other way to deal with the situation, I had her committed to Serenity Springs, a mental health facility in Virginia, and she's been there ever since."

He bowed his head, as if his past had finally defeated him.

"Why the lies?" Emma asked.

"I didn't want Liza to grow up knowing that her mother had tried to harm her," he said. "She held a knife to Liza's throat and threatened to slit it if I didn't let her leave and take Liza with her. I had no choice but to commit her. But how was Liza supposed to live with that? She was so young. I hoped she'd forget. Besides, I was afraid if it got out, people would always look at Liza like they suspected she was nuts, too."

"Did you ever tell Liza the truth about her mother's whereabouts?" Emma asked.

"No, I told her that her mother was missing and that I assumed she'd died in a boat accident," he said.

"Which is what you set it up to look like," Emma said.

"Do you have any idea the man power that was poured into trying to find your wife? I've read the reports. It was a massive effort."

"Yes, I know. Because there was no body found, I've had to live with the taint of having a missing wife for the past fifteen years," he said. "People treat you differently when your wife goes missing. No one says to your face that they think you killed her, but it's always there, always in the background like lousy elevator music, until Theresa. She was the first person who never looked at me that way. She believed from the first that my wife had gone missing, and she never made me feel like a bad guy. I love her so much. I'd do anything to keep her safe."

Emma drew in a deep breath. "Then you have to accept the fact that it is most likely Liza who tried to have her killed."

"What? No! Liza loves Theresa as much as if she was her own mother," Larry argued.

"Does she?" Emma asked. "Larry, you have to look at the evidence. Who had Toby's library card? Liza. Who checked out the materials that were found in the car with Chad Bauman? Liza. Larry, it's highly likely that she and Bauman have a connection and that she hired him to kill Theresa, knowing that she'd inherit millions when Theresa died."

"You're wrong, and I can prove it," he argued. "Liza has no idea that she's the beneficiary if Theresa dies. We never told her. And you can't prove that she used Toby's card. That could have been anyone."

"It wasn't," Lindsey said. "I saw her with it. I was there when she checked out the materials on his card."

"That doesn't mean she was the one who checked out the CDs for the dead guy," Larry said. "It could have been someone else."

They all stared at him until finally Robbie shook his head and said, "It wasn't someone else, mate."

"You don't know that," he said. "I believe in my daughter, and I will continue to do so until I draw my last breath."

"Fine, we won't argue about it," Emma said. "Supposing you're right, we still need to find her. If the attempts on Theresa's life have been done by someone else, we need to find Liza to keep her safe. So help us. Where would Liza go?"

Larry looked up at them, and his expression was bleak. "I don't know."

Lindsey watched from her office as Emma left with Larry. Robbie followed behind them as a sort of moral support, but Lindsey wasn't sure which one of them he was supporting. She felt for Larry, she did. It had to have been difficult to have his wife institutionalized, but at the same time, she felt like he could have avoided so much of this if he had just told the truth about her and her condition.

Sometimes the reality of things wasn't pretty or even vaguely attractive. Sometimes it was downright ugly and awful, but there was no hiding from it. Having been deceived before, Lindsey always preferred the truth, even if it wasn't flattering or kind, because one lie spawned so many more that it soon spread out of control until everyone within reach was caught in its sticky web and no one knew what was right and what was wrong anymore.

She shook off the macabre thought and finished out her day. She kept one ear glued to her phone on the chance that Emma called her with the news that they'd found Liza. No call came. Lindsey hated to think that Liza was the one behind the attacks on Theresa, but unless they could come up with some other reason why Chad Bauman, who had no known connection to Briar Creek or Theresa, had wanted to kill the tennis coach, then it seemed Liza hiring him to do her dirty work was the only answer.

No connection to Briar Creek. Lindsey couldn't stop thinking about the fact that Bauman was a stranger in town. Liza lived a quiet life here. If Bauman wasn't from here, how did she meet him? On a hunch, Lindsey went onto the internet and looked up Serenity Springs, the mental health facility that Larry had put Sarah in. If Lindsey hadn't been hallucinating the face in the window, if Sarah had somehow come here, could she have been the one who hired Bauman? And if she did, where did she find him? It would have to be the place she'd been for the past fifteen years. At the very least, it was worth a look.

The Serenity Springs website was very detailed, in peaceful pastels and a flowing font. The pictures showed a beautiful property in the rolling hills of Virginia. It

looked more like a plush resort than a mental health facility. Lindsey looked over the staff pages, clicking
through the doctors and counselors. When she got to the
list of intake specialists, she paused.

The third name on the list was Chad Bauman. She'd
never gotten a good look at the driver of Kayla's stolen
car, but the picture of the man smiling from her computer monitor was one of a twenty-something man with
a toothy grin and kind eyes. The coincidence was too
great. She reached for her cell phone, snapped a picture
of the screen, and sent it to Emma's phone with a text
explaining her search.

Emma had seen Bauman's body; she'd be able to confirm whether this was him or not.

Lindsey clocked out at the end of the day, knowing
that Sully had an evening boat tour and wouldn't be
home until later. That meant that she was solo that evening, so she hurried home to give Heathcliff his walk and
supper.

The April air was chilly, and she bundled up while
striding along the beach with Heathcliff. He chased
seagulls, and Lindsey laughed. Every single day, the boy
hit the beach at top speed, believing that if he ran fast
enough, he would achieve liftoff and catch one. And
every day, Lindsey laughed at his boundless optimism.

When he trotted back to her and leaned against her
side with his tongue hanging out and his furry chest heaving, she reached down and rubbed his fluffy head.

"You'll get 'em next time, buddy," she said.

As the wind whipped at her hair, Lindsey tried to push

all thought of the Milsteins out of her head. There was nothing she could do now. It was up to the police to find Liza. Only she could explain the library-card mix-up and her possible relationship to the deceased Chad Bauman and the second man who had recently tried to shoot Theresa.

Lindsey had a hard time accepting that the personable young woman she had come to like was actually cold-hearted enough to have plotted the murder of her future stepmother. A shiver rippled through her, and it wasn't from the cold wind whipping in from the water.

She had seen many despicable things over the past few years. She'd been witness to the horrible lengths people would go to keep a secret, seek revenge on a lover, or steal someone else's fortune. Truly, it had left her with a jaded view of her fellow man.

But then there were the people in her community who showed up every day, trying to make it a better place. Like Violet, who shared her love of the stage with the local community-theater troupe, and Milton, who taught yoga and ran the local chess club, and Nancy, who baked cookies for everyone for every occasion, brightening all of their days. Those were the people who kept her from giving up on humanity. When Lindsey looked around her, she knew which team she wanted to be on. The helpers.

Once the sun set, twilight came on quickly. Lindsey didn't want to linger out in the darkness, because that was usually when Heathcliff accidentally trotted off into the water and then required a bath. She was not up for that tonight. Heathcliff seemed eager to head home, too, as Lindsey broke into a jog and he was right beside her.

They were walking through the tall grass when Lindsey got the hinky feeling that someone was watching her. Thinking it was just the stress of the day, she moved a bit faster and could have sworn that whoever was tailing her did, too. She stopped abruptly in the middle of the path and glanced around at the tall marsh grass surrounding her. The shadows had gone deep, and there was an eerie stillness to the air, which had just held a strong breeze.

"Who's there?" she called.

No one answered. There was no sound, no movement, nothing but silence. She felt her skin prickle, and she turned and hurried back to the house with Heathcliff at her side.

They bounded up the steps and into the house. Lindsey closed and locked the sliding glass doors behind them. Heathcliff hadn't barked, so there couldn't have been anyone out there. He was so protective; he would have leaped at anyone who surprised him. Clearly, she was just being oversensitive because it had been a heck of a day.

Still, as soon as she began to draw the curtain, she felt a huge surge of relief. She pulled the heavy drape across the glass just as Heathcliff rose up on his hind legs. He barked and pawed at the glass. This was not his *I'm happy to see you* bark but rather his *Get off my lawn* cranky-old-man growl. It was fully dark outside now, and Lindsey couldn't see past her reflection in the glass.

She reached for the light switch to the left of the door

and snapped it on. Standing in the beam of the spotlight on the steps to the back deck was Liza Milstein, and she had a gun. Her face was pale, and she was shivering. Lindsey was sure she saw a tear course down her cheek. She was about to call out to her when Liza raised the gun.

Lindsey jumped. She grabbed Heathcliff by the collar and snapped off the lights on the inside of the house, not wanting to make them easy targets for Liza. Heathcliff struggled, fully intending to attack the stranger on his turf, and Lindsey had to snatch him up into her arms as she hurtled them both behind the kitchen counter, hoping the quartz counter and thick wooden cupboards could stop a bullet if need be.

Thud!

The sound of a gunshot never came. Lindsey held on to Heathcliff's collar with one hand while trying to peer around the counter. The sounds of a scuffle were distinct, and when she glanced outside, she saw Sully sitting on top of Liza.

"Let me go!"

Lindsey released Heathcliff and dashed for the door. The Norrgard twins pounded up the steps, with one of them holding a length of rope in his hands. Liza was bucking and fighting, trying to knock Sully off her, but he held on to her gun hand, not letting go. Lindsey swooped in and pried Liza's fingers off the gun. Sully flipped the young woman onto her front, drawing her arms up behind her back.

"Let me go!" she cried. "Do you know who I am? My

father will destroy you if he finds out what you've done to me."

"I sincerely doubt that," Stieg said. He grasped her arms so that Stefan could tie them with the rope.

"Yeah, you tried to have the woman he loves killed. No dad is ever okay with that," Stefan said.

Once her arms were tied, Sully got off her and grabbed Lindsey. He hugged her close, as if to reassure himself that she was okay.

"I'm all right," she said. But even she could hear that her voice sounded shaky.

"I was so worried we wouldn't get here in time," he said.

Stieg hauled Liza up to her feet. "Chief Plewicki should be here any minute. Shall we go wait out front?"

"Wait!" Lindsey said. She stepped out of Sully's arms and moved in front of Liza. "Why me? Why would you try to shoot me?"

"You're the only one who could prove that I had Toby's library card. If I got rid of you, there was no evidence. Duh," Liza said.

She tilted her chin up in defiance, but it was all for show. Lindsey had seen her shaking and crying. She didn't want to shoot Lindsey. In fact, Lindsey would bet big money she didn't want to be here, doing this, at all.

"Get her out of here," Sully said.

"Hang on!" Lindsey cried. She faced Liza, staring into her eyes. The young woman looked scared and not because she'd been caught. "It's her, isn't it? You're doing this for her."

An expression of surprise flashed over Liza's face, and then she scowled. "I don't know what you're talking about."

"Your mother is alive, and she's here, isn't she?"

Liza's eyes moved from side to side. She looked terrified. "I want a lawyer."

"Liza—" Lindsey began, but Liza cut her off.

"Leave me alone!" Liza cried.

There was nothing more to say. Stieg and Stefan escorted her off the deck and around the house, with Heathcliff barking at Liza all the way.

Lindsey leaned against Sully. "How did you know she'd come after me?"

"I didn't," he said. "I was getting ready to take out the dinner cruise, and I just got the feeling that something wasn't right. I knew I had to get to you as fast as I could. On my way, I ran into Stieg and Stefan, and they told me Liza had gone missing."

"And you just assumed she'd come after me?" Lindsey asked.

"You do have a magnetic field for trouble that is unequaled," he said. "That being said, I don't think she would have shot you."

"Intuition?" she asked.

"More like she tossed the gun down before I tackled her," he said. He looked rueful when he added, "She grabbed it again when I knocked her to the ground. Can't say I blame her, as I likely scared the snot out of her."

The sound of a siren wailing interrupted them.

"That'll be Emma," she said.

Heathcliff's howl answered the siren, and Sully smiled and kissed the top of her head. "Your guard dog wasn't about to let anything happen to you. I'm going to give that boy the biggest chew toy he's ever seen."

Lindsey laughed. She knew it was mostly relief but also the realization that she could have lost all of this—her life with Sully and Heathcliff, in their home. In the blink of an eye or, more accurately, the squeeze of a trigger, Liza could have made all of it go away permanently.

She slipped her hand into Sully's as they walked around the corner of the house to meet Emma.

She squeezed his fingers, silently telling him she loved him. His hand tightened around hers, returning the sentiment.

CHAPTER

17

BRIAR CREEK
PUBLIC LIBRARY

"Liza!" Larry Milstein climbed out of Emma's squad car and ran toward his daughter. "Are you all right?"

Liza whipped her head in her father's direction and snapped, "What do you care?"

Larry stumbled to a halt just a few feet from her. "What? I care—of course I care. I've always cared."

"Really?" she asked. "You cared so much that you lied to me my entire life about my mother being dead."

"Listen, it was for your—"

"Own good. Yeah, yeah, I'm sure," she said. "Too bad it's a lie. It wasn't for my own good. It was so that you could get rid of a wife you didn't want anymore."

"That's not true!" Larry insisted. "She was a danger to herself, and she was a danger to you."

"Liar! She said you would say that. She said you would make up horrible lies to keep me from her," Liza cried. Tears were coursing down her cheeks. "She's my mother. You had no right to take her away from me."

Larry's brow wrinkled with distress, but then the pragmatic businessman emerged to take charge of the situation. "I had every right. You are my daughter."

"Please," Liza scoffed. "Daughter? I am no more important to you than a piece of furniture."

"Where is this coming from?" Larry asked. "I don't understand. I've given you everything."

"Except my mother!" Liza screeched.

Emma stepped forward, obviously sensing that this was going from bad to worse.

"I was giving you a mother. I picked Theresa for you," he said.

A noise came out of Liza's throat that sounded almost like a feral growl. "You didn't pick her for me. You picked her for you."

"That's not true," Larry protested. Everyone looked at him. "Okay, it's a little true, but I would never have asked her marry me if I didn't think she'd be a wonderful mother to you."

"I. Have. A. Mother."

Larry looked at his daughter. Sadness pulled his features until his eyes drooped at the corners and his lips turned down.

"No, you don't, not really," he said. He reached up and pushed aside a hank of Liza's hair, exposing her throat. "You know this scar above your collarbone?"

"Where I cut myself when I was little?" she asked.

"You didn't cut yourself," he said. His voice was barely above a whisper. "Your mother did that when you were sleeping. She was holding a knife to your throat, threatening to kill you if I didn't let her leave and take you with her. She slipped. I think the blood surprised her, and I was able to knock her away from you. I couldn't let her take you. She couldn't take care of herself, never mind a child. After that night, I knew she couldn't be your mother anymore."

"She told me you just wanted to be rid of her because you were bored with being a husband and father," Liza said. Her fingers moved over the old scar as if its shape might have changed now that she knew the truth of its origin.

"Liza, you know that's not true," Larry said. "I know I traveled a lot during the weekdays when you were growing up, but I made sure I was always home on weekends, and I always made time for you. I even coached your soccer team, and I hate soccer."

He stepped close to his daughter and cupped her face in his hands. "Your mother can be wickedly charming. She makes you doubt yourself and everything you know to be true. When did you get in touch with her?"

"I didn't," Liza said. "She got in touch with me. She found me online. At first, I didn't believe it was her, but she knew so much about me and you . . ."

"Did you go see her in Virginia?" he asked.

Liza nodded. Her chin dropped to her chest, as if the burden of having her mother in her life had become too heavy to carry.

"What did she say to you?" he asked.

"She said she never wanted to leave me and that you forced her out. She said that if I helped her scare off Theresa, you'd give her another chance and we could be a family again," she said. She began to cry in earnest. "She told me she'd kill herself if she had to spend another night there away from me. She promised me no one would get hurt but then . . . Chad. And she told me I had to shoot Ms. Norris, and I . . . Oh, Dad, what do I do?"

Liza broke down into sobs, and Larry looked at Emma. She gave a small nod and then stepped forward and unbound Liza's arms. The twins shadowed her. If Liza had any nefarious plans to bolt, she had another think coming.

"Liza, where is your mother now?" Lindsey asked. She still couldn't get the face in the window out of her mind.

"She's in Virginia," Liza said. Her voice came out high and tight, and her gaze shifted to the ground.

"No, she isn't," Emma said.

Larry's head snapped toward Emma. "What are you saying?"

"When I got the divorce report from Lindsey, I did some checking and found mention of a Sarah Milstein performing in the Serenity Springs production of *The Sound of Music*. They even had her picture in the local paper. When I called Serenity Springs to verify that their Sarah Milstein was your Sarah Milstein, they told me that she'd been checked out of the facility by her daughter."

"Oh no," Larry said. He looked at Liza in horror. "You didn't."

"I . . ." Liza's face crumpled. "I didn't know what to do. She said she'd kill herself."

"The face," Lindsey said. "The face I saw in the window at your house. That was your mother."

"What?" Larry looked at his daughter in horror. "She was in our house?"

"I'm sorry, Daddy," she cried. "She said she wouldn't hurt anyone!"

"Tell that to Chad Bauman," Emma said. Her look was dark.

Liza swallowed and then started to sob.

Larry spun around to look at the twins. "Who is with Theresa?"

"Don't worry," Emma said. "I had Officer Kirkland take Theresa to a safe house."

"A safe house?" Larry asked. "What does that even mean? You don't know my ex-wife. She can convince you your favorite ice cream is vanilla even if you know you've loved chocolate all your life."

Emma frowned. "I am quite certain that she is safe and sound."

"Call," Larry urged her.

"I don't think—"

"I'm begging you," he said. "Call her and let me know she's okay."

Emma took out her phone and dialed a number. She put the phone to her ear. She looked at Larry. She looked

at the sky. She began to tap her foot. Finally, she ended
the call with a frown.

"No one is answering," she said. "I'm going over there."
She looked at the twins. "Stay with her. Do not let her out
of your sight." With that, she ran to her squad car.

Larry broke into a run and joined her, jumping into the
front of her car. Lindsey looked at Sully, and he nodded.

"Make yourselves at home," he said to the twins. Then
he looked at Lindsey and Heathcliff. "Come on."

They piled into his truck, with Heathcliff taking the
passenger window. Sully bolted down the driveway,
keeping Emma's squad car in front of him. They raced
through town, slowing down on Main Street and then
turning onto a small side street. Emma parked beside an
old brick building that used to house a bustling fish market but was now Lurie's Variety Store, where the locals
could pick up anything from shoelaces to beef jerky to
the odd appliance.

The shop was closed, but there was a light on in the
second-floor window above. Lindsey had always believed
that the second floor was used by the Luries, the owners
of the store, as an office and storage area. But since Emma
was here and there was a light on above, she had to assume this was the safe house. It was a good choice. She
never would have guessed. She rolled down the window
to give Heathcliff air while he waited and hopped out of
the truck. Sully did the same.

Emma and Larry were standing by the side entrance of
the building, where no windows looked down on them.
Emma motioned for them to huddle up.

"There are two ways to get upstairs," she said. "Through the shop or up the back entrance. I have the code to get into the shop. The Luries gave it to me so I could check on the shop as needed."

"I'll watch the back," Sully said. "If anyone comes down, I'll—"

"Call me immediately," Emma said. "Lindsey, Larry, I want you two to wait in Sully's truck."

"What?"

"No!"

Emma held up her hands. "This is not up for debate. Officer Kirkland is supposed to be up there with Theresa, but he's not answering his phone. I may very well have an officer down. I'm sorry, but accommodating you two is not the priority here. Sully is a former naval officer; he can handle himself."

Lindsey looked at her man, and she knew Emma was right. She didn't like having him in harm's way, but there was no denying that Sully was the most viable candidate to give Emma backup.

"You're right," Lindsey said. "We'll wait here."

She took Larry by the elbow and led him to the pickup truck. Larry looked like he would protest, but Emma was already approaching the side door and Sully was moving along the edge of the building to hide in the shadows at the base of the stairs in the back.

Lindsey climbed into the driver's side of the pickup truck while Larry took the passenger seat. Heathcliff, who'd been sprawled, popped up to a sitting position so he could lick Lindsey's face.

"It's all right, buddy," she said. "Sully will be just fine. I promise."

She wasn't sure whether she was trying to reassure herself or the dog. She suspected it was herself.

"I can't stand this," Larry said. "What if something has happened to Theresa? I'll never forgive myself for getting her mixed up in this mess."

"There's no way you could have known," Lindsey said.

"Yes, I could have," he argued. "I should have been more vigilant. I promised myself when I made Sarah go away that I would never ever let her get to Liza, and yet she did."

"What do you think she wants?" Lindsey asked. "I mean, do you believe that she is trying to get the three of you to be a family again?"

"No, that would never ever happen," he said. "She has to know that after what she did."

"The knife?"

Larry's mouth tightened. He looked like he was going to refuse to talk about it. Then he turned to her, and Lindsey could see the stark fear and hurt in his gaze.

"When she held that knife to Liza's throat, she told me she would kill her if I didn't give her everything she wanted," he said. "At the top of her list was a divorce and full custody of our daughter. She actually thought I would just give away my only child to a woman who was holding a knife at her throat. I took Liza to the emergency room, had her stitched up, and within a day, I had Sarah shipped away for evaluation.

"They came back with a doozy of a diagnosis, all of which essentially means that she is incapable of forming an emotional attachment to anyone or anything. That's one of the reasons she is so good at manipulating others. She can see what people want or need; she can use their vulnerabilities against them to get whatever she wants. Frankly, she's terrifying. I had no choice but to have her institutionalized. I found the best facility that I could—"

Creak.

The passenger door to Sully's truck was yanked open. Standing on the other side of Larry was the woman Lindsey had seen in the window of the house. Sarah Milstein.

Sarah shoved Larry hard in the shoulder, pushing him across his seat. "Move over, husband. We've got to go."

"Sarah! What have you done?" Larry balled up his right fist, looking like he was going to take a swing at her. She lifted a handgun and pointed it right at his nose.

"Relax, your lady love is fine," she said. Her voice was full of derision. "Can't say the same for the policeman who was with her, but—" She shrugged. Her gaze moved to Lindsey, who was holding on to Heathcliff's collar. "You're still alive? Pity." She looked at Larry and shook her head. "That daughter of ours. She had one job to do."

"You sent her to kill me," Lindsey said. The words made her breathless, and she had to force herself to breathe normally.

"Yeah, well, Mom is on the job, but it looks like Liza will have to take the fall for it all," Sarah said.

"Why are you doing this?" Larry asked. "I mean, I get why you're coming after me, but why Theresa—"

"Do you want to know, Larry, really?" she asked. "Revenge. Do you have any idea what it's like to be locked up and held against your will, day after day, with every day bleeding into the next while you live on a constant diet of pills that make you feel as euphoric as a ball of lint? I spent every single day planning my revenge, and now it's here."

Lindsey thought her heart was going to beat right out of her chest. She slid her left hand down to the seat, trying to get to the door handle. If she could open it, she might be able to tuck and roll around Heathcliff and get them both out of there.

"You can't blame me. What choice did I have?" Larry snapped. "You threatened our daughter at knifepoint."

"*What choice did I have*?" Sarah mimicked him. "Quite simply, you should have given me what I wanted."

"Over my dead body, I'd let you take Liza," he said. "You are unfit to mother a rock, never mind a child. I mean, for God's sake, you had her point a gun at a librarian, a woman she considers her friend."

Sarah's gaze moved to Lindsey, and the look in them was one of sheer, undiluted hate. Lindsey stopped feeling for the door handle. She didn't blink. She didn't breathe.

"Well, since baby girl couldn't do it, I'll just have to take care of the librarian for her," she said. "See? I am a good mother."

"You're a nightmare," Larry said. "You always have been. Liza isn't your daughter anymore. She's mine, and I will protect her from you until the day I die."

"That can be arranged." Sarah's gaze swept back to

him, and she hissed, "I'm going to kill you, Larry. I'm going to shoot you right between your beady little eyes."

"Where's the chief of police?" Lindsey asked. She saw Sarah's finger twitch on the trigger, and she had to stifle the scream that clawed up her throat.

Sarah looked at her as if she'd forgotten Lindsey was in the car with them. Then she blinked as if pulling Lindsey into focus.

"When I saw the chief enter the shop, I knew I'd have to sneak out before I could finish the job—well, most of it anyway. At least I took one cop out," she said. She waved the gun at Lindsey and the steering wheel. "Start the truck."

Lindsey felt her chest compress. The cop she mentioned had to be Officer Kirkland. Lindsey had shared quite a few adventures with him. The tall, lanky redhead was always quick with a smile and eager to take on any case that came across the front desk of the Briar Creek PD. She couldn't bear the thought of anything happening to him. Heathcliff must not have liked it either, because with an abrupt yank against Lindsey's hold, he lunged across Larry at Sarah with his teeth bared. Sarah turned her gun on the dog, and Lindsey felt her heart stop.

CHAPTER

18

BRIAR CREEK
PUBLIC LIBRARY

For the second time in one night, Lindsey grabbed her dog, hauling him down and trying to block him with her body from a gunshot. It never came. Instead, there was a sickening crunch, a thump, a groan, and then nothing.

The door on the driver's side was jerked open, and there was Sully. Lindsey raised her head and blinked at him. Then she whipped around and looked at Larry. He was shaking out his fist while Sarah was slumped against the passenger door, unconscious.

"I've never hit a woman in my life," he said.

The door on the other side of Sarah was jerked open, and she slid out, her body limp. Emma was there and grabbed her before she hit the pavement. Larry climbed out after her, retrieving the gun that Sarah had dropped on the truck floor when he hit her.

Lindsey let Heathcliff jump out and then followed him. She hugged Sully tight, absorbing his strength and his warmth for a moment before walking around the front of the truck to join the others.

"Theresa? Is she okay?" Larry asked Emma. He sounded as if he was afraid of the answer, and given how ruthless Sarah had been, Lindsey didn't blame him. She clenched her muscles, anticipating news she did not want to hear.

"She's fine," Emma said. "She's upstairs with Officer Kirkland, who was shot."

Lindsey gasped, and Emma shook her head. "Don't worry. It's not life threatening. When I couldn't find Sarah in the building, I came down to meet the ambulance. I didn't realize she was in the truck with you until I saw Sully creeping up on the vehicle."

"I heard her force her way into the truck," Sully said. "But I saw she had a gun, and I didn't want to scare her into shooting anyone."

"Good call," Emma said. She glanced at Lindsey and Larry. "What did she say to you?"

"She said she was going to kill Larry and me," Lindsey said. "Then Heathcliff jumped at her, and she turned the gun on him and Larry knocked her out."

"She saw you come into the shop, and she sneaked out," Larry said. "She wants revenge on me for putting her away. This is all my fault."

"No, it isn't." Lindsey grabbed his arm and squeezed it. "You may have made some poor choices, but you did the best you could at the time and you saved my dog."

The corner of Larry's mouth turned up just a little. He nodded and then turned to Emma. "Can I go see Theresa?"

Emma glanced from him to the building. "All right, but we have to remain vigilant. Whoever Sarah hired to kill Chad Bauman and take over his hit man duties is still out there."

"No, she isn't," Sully said. He gestured at Sarah. "That's your shooter. She killed Bauman, and then she went gunning for Theresa herself."

Both Lindsey and Emma gave him wide-eyed looks.

"How'd you figure that?" Emma asked.

"We saw the yellow sweatshirt that she's wearing in the back of the muscle car that was parked in the woods," he said. "She's the one who drove through town at top speed, chasing Theresa and the twins. The shooter is her. I'm betting ballistics will prove it."

"He's right," Lindsey said. "I remember the sweatshirt, too. It has to be her."

"Oh God, she was the one shooting at Theresa? I have to go see her now," Larry said. He ran into the shop, banging the door behind him.

Sarah groaned. Emma knelt down beside her and rolled her so that she could fasten handcuffs on her wrists behind her back. Sarah's eyes blinked open, but then she shut them and began to moan.

"You can't arrest me," she said. "You have to send me back to Serenity Springs, where I can get treatment."

"You shot one of my officers," Emma said. "You're not going anywhere until you answer for that and the murder of Chad Bauman."

Sarah opened one eye and stared at her. "You can't prove anything. Liza was the one who paid Chad Bauman out of her trust fund, she was the one who got me out of the nuthouse, and she was the one who wanted to kill Theresa so she could cash in on the life insurance policy that Larry took out on Theresa for Liza."

"That's a lie," Lindsey said. Whether Sarah was crazy or not, the fact that this woman would let her daughter take the fall for her own reprehensible behavior made Lindsey furious. "Liza didn't know about the policy, but I'm betting you did, because Larry likely had one on you, too, for *his* daughter, am I right?"

"Shut up!" Sarah snapped.

"You lied to Liza, too, telling her you were going to kill yourself, convincing her you were just trying to run Theresa off when you really planned to kill her so that Liza would inherit and you could help yourself to Liza's inheritance."

"I said shut up!" Sarah bellowed. Her face was bright red, and her breath was heaving in and out as if she'd run a long distance. "He owes it to me—hell, the kid owes it to me. If I'd never had that lousy brat, I could have murdered Larry in his sleep, inherited a fortune and disappeared, but no, I had to get knocked up, and then when I couldn't take it anymore, he sent me away."

Emma stared at Sarah with contemptuous disdain, while Lindsey found herself leaning closer to Sully, as if his goodness was a buffer from the horror that was this woman.

"Why did you threaten to take her, then?" Lindsey asked. "Why did you want custody?"

"Because she was my cash cow for life," Sarah said. "As long as I had her, I was set. I could milk Larry for anything I wanted."

Disgust left a bad taste in Lindsey's mouth. Perhaps Sarah was mentally ill, as Larry had said, but she was also evil personified.

"That's what you thought of me? As a meal ticket?" Liza stepped out of the shadows, flanked by Stieg and Stefan. "You lied to me. You told me my father had put you away because he was tired of being a husband. You threatened to kill yourself. And . . . and you said you had nothing to do with shooting Chad. But it was you, wasn't it?"

Sarah rolled her eyes as if she couldn't abide Liza's drama. "Chad was a total disappointment. I mean, how hard is it to hit someone with a car or hold a pillow over their face? Honestly, I should have known when I offered him money to break me out of Serenity Springs and he couldn't figure out how to do it that he wasn't too bright. Still, he took the money to do the hit on Theresa without fussing. I should have hired a professional."

"You told me he was just going to scare her off so that you'd have a chance to win Dad back." Liza wobbled on her feet, and both Stieg and Stefan steadied her. "All of it, every word you uttered, was a lie."

Sarah looked at her daughter and couldn't even hide the malice she felt. "Look at you, all grown up and still a pain in my ass. Why? Why would I ever want you or your father? You're pathetic."

With that, she slumped to the ground as if she'd

fainted. Emma wasn't having it, and she dragged the woman up to her feet. Sarah's head lolled as if she was unconscious, but Emma refused to play.

"Stop it!" she snapped.

She forced Sarah to stand, held her arm in a firm grip, and half dragged, half pushed her toward her squad car. She put her hand on Sarah's head and folded her into the back seat, then she slammed the door.

"Sully? Keep an eye?" she asked.

"Of course," he said.

Emma hurried off to meet the ambulance that had just pulled up behind them. Lindsey knew she was worried about Officer Kirkland and wouldn't rest until she knew he was going to be okay.

The EMTs and Emma hurried into the shop while Lindsey and Sully kept watch over Emma's squad car. Sarah booted the door, demanding that they release her. She threatened to kick the window out, she swore she would harm herself, and when they ignored her, she threatened their lives.

Sully took his phone out and began to record her. She immediately stopped. Instead, she curled up into a ball and began to rock back and forth. Lindsey got the feeling she was plotting something. The conniving look in her eyes was unnerving, and Lindsey shivered. Sully put his arm around her and pulled her close as if he thought she was cold. She was grateful for both his strength and his warmth.

A quick glance into the back of the car, and she saw Sarah watching them. She knew that Sarah suffered from a mental illness, but there was no changing the fact that she'd taken a life, and given the chance, she would have taken another. When Lindsey glanced over at Liza, she was sitting on the curb with her head down on her folded arms. She looked as if she was sobbing while Stieg and Stefan stood beside her, clearly not knowing what to do.

"Thanks, Sully." Emma reappeared with the EMTs behind her.

Officer Kirkland was on a stretcher. As they passed by Lindsey to get him loaded into the ambulance, she reached out and grabbed Kirkland's hand.

"Hey, I'm really glad you're all right," she said. It was hard to talk around the lump in her throat, but she swallowed hard and managed it.

"Me, too," he said. His freckles stood out against the pallor of his skin. He squeezed her fingers and said, "Got a hell of a story out of it though, didn't I?"

"And probably a scar." Lindsey laughed.

She leaned over the side of the stretcher and kissed him on the head. Kirkland flushed pink and grinned. The EMTs loaded him into the back of the ambulance and closed the doors.

Just then Larry emerged from the shop with Theresa in his arms. His eyes were damp, and it was clear to Lindsey he was overcome with relief that the woman he loved was safe. Theresa rested her head on his shoulder, obviously relieved to be alive and well.

She lifted her head and searched the area. Lindsey wondered whether she was looking for Sarah, afraid she'd be attacked again, but she wasn't. Instead, her gaze settled on Liza. The compassion in her eyes made Lindsey blink. She wasn't angry at her future stepdaughter; rather, she was worried.

"Liza, are you all right?" Theresa asked. She flailed in Larry's arms as if she'd run to Liza if she could.

Liza lifted her head from her arms, saw Theresa trying to get to her, and promptly burst into big, gutwrenching sobs. "I'm sorry. I'm so, so sorry."

The Norrgard brothers stepped back, making room for Larry and Theresa. Larry lowered Theresa until she was on the ground beside Liza.

Theresa opened her arms, and Liza fell against her. "Shh. Hush now," Theresa said as she stroked Liza's hair. "It's all right. You're safe now."

Liza leaned back and looked at her. "How can you forgive me? I could have gotten you killed. I probably did get Chad killed by signing her out of that facility. Mom—Sarah—told me he was robbed and that the shooting had nothing to do with us, but it was her. She killed him, and she tried to kill you when she told me she was only going to scare you off. And then she wanted me to kill Ms. Norris, because she said she knew too much and I was going to be sent to jail, but I couldn't do it."

"I know, baby. I know." Theresa pulled her back into her arms and let her continue to cry. She rocked Liza gently back and forth and then kissed the top of her head.

"When you and Dad got engaged, I just . . . I lost my place," Liza sobbed. "And then Sarah found me and convinced me that we could be a family again—oh God, I was so dumb. I thought I'd finally have my mom, but she isn't, she wasn't, she never could be—"

"You have a mom. You'll always have a mom, assuming you still want me, that is," Theresa said. Her voice was thick, and Larry, who knelt behind her, propping her up, was openly crying.

"Yes, oh please, if you can forgive me, I'd love for you to be my mom," Liza said. "For real."

The rest of them watched as the small family took the first steps toward mending. Emma locked the door to the variety store and strode toward her car. She punched Sully on the shoulder as she passed.

"Thanks for keeping watch," she said. "I'm taking Sarah into the station. Can I count on you two to come and give your statements?"

Lindsey felt her lips twitch. Only Emma could ask a question that wasn't a question at all.

"We're right behind you," Sully said.

Emma nodded. She said the same thing to the Milsteins and the Norrgard brothers. Then she climbed into her car and drove off.

Stieg and Stefan helped Larry load Theresa and Liza into the oversize SUV and followed Emma. In moments, it was just Sully, Lindsey and Heathcliff standing on the sidewalk, catching their breath and regrouping. At least, Lindsey thought that's what they were doing.

"Come on, let's get some air," Sully said. He took her hand in his and started to walk toward the center of town.

"Where are we going?" Lindsey asked.

"To the pier."

Lindsey patted her thigh, signaling to Heathcliff to follow. He bounded alongside them, his tongue hanging out of his mouth. He looked happy, and Lindsey envied him for his doggy resiliency and the fact that he had no idea what could have happened back there.

She let go of Sully's hand and slid her arm around his waist. The night air was cool, and she wanted to absorb his warmth and at the same time feel sure of him, of them, of the life they were going to carve out together.

They passed the Blue Anchor and the sound of Charlie Peyton's band, rising and falling as the doors opened and closed as people came and went. Down the pier they strolled, all the way to the end, and stood beneath one of the overhead lights. The few islands out in the bay that had power had their lights on, which were reflected in the gentle waves that lapped their way toward shore.

Sully turned to face her. He reached into his pants pocket and pulled out a ring. It sparkled in the lamplight, and Lindsey glanced from it to him.

"I had a whole speech prepared," he said. "It was a sales pitch, really, on why you should say yes and become my wife, but after the events of the evening, I can't remember a word of it, except this." He paused and lowered himself to one knee. Heathcliff, as if suspecting something big was happening and wanting to be a part of it, sat beside him, swishing his tail across the rough wooden planks.

"Lindsey Norris, I love you with all that I am and all that I will ever be. I want to ask you officially this time, with a ring to seal the deal, will you marry me?"

"Yes, yes, yes."

She dropped to her knees and threw herself into his arms, kissing him as a tear coursed down her cheek. Sully returned her kiss and then pulled back so he could take her hand and put the ring on her finger. It was an emerald-cut diamond surrounded by smaller diamonds, and it was a perfect fit.

"It was my grandmother's," Sully said. "She was a well-read, sassy woman, so I know she'd be thrilled with my choice of bride."

Lindsey laughed and wiped the tears off her face. She stared into Sully's bright blue eyes and considered herself the luckiest woman in the world, predawn whistling and all.

CHAPTER

19

BRIAR CREEK
PUBLIC LIBRARY

I t was Lindsey's turn to make the food for crafternoon
Thursday. She'd wanted something festive but healthy,
so she'd gone with avocado and goat cheese grilled sandwiches, pear salad, and flourless chocolate cake with a
dusting of confectioners' sugar for dessert. The group
was discussing *My Life on the Road* by Gloria Steinem,
a nonfiction book for a change of pace, and they were
finishing the string bracelets Paula had been trying to
teach them to make for a while. No one seemed to be able
to manage the square-knot closure. In fact, Lindsey's
looked more like a web of knots than a bracelet, but
Paula assured her that she could fix it.

The first to arrive was Beth. She was wearing striped
overalls, an engineer's cap and a red bandana around her
neck. No one could carry off the train look like Beth.

"All aboard for crafternoon," Lindsey said.

Beth pulled a large wooden whistle out of her pocket and blew into it, imitating a train's whistle perfectly. Then she laughed. "I love my job."

"Come on and eat. You must be starving after story time," Lindsey said.

"I am! Reading Virginia Lee Burton's *Choo Choo* always makes me hungry, or maybe it's the pretending to be a huge train with thirty three-year-olds hanging off me that does it—hard to say."

Beth hurried to take the plate Lindsey offered her just as Paula, Violet and Nancy entered the room. Lindsey handed Beth a glass of lemonade, but when Beth reached out to take it, she gasped.

"Oh my God, is that . . . are you . . . it is! You and Sully are getting married, aren't you?" she cried.

"Huh?" Lindsey followed the line of Beth's gaze to her hand. Oh yeah, her ring. The one Sully had put on her finger a few days ago, the same one she'd caught herself staring at repeatedly as the sunlight made the diamonds sparkle and shine. "Oh, that."

"That?" Nancy came hustling up to the table. She grabbed Lindsey's hand and turned the ring in the light. Like a chorus, all of the women oohed and aahed. "That is stunning."

"Dazzling," Violet agreed.

"Gorgeous," Paula breathed.

"How could you not have texted me the minute it happened?" Beth cried. "Oh, the betrayal. How long have you been engaged exactly?"

"Well, he proposed the night we chased Sarah Milstein in her red sports car into the woods," Lindsey said.

"Ah." Beth gasped. "But that was days ago."

"Well, things were crazy, and I wasn't sure, but then he asked again and—"

"He put a ring on it," Paula said.

"Yes, he did," Violet said.

"Does this mean what I think it means?" Beth put her cup and plate on the table and started to bounce on her feet as if she couldn't contain her excitement. Up and down, up and down, like a super-bouncy ball.

The smile that parted Lindsey's lips was impossible to hold back. "Yes, there's going to be a wedding, and yes, you're my matron of honor."

"Woo-hoo!" Beth cried. Then she let out a girly "Squeeee!" and ran around the table and grabbed Lindsey in a hug that strangled. The brim of her engineer's cap clipped Lindsey in the temple, but she didn't mind. She knew Beth's exuberance was just a part of who she was.

Charlene La Rue and Ms. Cole joined the crafternooners. Charlene congratulated Lindsey with a warm hug and complimented her ring, and then, to Lindsey's surprise, Ms. Cole gave her a bracing hug as well and said, "Well, it's about time."

All the crafternooners paused to stare at her, and Ms. Cole waved a hand and said, "Oh, please, I knew the first time they laid eyes on each other that they were made for each other. I just didn't think it would take them this long to figure it out."

Nancy choked out a laugh and gave Ms. Cole a hug. Violet did the same, and Lindsey grinned. She loved the camaraderie in this group.

"So, have you set a day for the wedding?" Charlene asked. "You'll have to send out save-the-date notices, because I am not going to miss the wedding of the year in Briar Creek."

"Agreed," Beth said. Then she frowned. "Wait, I thought my wedding was the wedding of the year."

Sensing disaster, Lindsey said, "It was, and since we won't get married for at least a year, ours will be the wedding of the year next year, if not the year after that."

"Oh, well, all right then," Beth said. She picked up her plate, bit into her grilled cheese, and smiled. Then she looked worried. "But you shouldn't wait too long to get married. We're getting up there, and if you're going to start a family, you need to get on that."

"So to speak," Paula said.

Violet snorted, and Charlene rolled her eyes at her mother. Lindsey tried to smile, but it felt like a grimace, especially when she felt all eyes turn her way.

She was certain they were looking for her to give a hint about whether she and Sully wanted to be parents. She had barely wrapped her head around planning a wedding, never mind sharing her more personal plans for the future, which presently did not include children.

"So, did you know that Gloria Steinem broke out as a reporter when she went undercover as a waitress at the Playboy Club?" Lindsey asked.

"And there she goes, changing the subject from her personal life," Violet said with a laugh.

"Nice to know marriage isn't going to change her," Nancy said. She glanced at Lindsey and said, "And I did know about that. I remember my mother reading 'A Bunny's Tale' in *Show* magazine and being scandalized. Well, she acted scandalized. It came out in the May and June issues in sixty-three, and my mother was chomping at the bit for the June issue."

"That was the same year *The Feminine Mystique* and *The Bell Jar* were published," Violet said. "Those were some wild times."

Lindsey watched Nancy and Violet exchange a knowing look. She wondered whether the world was what they thought it would be on the other side of their youth—but then, did anyone's life work out as they expected?

"Speaking of wild times, how are things working out for the Milsteins now that Sarah has been charged with the murder of Chad Bauman and the attempted murder of Theresa Huston?" Paula asked.

"They are moving ahead with the wedding," Lindsey said. "And according to Theresa, they've decided to postpone their big honeymoon until they can take Liza with them."

"I saw Liza the other day, and she looked, well, like someone who has just suffered a severely traumatic experience," Paula said. "And having been the center of a homicide investigation myself, I could relate."

"Poor kid," Beth said. "She spent her whole life wondering what happened to her mother, and then out of the blue, her mother finds her and manipulates her with a pack of lies and makes her an accessory to murder."

"I heard they are working with the district attorney," Charlene said. She poured herself a glass of lemonade. "She'll likely be cleared so long as she testifies against her mother."

"Oh, that's awful," Violet said. She glanced at her daughter. "You'd never testify against me, would you?"

Charlene studied her mother over the rim of her cup. "Do you even have to ask?"

Violet grinned. "That's my girl."

"What's truly tragic is that the whole thing could have been avoided. Chad Bauman would never have been swept into this by Sarah if Liza had known about her mother's mental health. Larry should have told her the truth," Nancy said. She shook her head. "Lies will always rise to the surface."

"Like dead bodies," Ms. Cole said. They all looked at her, and she shrugged. "What? It's true."

"Yeah, and really grisly," Lindsey said. She held up a plate. "Grilled cheese?"

"I'll take that!" Mary Murphy, the final member of their crafternoon group, came into the room. She had Josie strapped to her front and the baby bag slung across her back. She dropped the bag onto the floor and looked at the group. No one volunteered to take the baby, as they had all loaded up their plates with sandwiches.

This did not slow Mary down, not even a little. She approached the table, hefted baby Josie up and out of her sling, and thrust her at Lindsey.

"Here you go, Auntie Lindsey," she said. She had heard about the engagement a few nights before, when Sully and Lindsey had called their families. "Have some quality time with your soon-to-be niece."

"I . . . um . . . are you . . . is that . . ." Lindsey stammered, but it was no use. Mary plunked the baby into her empty hands, and Lindsey grabbed hold of Josie, pulling her in tight so as not to drop her.

Mary loaded up her plate and began to gab with the other ladies about Gloria Steinem and how fabulous it was to listen to an audiobook while she had Josie in the jogging stroller and was running along the beach, trying to shake the baby weight.

Lindsey stood paralyzed. The baby hadn't made a peep. Surely she should be wailing in protest by now. Didn't she have any survival instincts? She had to know Lindsey was the last person in this room—heck, in this whole town—who should be holding a baby.

She heard a little snuffle and tipped her head down so she could see the baby. Josie was blinking up at her with big bright blue eyes just like her Uncle Sully's.

"Hey, there," Lindsey said. Her voice was barely above a whisper.

Josie's eyes met hers, and her toothless mouth moved up into a wide smile. Lindsey let loose the breath she'd been holding and found herself smiling back at the baby. Josie blinked, and her smile got wider. Then she thrust a chubby fist into her mouth. It was the most ridiculously adorable thing Lindsey had ever seen, and she laughed.

"All right," she whispered. She rested her cheek on the

baby's soft, downy head. "Maybe babies aren't so bad after all. I'm not saying I want any, mind you, but you smell pretty good and you have your uncle's eyes, so this is actually not . . . horrible."

She lifted her head and glanced back down at the baby. Josie cooed and then grinned at her, and Lindsey smiled back. Well, okay then.

Guide to Crafternoons

What's a crafternoon? Quite simply, it is when a group gathers to discuss a book they've all read or listened to, share food (always food) and do a fun craft. If you want to host your own crafternoon, here's a handy guide to get you started.

Readers Guide for
A Tree Grows in Brooklyn

1. Do you think the Nolans are an accurate portrayal of a struggling family during the early twentieth century in Brooklyn? If so, why? If not, why not?

2. What does the tin can nailed down in the back of the closet represent to the family?

3. What do you consider to be the overall theme of the book? Why?

4. What are the dreams of the different family members— Johnny, Katie, Francie and Neeley? Do you believe they will achieve them?

5. What do you think Francie's future holds for her?

Craft:
Adjustable String Bracelet

Waxed polyester thread (any color)
Scissors
Ruler
Lighter

Using the ruler, measure nine pieces of string, cutting each so that it is five inches long. Place them together and then cut two ten-inch lengths of string. Using one ten-inch length, tie the ends of the nine five-inch lengths of string together in the middle of the ten-inch piece of string. There should be a quarter of an inch of the ends sticking out of the knot. Tie two knots to keep it secure. Using your lighter, very carefully use the small flame to melt the ends of the nine five-inch lengths of string. This keeps them from slipping out of the knot. Now take the other ten-inch length of string and do the same on the other side, tying the nine five-inch lengths of string together.

Now take the two ends of one of the ten-inch strings and twist counterclockwise so that when released the two strings will wrap tightly around each other. Tie off at the end, and use the lighter again to melt the wax and keep the knot from untying. Repeat the process with the other ten-inch length.

Now the final step: Cut a five-inch length of string, and make a square knot (five loops is good) around the two twisted lengths of string. This allows the bracelet to be adjustable. Again, very carefully melt the ends of the square knot to keep the knot from untying.

Recipes

GOAT CHEESE AND AVOCADO GRILLED CHEESE

½ cup pesto
1 loaf sliced whole-grain wheat bread
10 slices of mozzarella cheese
1 bunch of spinach leaves, washed and dried
2 avocados, sliced
1 cup goat cheese, crumbled
3 tablespoons olive oil

Assemble each sandwich by spreading the pesto on a slice of bread and layering a slice of mozzarella, a couple of spinach leaves, two slices of avocado and a sprinkle of goat cheese on top. Top with another slice of bread and gently press down, sealing the sandwich. Heat the olive oil in a skillet on medium heat, making sure the oil coats the pan. Cook each side of the sandwich until golden brown. Remove from heat and cut corner to corner in triangles. Serve while warm. Makes 20.

GAZPACHO: COLD TOMATO SOUP

4 large, sweet tomatoes
1 cucumber, halved and seeded, not peeled
2 red bell peppers, seeded
1 red onion
3 garlic cloves, minced
3 cups (24 ounces) tomato juice
¼ cup good olive oil
¼ cup white-wine vinegar
½ teaspoon sea salt
¼ teaspoon ground black pepper

Chop the tomatoes, cucumber, bell peppers and onion into 1-inch cubes. Put each vegetable into a food processor, one at a time, and process until coarsely chopped. Add each processed vegetable into a large bowl, then mix in the garlic, tomato juice, olive oil, vinegar, sea salt and ground pepper. Mix well and chill for 2 hours before serving.

FLOURLESS CHOCOLATE CAKE DUSTED WITH CONFECTIONERS' SUGAR

12 ounces semisweet or bittersweet chocolate, chopped
1½ sticks unsalted butter
¼ teaspoon salt
6 large eggs, room temperature
1½ cups granulated sugar
Confectioners' sugar

Preheat oven to 325 degrees. Grease a 9-by-2-inch springform pan. In a large microwave-safe bowl, put the chocolate, butter and salt. Melt in the microwave for 90 seconds. Stir and microwave again, in 1-minute intervals, until completely melted. In a separate bowl, beat the eggs and sugar with a mixer until light and thickened, about 8 minutes. Fold the melted chocolate into the whipped eggs until evenly combined. Pour the batter into the springform pan and bake about 1 hour and 25 minutes, until a toothpick inserted into the cake comes out damp but not runny. Remove cake from the oven and cool on a rack.

Once the cake is cool, carefully remove from the pan and sift a light layer of confectioners' sugar over the top.

Turn the page to read an excerpt from
Jenn McKinlay's next Library Lover's Mystery . . .

WORD TO THE WISE

Coming in September 2019

"Too meringue, too low-cut, holy bananas, too high-cut!" Lindsey Norris sat at the reference desk of the Briar Creek Public Library and clicked through a website full of wedding dresses. Her mother had sent her the link in an email and wanted to know what sort of dress Lindsey was thinking of wearing for her upcoming wedding. Too many choices. There were just too many. She felt herself starting to melt down, so she closed the website. She'd get back to her mother on this soon. Really, she would.

It was the height of summer in Briar Creek, and she had a good five months before the wedding. It was going to be a very small holiday ceremony out on Bell Island, one of the Thumb Islands that made up the archipelago of over one hundred islands—some were just big rocks—in the bay off Briar Creek's shore. Her fiancé, Captain Mike Sullivan, had asked that they get married on the island where he'd grown up, and Lindsey couldn't think of a more romantic place to say "I do." So the location was a go. It was all the other details that were killing her.

Click click click.

Lindsey turned around to see a bat fluttering through the book stacks. She was a pretty big bat. With large ears pointing up from a wide headband and enormous pale gray wings made out of an old bedsheet and some wire, she fluttered her outspread arms while holding a mango in one hand. She also had merry eyes and shoulder-length dark brown hair and answered to the name of Beth Barker. She was the Briar Creek children's librarian, and she was leading a parade of toddlers and their parents through the library, all fluttering their "wings" and making clicking noises.

Lindsey propped her chin on her hand as she watched the little bats flutter by. She met Beth's happy gaze and said, "Practicing your echolocation, Stellaluna?"

Beth grinned and said, "Naturally, then it's back to the bat cave to read *Nightsong* and *Bat Loves the Night*."

"Flutter on," Lindsey said.

"Will do. Don't forget crafternoon is today," Beth said. "We're making tin can lanterns. And for the food, I ran with the Chicana theme since we are discussing *The House on Mango Street*."

"Can't wait. I love that book," Lindsey said. Which was true, plus she had also seen the food that Beth had brought for lunch, and there were quesadillas, mango smoothies and flan. There was just nothing better than flan on a hot summer day.

"Okay, little bats," Beth said. "Let's get back to the cave. *Click click.*"

Lindsey watched as Beth led her colony of bats and their parents back to the story time room. Then she glanced at the circulation desk to see Ms. Cole watching the commotion over the top of her reading glasses. Nicknamed "the lemon" for her occasional puckered disposition, Ms. Cole had come a long way since Lindsey had been hired as the library director several years ago. Instead of chastising Beth, she simply heaved a put-upon sigh, which was encouraging.

The lemon had lightened up on late fees, beverages in the building and the exuberance of the story time regulars, but the one policy on which Ms. Cole did not bend was noise. She was a shusher of the first order, and Lindsey was surprised she hadn't hissed at Beth to keep it down. Instead, Ms. Cole put her left index finger over her left eyelid as if trying to prevent it from twitching. Lindsey glanced down at the top of her desk to keep from laughing.

"Excuse me."

Lindsey turned her head to see a man standing at the corner of her desk.

"Hi, may I help you find something?" she asked.

"I hope so," he said. He sounded worried.

The man was middle-aged with just a hint of gray hair starting at his temples. He was wearing a short-sleeved collared shirt in a muted plaid with navy pants and brown shoes. He looked to be somewhere in his mid to late forties, but his forehead had worry lines going across it and his blue eyes looked concerned.

"Well, let's give it a try," Lindsey said. She gave him a reassuring smile. "Tell me what you need."

"I grow roses," he said. "But I'm new to this area, and I'm not sure that my garden can survive the drought we're having. Do you have any books on growing roses specifically along the shoreline or in drought conditions?"

"Thanks to our local garden club, we have an excellent collection on that subject," Lindsey said. "I'll see what's available."

"Thank you," he said.

Lindsey searched the online catalog, limiting the results to the items that were currently available. She found three books on roses, but they weren't specific to the region. Still, they might have something in them about dealing with drought conditions. She noted the call numbers and then did a quick check of the local community webpages that they had bookmarked on the reference database by organization. She found several local gardening groups and one that specialized in roses. She swiveled the monitor on its base so her patron could see it.

"We do have some books in, but they aren't specific to the area," she said. "However, there is a local rose club, and I am sure they can help you with your concerns about the current drought. Would you like me to write down their contact information for you?"

"Yes," he said. "Thank you. This is great."

Lindsey smiled. She took a piece of scratch paper and wrote down the name of the chapter president and her email address and phone number. She handed that to the man and then rose from her seat and said, "Let's go see what's on the shelves."

As she led him through the stacks of books, she asked, "So, you're new to Briar Creek?"

"Yes, my wife and I just moved here a few months ago," he said. "Just in time for me to plant a rose garden, but then this dry spell hit."

"It's a bad one," Lindsey said. "I've only been here for a few years myself, but the locals tell me that they've never seen anything like it."

"I hear the town is planning to ration water," he said. The lines in his forehead deepened.

"There has been some preparatory talk about that, Mr. . . . um, I'm sorry," Lindsey said. "I didn't introduce myself. I'm Lindsey Norris, the library director."

She held out her hand. The man stared at her and then her hand for a moment, and she wondered whether she had offended him.

"Aaron," he said. "Aaron Grady. It's nice to meet you." He clasped her hand and gave it a firm squeeze before letting go.

Lindsey smiled and continued along the shelves until she reached the gardening section. She followed the Dewey Decimal numbers until she found books specifically about roses. The three books the online catalog had listed were there, as well as two more that she hadn't seen. She pulled them from the shelf and turned to find

Mr. Grady right beside her. He was a bit too close, making her feel crowded, so she eased back a step. Instead of looking at the books she was holding, he was staring intently at her, with his hands down by his sides.

She'd had this sort of patron before, and they always amused her. They asked for books and she showed them the books, but when she took the books off the shelf, they didn't reach for them. They just stood there. Lindsey often wondered whether they thought she was planning to read the books to them. She usually broke the stalemate by forcibly pushing the books at them.

"Here you are," she said. She handed him the stack, keeping the most recently published book so that she could check the index. She flipped to the back and scanned for the word *drought*. The book referenced several pages on it, so she opened the book to those pages and skimmed the content. It listed different methods to maintain roses in a drought situation and even included a watering schedule. She handed Mr. Grady the open book and said, "This one looks like it will answer your question."

The lines that had been deepening on Mr. Grady's forehead eased, and he gave her a closed-lip smile as he took the book and studied the pages.

"This is perfect," he said. "Thank you so much, Lindsey."

"You're welcome," she said. "Let me know how it goes, and if you have any more questions, I'm happy to help."

He smiled at her again, and Lindsey turned and headed back to the reference desk. She was relieved one of the books had answered Mr. Grady's questions. She always felt like it was a win when she could get a patron the answer they needed.

Back at the desk, she found Laura Hogan waiting for her. She was a tiny little thing but had the biggest heart in Briar Creek. She came in every week with her dog, Buck, and together they helped elementary school students who were struggling with learning how to read. Buck was a reading-therapy dog; essentially he sat on the floor with a student and listened while the child read aloud to him.

Buck was a beautiful black and brown dog with long legs and the softest ears Lindsey had ever felt. He was great friends with her dog, Heathcliff, and the two of them cavorted and carried on when they met up at the dog park. As soon as Buck saw Lindsey, he started wagging his tail and let out a small whimper.

"Sorry, Buck," she said as she scratched his ears. "Heathcliff isn't here. It's just me." She glanced up at his human, who was smiling at her. "Hi, Laura, how are you?"

"Great, I'm looking forward to today's reading," she said. "We're halfway through *Gregor the Overlander,* and I can't wait to hear what happens next."

"The room is all set up," Lindsey said. "I'll just walk you over and unlock it for you."

"Thanks," Laura said. She patted her thigh, and Buck fell in beside her as they crossed the library to one of the study rooms. Lindsey unlocked the door and pushed it open.

"Lindsey!"

They both turned to see Mr. Grady hurrying toward them. Buck's ears went back and he growled low in his throat. Laura grabbed him by the collar and held him still.

"Weird," she said. "He's never done that before."

"He's likely more used to children," Lindsey said. She stepped forward and intercepted Mr. Grady so Buck wouldn't get more protective. "Yes, did you have another question?"

"Yes, actually," he said. He looked sheepish as he clutched the rose books to his chest. "I don't have a library card. Is it possible for me to check out these books?"

"Absolutely," she said. "I'm sorry—I should have explained. To sign up for a card, we just need proof of your local residence, and then Ms. Cole at the circulation desk will sign you up and you'll be able to check out."

"I can do that," he said. He gave her a small smile and then backed away, watching her as he went.

Lindsey turned back to Laura and Buck. "Can I get you anything? Coffee? Water? Dog biscuit?"

"Coffee would be fantastic," Laura said. "But no treats for Buck, thanks. He's on a diet."

"Coming right up," Lindsey said.

She turned and headed for the staff break room. She grabbed a cup of coffee for Laura and a bowl of water for Buck. By the time those were delivered, her desk replacement, Ann Marie, had arrived, and Lindsey went to the back of the library, where her favorite activity, Thursday crafternoon, was held.

She brought her well-loved copy of *The House on Mango Street,* in which she'd stuck several sticky notes to mark the particularly pertinent passages she wanted to share. As she pushed open the door, she found that she was the last to arrive.

Beth was standing behind the table, dishing out quesadillas, while Nancy Peyton and her best friend, Violet La Rue, were seated on the couch, holding full plates. Paula Turner, one of the circulation attendants, was pouring out the smoothies while Mary Murphy, Lindsey's soon-to-be sister-in-law, was standing with her baby, Josie, on her hip. Mary was swaying back and forth in her mama's stance while trying to eat. Lindsey headed right for her and held out her arms.

"I'll take her," she offered. Mary gave her a grateful look and handed off the baby.

"Thank you," she said. She studied Lindsey for a second, and then she grinned. "You look good with a baby in your arms."

Lindsey pressed her cheek to Josie's soft hair and laughed, "I said I'd hold her, not that I wanted any of my own."

"We'll see," Mary said. Then she grinned, a wide, warm smile just like her brother's, and sank into a nearby chair.

Lindsey moved around the room with Josie in her arms. A few months ago, she would have avoided holding her future niece as if she carried the plague. Lindsey wasn't really baby friendly, or she hadn't been until this kid came along. But Josie had the same sparkling blue eyes as her uncle, and her hair was already beginning to thicken into a cascade of dark curls just like his, and Lindsey had to admit she was smitten.

While Josie tugged on Lindsey's long blond curls, she joined Beth by the table and glanced at her friend. Beth had ditched her bat wings and the headband with the big ears. There was something about her that looked ethereal and lovely. She was watching Josie as if trying to understand the inner workings of her little mind.

Lindsey glanced from Beth to Josie and back. It occurred to her that she'd seen only one person glow like that before, and it was Mary when she was pregnant with Josie. Her eyes went wide, and she looked at Beth and said, "Oh my God, you're pregnant!"

She hadn't meant to say it so loud, and she cringed, aware that her guess could be wrong but also that Beth may not have wanted to share this news just yet. The entire room went quiet, and everyone turned to face them. Beth turned a deep shade of pink and then grinned. "How did you know? Am I showing already?" She hugged her belly. "Or is it my nose? Is it wider? I heard noses get bigger when a woman is pregnant."

"Another baby," Nancy said. She clapped her hands in delight. She tossed her gray bob, and her merry eyes twinkled as she turned to Violet and said, "You owe me five dollars."

Violet tutted. "That was a sucker's bet. We knew she'd get pregnant. I just thought it would be after summer."

A retired stage actress, Violet was still a great beauty with dark skin, high cheekbones, and a full and generous smile. She opened her purse and pulled out a five-dollar bill, which she slapped into Nancy's hand.

"You were betting on me?" Beth asked. She stared at the two women in amusement. "That is hilarious. What else are you two gambling on?"

Nancy and Violet both looked down at their food. As one they took bites of their quesadillas, and through a mouthful, Nancy mumbled, "Can't talk. Eating."

"Hmm-mmm-mm," Violet hummed in agreement.

Beth shook her head at them and then turned to Lindsey. "They are not fooling me one bit. You?"

"Not for a second," Lindsey said. She was about to question them when Nancy spoke first.

"Did you think the lead character, Esperanza, was aptly named?" Nancy asked.

"Yes, because it means *hope*," Violet said. "And her story is one of hoping for a better life."

Beth looked at Lindsey. "Those two are starting the book discussion instead of gossiping? They are definitely up to something."

"Agreed." Lindsey propped Josie on her hip and took a bite of the quesadilla Beth put on her plate. The tortilla had a little crunch, and stuffed with seasoned chicken and melted cheese and topped with *pico de gallo*, it was perfection. She turned to Beth and said, "This is amazing."

"Thank you," Beth said. "Aidan's grandmother is from Mexico, and she's been teaching me how to make some of his favorites. He's better at it than I am, but I think I might have finally nailed the quesadilla."

"Yeah, you did," Mary said. This was no small praise,

given that Mary owned the Blue Anchor, the only restaurant in town.

It was Paula who cracked the two older women. Having finished her lunch, she started to put out the craft supplies. While giving side-eye to Nancy and Violet, she asked, "So, if a library clerk wanted to get in on the action, what would she be betting on?"

Violet pointed to her mouth in a gesture that said she was still chewing. Nancy, having finished her food, was left to consider whether she should answer or not. The lure of having one more purse in the pot won.

"Nothing, really," she said with a shrug. She glanced at Ms. Cole, who had just arrived since she'd had to wait for another staff person to cover the circulation desk. "Do you ever gamble on silly things? You might want a piece of this."

"No," Ms. Cole said as she filled her plate. "Thank you."

Paula, who was Ms. Cole's assistant on the circulation desk, just smiled, clearly not surprised by her answer.

"We may have debated the possibility that Lindsey was going to elope for her wedding," Nancy said. She looked inquisitively at Lindsey. "So, care to tell us who owes whom a fiver?"

Josie grabbed a fistful of Lindsey's hair with her chubby fist and stuffed it into her mouth. She made a squinched-up face, which made Lindsey laugh because hair—ew.

"No, I don't. Did you know that author Sandra Cisneros is a Buddhist?" she asked the group.

Beth shook her head. "Nice try. There's no way you're going to change the subject on this one."

"I had to give it a go," Lindsey said.

Paula tossed her green braid over her shoulder. She was the hippest library staff member, with a sleeve of tattoos and colorful hair that she changed when the mood hit her. So far it had been purple and blue. Lindsey realized that if Paula ever went natural, she might not recognize her.

"Would you really elope, boss?" she asked Lindsey. "I mean, you only get married once."

"Statistically, that's not true," Ms. Cole said. When Beth gave her an exasperated look, Ms. Cole shrugged. "Fifty percent of marriages end in divorce."

"I'm not going to elope," Lindsey said. "In fact, my mom is coming to town in a few days, and we're going wedding-dress shopping. Also, Sully and I are having a small ceremony on Bell Island in his parents' backyard."

"Oh," Nancy said. She looked cranky and slapped the five-dollar bill back into Vi's hand.

"Nancy!" Lindsey cried. Then she laughed. In truth, she would have bet she'd elope, too. Being an introvert, Lindsey wasn't really into the whole princess-for-a-day thing, and she was finding even the planning of a simple wedding to be a bit much.

"How small?" Nancy asked.

"Don't worry," Lindsey said. "You're all invited."

Josie made a hungry garble, and Mary immediately held up her arms. Lindsey handed over the baby, and they all moved to the craft table, where Paula had laid out the materials for this week's craft.

She'd put towels down on the table, and a tin can with water frozen inside of it was placed at each seat. Picking up an awl and a hammer, she demonstrated how to punch a hole in the can.

"Once they're finished and dry, you can paint them or not, then put a candle in them or tiny little battery lights. You can make a pattern or just punch random holes in them. The ice will keep the cans from denting while you tap in the holes, but you want to work fast so the ice doesn't melt, or you'll be sitting in a puddle."

The next few minutes were spent with everyone punching holes in their cans. Lindsey, who was not crafty at all, discovered that there was a certain stress release to be found in tapping the awl through the metal to make a hole. She decided on a starburst pattern and was actually eager to see how it would come out when the ice melted. It occurred to her that these would make really cool centerpieces for her wedding.

She blinked. This was the first time she'd gotten excited about something for the wedding. Did this mean she was about to morph into a bridezilla? She scanned through all the things she had to do for the wedding. Nope. She still wasn't that jazzed about all the work involved. Okay, phew. Maybe she just liked punching holes in the can. It was rather therapeutic.

Her thoughts strayed to the book they'd read. She glanced around the table. The heroine in Cisneros's book wanted to escape Mango Street, her neighborhood in

Chicago, and desperately longed for a house of her own. Lindsey glanced around the table and wondered whether all the women here felt the same way.

"What did you think about Esperanza's desire for her own home?" she asked.

"I thought it was very relatable," Nancy said. "When Jake and I bought our house, he insisted that the house be put in both of our names. He wanted to be sure it became mine in case anything happened to him. He was afraid one of his brothers would try to take the house, claiming I couldn't handle it by myself. Pfff."

She looked irritated for a moment and then sad, and Lindsey knew the memory of losing her captain husband when his boat went down during a storm haunted Nancy to this day.

"I was a single young woman in the early seventies, and while I didn't much care about owning a house, I did want to get a credit card in my own name," Violet said. "It wasn't allowed. Even though I was starring as the lead in a Broadway play, a woman had to have a husband to get a credit card. Huh. Now I have ten."

"I know what it's like to want to leave your past behind you," Paula said. "But I don't know that you really can. It shapes you, whether you like it or not. I think Esperanza learns that in the book. No matter how far she goes, Mango Street will always be part of her, even after she leaves."

"Sort of like Briar Creek and the Thumb Islands," Mary said. "I could travel anywhere in the world, but the years I've spent here have made me who I am. When I read the book, I realized how lucky I am to live here."

"I couldn't agree more," Ms. Cole said. She was tapping away on her tin can, and Lindsey glanced over to see the pattern she was making. It was the outline of an open book.

"That's brilliant," Lindsey said. She pointed to Ms. Cole's can, and the rest of the crafternooners took a look. As they heaped on the praise for her cleverness, Ms. Cole blushed a faint shade of pink. It looked pretty cute on her.

"Lindsey."

Lindsey glanced at the door to see Ann Marie there. She was holding a small piece of paper in her hand.

"This was left for you," Ann Marie said. She came into the room and handed Lindsey the note. "The patron wanted to give you the note himself, but I explained that you were at lunch."

"Oh, thanks," Lindsey said. She opened the note. In a small, tight script it read, *Lindsey, Thank you so much for your assistance today. I enjoyed our interaction and appreciate your help more than I can say. Fondly, Aaron Grady.*

"What does it say?" Ann Marie asked.

Lindsey glanced at her. "It's just a thank-you from Mr. Grady."

"The guy with the rose bushes," Ann Marie said. "He told me how your excellent research was going to save his precious roses."

"Well, that was thoughtful," Ms. Cole said.

"I don't know," Ann Marie said. "Maybe I'm paranoid because I read too many women-in-jeopardy thrillers, but I got a weird vibe off him."

"He seemed okay," Lindsey said. "A little socially awkward perhaps, but there's no harm in that. Right?"

"If you say so," Ann Marie said. With a wave, she exited the room.

"Looks like you have an admirer," Nancy said. She winked at Lindsey.

"What can I say?" Lindsey asked. "I give good reference."

"Wouldn't it be nice if all of our patrons took the time to write such nice notes?" Beth asked.

"Yes, because manners matter," Ms. Cole said. No one argued the point.

Ready to find
your next great read?

Let us help.

Visit prh.com/nextread

Penguin
Random
House